PRAISE FOR ANNE MARSH

The Hunt

"*The Hunt* marks Anne Marsh's debut novel and what an entrance! I was completely hooked from the first paragraph all the way through till the end. Ms. Marsh shows a true gift in weaving fun and charismatic characters that will leave you wanting more of her Hunter's Mate romances."

—ParaNormal Romance Reviews

"Marsh quickly draws you in and then shoots you down a dark and twisty tunnel . . . the pace keeps the reader motivated to find out what happens next."

—*RT Book Reviews*

"This book has an interesting concept, magical temple guardians that can change back and forth between man and cat . . ."

—Night Owl Romance

"This story is filled with submission, humor, and lots of excitement . . . an excellent read, from author Anne Marsh."

—The Romance Studio

"Funny and explicit, *The Hunt* will tempt the most fin-cky reader into an afternoon of reading delight."

—Fresh Fiction

TAKING THE PLUNGE

"You let me in," he promised, "and I'll make it good. I'll give you whatever you want, *dushka*. No questions. No explanations." He trailed the sword-roughened pads of his fingers down the bare skin of her arm and leaned forward. The hair she'd unbound slid around them, sealing them into a dark, decadent world of pleasure. The spicy scent of male and sex surrounded them.

"For a price," she said, desperate to shake off his erotic spell.

"Everything has its price, *dushka*," Brends whispered against her ear.

She needed *this*. She needed him. She wasn't going to find her cousin on her own, not before the killer did. Brends, on the other hand, could. She wished she wasn't so attracted to him. If they bonded, he'd have an inside track straight into her head. He'd be able to connect to her. Communicate with her.

"And?" Her voice sounded dry. As if her throat was closing up.

"If the killer were to come for you," he eyed her closely. "I'd know. I'd be right there."

"You want to use me as bait."

To give him credit, he didn't hesitate. He gave her the truth, although she supposed it only helped his cause. "Yes."

She might be able to help stop this. And stopping this was the right thing to do. Before she could rethink her decision, she said it. "Yes. Bond with me, Brends."

Other books by Anne Marsh:

The Hunt

ANNE MARSH

BOND WITH ME

Dorchester
Publishing

DORCHESTER PUBLISHING

July 2011

Published by

Dorchester Publishing Co., Inc.
200 Madison Avenue
New York, NY 10016

ISBN 13: 978-1-4285-1108-8
E-ISBN: 978-1-4285-0922-1

The "DP" logo is the property of Dorchester Publishing Co., Inc.

Printed in the United States of America.

ACKNOWLEDGMENTS

It seems unfair that only the author's name appears on the cover of a book when so many other people play important roles in getting the book written (and rewritten) and out the door. My fabulous agent, Roberta Brown. The amazing editors at Dorchester. My family, Zoe, Ethan and Louis. A book really is a group effort and I appreciate each and every one of you.

Special thanks go to Jen, who had no idea she'd spend our girls' weekend licking envelopes shut; to Beth, who convinced an entire Duke psychology department to wait for the "erotic Goblin novel" (yeah, this is that book); to Marge, who always turns my books face out on the Borders shelves; and, last but not least, to the small army of folks my mother-in-law strong-armed into buying and reading my first book. Roger David Lee—you rock, and I'd love to meet you.

BOND
WITH ME

THE FALLEN

The first rebellion that disturbed the Heavens was unthinkable. The rebels were Dominions, guardians and angel warriors bred to defend the Heavens' throne. To die for it. And yet the other angel castes handed the archangel Michael incontrovertible proof that the grisly killings sweeping through the Heavens were the work of these same Dominions.

When the killings continued, Michael knew that he must make an example of the rebels and their leaders. The rebels undermined his authority, and worse, his lieutenants whispered, the rebels accused Michael of the very killings of which the Dominions themselves stood convicted. Nothing like this had ever disturbed the perfect fabric of Michael's Heavens.

What the archangel devised then was the cruelest punishment imaginable. He ordered the rebels stripped of souls and wings and cast out of the Heavens. The Fallen were thrown down to Earth, and to make sure that they learned their lesson, Michael cursed each to live as a Goblin, half man and half beast, one half eternally at war with the other. Whenever the man's control slipped, the beast would emerge, a predator driven to devour human souls to feed the man's need for the soul he had lost. Michael held out just one hope of salvation: if one of the Fallen found his soul mate, the one female who could redeem him and teach him love and light and peace, that Fallen would regain his wings, his soul and the Heavens as soon as he truly knew what it meant to love.

Three thousand years later, in the year 2090, no one had ever reascended, and the Fallen no longer believed in the promise of soul mates.

ONE

As far as the human residents of M City were concerned, G2's was one damn sexy club, the sort of place you visited when you were in the money and feeling very, very lucky. You put on your best dancing clothes, flashed whatever cash you had and got ready to bargain very, very hard. Because only the select few were ever invited inside.

Prowling past the queue of waiting humans, Brends Duranov scented hope, anticipation and outright desperation seeping from the waiting mob of would-be revelers. Cross that plush velvet line, take the first step inside the club, and who knew what could happen? Humans believed that his Goblin ability to make a wish come true was worth any price.

Brends knew better.

The hot interest, the even headier cocktail of their individual souls, teased his inner addict. What he wanted—what he *needed*—was lined up and waiting for him. All he had to do was stretch out a hand and choose. Pick a female and make her his dark offer: bond with him, swear to serve his every desire, and receive one favor. She could name anything at all and he'd deliver. All she had to do was serve him, in bed and out, letting him drink of her soul through their bond. He'd taste all the light and goodness she had stored inside her soul, until she was drained and lifeless—or insane.

The fantasy was that in serving him, they served themselves.

That's what those females standing on the other side of the paltry velvet rope were *really* waiting for. That was the chance for which they'd come, why they'd put on their four-inch heels and were staring at him with those needy eyes.

He scanned the crowd, looking for one human in particular. She'd stalked him at the club for the last three nights. Her honey-and-musk scent was just as much of a turn-on as the thought of her long, supple fingers stroking his cock. He could feel himself hardening even now.

But the woman was nowhere to be found. And suddenly he had no appetite for anyone else. He wasn't bonding with anyone. Not tonight.

She didn't want him.

"My liege?" The bouncer closest to the door looked startled at the pause in Brends's long, sure prowl toward the front doors of G2's. He'd never stopped before. The women waiting in line pushed closer to the rope.

He growled something that must have passed for a greeting, because the bouncer held the door open so he could pass through it. He jabbed the elevator button almost hard enough to punch through the brass panel, cursing silently. It was just as well the unknown female had wised up and left his club the hell alone. He couldn't afford to make the same mistake twice.

When he stepped out of the private elevator, letting the doors glide smoothly shut at his back, the thumping beat of prog music hit him like a blast between the eyes. He quickly moved to the quieter VIP section and the corner table reserved solely for his use. Tonight someone was there waiting: the male who'd called him here. His sire.

Zer was a soldier first and foremost, a tall, broad-shouldered shadow whom humans gave a wide berth. No one crossed Zer. A band of black tattoos circled his thick wrists, and his jet-black hair was bound back in a long queue. Even at rest, he looked ready to pounce. Zer never let down his guard, never relaxed. He didn't believe in mercy. Probably had never received any himself, if the nicks and scars on his face were any indication. He nodded a curt greeting in Brends's direction. His movements held the lethal grace of a snake, a cobra poised to strike.

"You've seen the newspapers?" Zer tossed the question out casually, as if he and Brends had been parted for minutes rather than months. Rumor had it that Zer had been tracking down a rogue Goblin who didn't want to be sent to the Preserves.

Near-immortal, the longer a Goblin lived, the harder it became for him to ignore the raw hunger for emotions that constantly tormented him. The man survived by judiciously feeding that thirst by bonding with a willing human, but the beast locked away inside him was a predator who yearned to devour the very soul that sustained it. Sometimes, the beast overpowered the man, and other times, the man Changed for reasons of his own.

When Michael pushed them out of the Heavens and down into the human world, he'd taken the time to rub a little salt into those wounds. Not only had he ripped off their wings, leaving a psychic wound that no amount of time could heal, but he'd stripped them of their softer emotions as well. Since they'd acted like beasts, he'd said, they could live like beasts. They'd experience hunger, pain, fear, rage, the keen desire to hunt and track and tear. He'd condemned them to a lifetime as feral predators—but with an inescapable hunger to be *more*. And the only way to get that "more" was vicariously. Bond with a human, and the Goblin could feel everything that human felt. Or rather, the Goblin preyed on the human's emotions, drinking them down like a vampyr did blood. Sooner or later, the human had nothing left. Most of them went mad.

Now the human papers had been reporting savage Goblin kills along the eastern edge of the empire, and public sentiment was turning against them. Any rogue Goblin who couldn't control the Change and his thirst for human souls had to be dealt with. Quickly. No surprise their sire had taken on the job himself.

A dancer shimmied dangerously close, the sweet, powdery scent of her perfume teasing Brends's senses. She smelled good. Good enough to eat. Tonight's hunger was worse than yesterday's. The itch to drink deep from a human and savor the complex taste of a soul slowly changing from light to dark was almost impossible to ignore. Brends had spent centuries ignoring the thirst, however; he'd survive one more night.

Still, the hunger put him on edge, made him tenser, terser than usual, so he wasn't in the mood to exchange small talk with his sire.

His sire had called. Brends had come. Now he just

wanted the damn bastard to get on with his business so he could return to his office and see if *she* had decided to come after all.

Hell, the plans he had to make her come. A small smile quirked the corner of his mouth. If she gave into her curiosity—and instinct told him she would—she wasn't leaving his club until he'd had a good, long taste of the secrets she was keeping from him. What he hadn't decided was where he would start. Would he tease her, tantalize her mouth, her neck, her breasts until she begged? Maybe he'd get straight to the point, spreading her creamy thighs and lapping at that juicy sex like she was dessert and he was a starving man.

Zer coughed. "When you said you would meet with me here, I thought your terms included listening."

Hell. He forced his attention back to the male sprawled across from him, nodding his head in curt apology. A knowing glint appeared in his sire's eyes. Zer knew how long Brends had held out, refusing to take a new bonded. Had to know just how hot and demanding the thirst riding him was.

The bastard was enjoying every minute of it.

"We've had a situation on our hands for months now. We've been losing human females, but now we're losing brothers—and not just to the thirst, either. They're going out to fight, and they're not coming back. Someone has finally got his shit down and he's killing our kind." Zer steepled his fingers over his broad chest, trying and failing to look like the chance to kick some serious ass didn't delight him. Shit, none of them liked losing their brothers—and Brends knew that they would exact every bit of revenge for their deaths that they could—but you didn't survive by mourning your dead and hiding in the past. What you did was fight back. Hard.

The pleasure faded from Zer's face. "There was another death just this week. We've got a rogue with a taste for blood on our hands here. He keeps killing, and we won't be able to keep it quiet."

"If the killer's one of ours who's gone rogue, we'll take care of it. We always have. MVD knows that." Not to mention that MVD, the human policing unit, wouldn't be equipped to deal with a rogue. Last time they'd tried, there'd been a sudden number of openings in the unit. And not due to a rash of retirements, either. While Brends didn't particularly care one way or another if the human population declined, this kind of mess had a bad habit of biting one on the ass if left unchecked.

So he'd clean it up. Big deal. He'd tracked hundreds of rogues; this one wouldn't be any different. It was bad policy to interfere with MVD investigations until you were damn sure of your facts. There was always fallout from stepping on MVD toes, even though Brends would have been perfectly content to settle matters by slitting a few throats. The solutions that had worked two thousand years ago were too brutal by today's standards, so he'd give diplomacy a whirl first. See what he could dig up.

"It could be another paranormal," Zer suggested. The Goblins weren't M City's only paranormal residents—just the most visible. There were vampyrs, banshees and any number of other dark creatures.

"But you don't think so."

"This one's killing for the pleasure of it." Zer drummed his fingers on the table. "There's a pattern here, but we're not seeing it."

"So let's review," Brends suggested. "His first kill was a tourist. We always figured wrong place, wrong time, just another human who stuck her nose where it didn't belong."

"Old M City family, that second one," Zer observed. He traced a pattern around his fingers with the blade. One wrong move and he'd be missing a digit, but Zer never made a wrong move. A good male to have at your back, and that was why so many of them had followed him all those thousands of years ago. Why they still did. When you looked into Zer's eyes, you believed. You had to.

"She knew M City. She had a human husband."

"Stocks and bonds." Zer nodded. He already knew this information. They both did, but some patterns weren't obvious at first glance. Talking it through helped. "Loaded even by most standards. If she wasn't tucked up in their town house, she was ferried around by limousine. Private planes."

Not bad protection for a human. Nowhere near as good as what Brends provided, but it should have been adequate. "And yet they found her three miles away from her bodyguards. In a negligee."

The press had had a field day with that one. The red negligee had been very expensive, very scanty and very bloody. Someone had ripped the socialite open from sternum to pelvis. Unfortunately, humans had been first to the scene for that one and the pictures had leaked before the Goblins could do anything.

"Then two more."

"That we know about."

Brends turned the facts over in his head as he scrolled through the collection of gory crime-scene video playing on the slim silver vid-player Zer tossed him.

"They're all human."

Zer shot him a look. "Obviously."

"And all female."

"Yeah. Ages?" Zer had clearly been down this avenue himself. More than once.

"Nothing too close—all within a ten- to twelve-year range of each other. No similarity in their appearance, either. Blondes, brunettes, hell, the bastard even threw a redhead in there."

The only obvious similarity was in the coroner's report: the same blade had been used to gut the women. The coroner had noted the distinctive edge.

"What about the weapon? Can we trace that?"

They could try, but M City was ass deep in illegal contraband. Finding one knife would be like looking for a needle in a haystack. More important was the kind of strength it had taken to pull an edge like that—hell, any edge—through a human body. The murderer had split those bodies clean open like a hunter gutting his kill. He'd severed bones. Then repeatedly stabbed the chest cavity.

"Sick bastard."

"Yeah." Brends poured amber-colored liquid into a glass. "So he's probably one of ours. He's got the blade. He's got the strength. I'll take care of it."

Two

The throbbing beat of the club music jarred Mischka Baran straight down to her bones. G2's wasn't a place known for subtlety. An almost visible wave of sound bowed out of the club's deceptively chic entrance, an aural onslaught that pushed against her skin and crawled straight inside her mind.

So what if she didn't like the music? She wasn't here to have fun, and if the mere thought of stepping through that doorway had her palms sweating and her heart racing, well, that was her secret, wasn't it?

The sheer quantity of gyrating human bodies crammed into the club let her disappear in seconds, despite the panic that almost had her hyperventilating. No, the real surprise was that G2's was precisely the sort of place she'd expected. Rumor hadn't exaggerated it at all. Reflected in the psychedelic panels set into the ceiling, the writhing crowd of dancers moved in rhythm to the pounding music. Some sort of computer-synthesized dance music. A DJ spun well above the crowd. Mischka slid up to one of the glass and chrome bars and eyed the approaching bartender.

Probably human, she decided. Definitely not Goblin, based on what she'd learned from her research. He was neither tall enough nor brutal looking enough. Instead, his features were finely chiseled, a smooth, straight jawbone that was almost too pretty to be masculine. A looker, sure, but almost as certainly human. Paranormals had a certain stamp to them she'd learned to read. Their faces reminded her all too easily of the cruelty that frequently lay beneath their surfaces. The few she'd met in person had been all about murder and mayhem.

Right. The sooner she had answers, the sooner she could turn tail and run. Whipping out her vid-player and an old-fashioned yellow pad, she ran her eyes down the list she'd made just so she couldn't chicken out. Someone in this club had seen or heard of her cousin, Pelinor Arden, and all she had to do was find that someone. Logic suggested she start with the bartender.

"*Oranzh* juice," she ordered when the bartender cocked an eyebrow in her direction. Her budget might just stretch to a juice in a place like this, and without a drink of some sort in her hand, she could forget any hope of blending in with the crowd. Hell, she already felt overdressed. Her classy little black number stopped two inches above her knees, but a discreet assessment of the dancers warned her that was about six inches too far past her ass for this crowd. Everywhere she turned, skin was on display. Other eyes slid over her, assessing, dismissing her. She wasn't competition for what *they* wanted.

No fallen angel would look twice at her.

Fine with her.

Mischka was counting on the fact that her cousin, on the other hand, was never overlooked. You simply didn't forget Pell if you'd met her. You couldn't. At first glance, she just seemed so clean-cut and ordinary.

Straight, shoulder-length brown hair stared up at her from the vid-player. There was just the faintest bit of curl to the ends. The high, clean arch of her eyebrows made it seem as if she were looking directly at Mischka. The still image didn't capture the energy trapped in that slim, taut body. Yeah, her cousin was forthright. Clean. Down-to-earth. And then that puckish, whimsical sense of humor hit you right between the eyes, and she reeled you in and you were both laughing. Pell was fun. People simply liked being around her because she enjoyed them. She enjoyed everyone. Which was why Mischka was so horribly afraid her cousin had struck a bargain with the devil.

When the bartender slid the drink across the bar to her, she wrapped her fingers around the cool tube and placed the vid-player down on top of the gratuity before he could palm the cash. "I'm looking for someone."

The juice was cold and artificially sweet. She would have preferred to drink straight from the bottle—after breaking the seal. But that was clearly not high-class enough for this club. Lucky her. Still, the juice was wet and her throat was dry. And she'd already paid for it.

The bartender's pale eyes flashed with irritation and weary acceptance as he leaned in to make himself heard over the music. "No," he said before she could so much as press the play button. His hand slid off the slim stack of bills and he started to turn away. "I can't help you."

"You don't even know what I want," she argued.

"Cash. Vid-player. Dressed to the nines but conservative. Not too flashy." He indicated her outfit with a nonchalant jerk of his thumb. "You're hunting one of *them* and you're looking for the inside scoop. I can't help you. Once your boyfriend, sister, best friend, whoever"—he shrugged—"has made a pact with one of those devils, there's nothing I can do. All I do is pour the drinks."

Did she really look *that* out of place? "I need to find my cousin."

"Sure. That's what they all say. And I'll bet you think she was dragged kicking and screaming into this club. That there's no way she knew what she was getting into, because she's not that kind of girl."

Well, yes. But it was true. And even if it hadn't been, she wasn't going to just abandon Pelinor because she'd made the mistake of a lifetime.

"Is there a posse of relatives behind you?" The bartender's eyes looked over her shoulder and she wondered if he was reaching for a panic button. "Did you bring the big brother or the irate boyfriend with you?"

During that last, unforgettable family fight two weeks ago, her cousin had yelled she was going out. Back to the club. And that she'd damned well bond with a Goblin if that was what it took to get the family off her back. Pell might not appreciate her parents' old-fashioned moral values—or that they refused to stop inviting a steady parade of stockbrokers and doctors to their Sunday family dinners—but Mischka wouldn't let her cousin throw away that kind of love and support. Hell. She would have given anything for her own parents to still be around to badger her with impossible blind dates and embarrassing recitals of her imagined virtues.

Pell just didn't know how good she had it.

"I left them at home," she said, placing both hands on the bar's top where he could see them. "It's just me. I figure it will take the rest of the family another week before they get over the upset"—not to mention mouthing useless aphorisms about making your own bed and lying in it—"before they all beat a path to your door. You could save yourself some grief, Serge." She read his name from the silver name tag pinned precisely to his well-ironed Gucci shirtfront. The club's owner hadn't stinted on the uniforms for his human hirelings; they were as expensive and well manicured as the club walls. Although the walls probably meant more to the owner. Goblins tended to think of their human neighbors as disposable.

"Just look at the vid for me," she coaxed. "You can tell me if you've seen her. Nothing more, I promise," she said when Serge flushed.

"You won't like what I say either way," he grumbled, but she could sense he was weakening. He'd look, if only to get her the hell away from his bar before she could cause a scene. She shot him the deliberately teasing look she'd seen Pelinor use a dozen times in an evening and he caved. "All right. Hand it over."

She slid him the sleek silver unit and watched as her cousin's puckish, mischievous face appeared on the thin screen. Even upside down, her cousin radiated life. Her husky voice chattered animatedly with someone off-screen, telling one of her favorite travel stories. Pell had itchy feet, her mother claimed affectionately. You couldn't nail the girl to one spot; she'd be out and about before a week was up. The young woman on the screen, however, was describing an exotic beach, a particularly effective alcoholic concoction and a close encounter of the paranormal kind that Mischka was fairly certain her aunt had never heard.

Vintage Pell.

She almost missed the tension in the bartender's shoulders. Hastily, he dropped the vid-player back onto the counter.

"No," he said quickly. Too quickly. "I don't recognize this one."

This one? Just how many women came into G2's and hooked up with paranormals here? He hadn't been shocked by the possibility. He hadn't so much as turned a hair—until he'd seen the vid.

"You recognize her, Serge. You've seen her in here."

He didn't answer, so she leaned closer. Pell would have known how to wrap this man around her finger, would have known how to flirt the damn answer out of him. For the hundredth time since Pell's disappearance, she wished she could *be* her cousin. That she had the guts and the courage to bend the rules. To live a little and find out, just once, what it was like to be the bad girl.

Instead, here she was, on cleanup duty yet again.

"Look," he sighed, "you don't want to know, trust me. She'll probably show up in a few weeks or months and then you can all put this behind you. But if you ask questions now, you'll get answers you might not want to hear. Things won't be the same."

She knew that; that was why she was here. "Tell me," she said, not letting go of his gaze. He'd have to say no to her face, that was for damn certain. She wasn't letting him slide off the hook easily.

"Fine." He shoved the vid-player back at her and this time she took it. "Yeah, I've seen her. She's pretty much a regular in here. Sometimes, she came in with a bunch of other women. Some of them were known Goblin junkies, women who'd hook up quick and easy with one of *them* for a night. Maybe two. For little favors, you understand. Nothing big. Maybe a promotion at work, that kind of thing."

She'd heard of that.

"Most of them, though," he continued, "were virgins in that sense. Oh, they were interested, sure, but they hadn't sold their souls yet. We had a pool going," he admitted, "about how long it would be before the next one sold out and who would go first."

Lovely. Her cousin had been a set of cheap odds.

"Pelinor?"

"That her name? Lovely girl. She was friends with one of *them*. Weirdest thing," he said thoughtfully. "Never seen that happen before, specially not here at G2's. That Goblin would just sit and talk with her, maybe dance. He bought her drinks."

"But she wasn't seeing him."

"No, not if by *seeing* you mean was he fucking her senseless. And he wasn't drinking her soul. Not the last time she was in here two weeks ago, at any rate."

"And?"

"And nothing. It was a busy night. That was the last time I saw her, and you asked. I haven't seen her— or him—since." He palmed the stack of bills and two days' salary disappeared into his expensive slacks' pocket. "You ordering another drink?"

She pushed. "You know his name?"

"Nope. Friend of the owner, though." He shrugged.
"You got the balls, you ask Brends Duranov if he's seen
your friend. That kind sticks together, though, and he's
not going to care if his friend drank your friend dry.
Look," he sighed, "it's a tough break, I know, but take
it from one who knows. You go home and you wait.
Your cousin will probably come home when she's good
and ready. And even if she doesn't, there's nothing you
can do. You're only human." His eyes went flat and lost.
"And they're not. You can't ever forget that *they're* not
human."

Amazing what jersey did for a female's ass.

Watching the ice princess sweet-talking his bartender, Brends admired the wicked cling of her dress
and debated whether she understood the effect it had
on her male audience.

Probably not.

Growl rumbling in his throat, he dragged her scent
deep into his lungs. He'd found his mystery woman, the
woman who had haunted his dreams for three nights
running and whom he'd scented outside his club.

So why she was here?

Sure, G2's drew some strange birds, but most of
them looked like they were enjoying themselves. Or
trying to. She'd ordered a damned juice, for Christ's
sake, and then left the ten-dollar beverage on the bar.
As if so much as taking a sip inside his club might con-
taminate her. On some level, he knew he was being
unreasonable. Maybe she was just another human female out slumming, making a quick little visit to taste
the Goblin wares and rack up stories for her friends

back home. A dare, maybe. Or a little gesture of rebellion. He'd seen the type. Made sure they got what they wanted—and that they paid the appropriate price for their pleasures.

It was almost witchy, though, the way the straight black sheet of hair fell around her face, parting smoothly around the strong line of her jawbone. Looking down on her from his hidden observation point three flights up, he could see the white line of her part marching across her skull.

Perfect. Every hair in place.

She walked with a sense of purpose, an almost feline prowl that had taken her straight across his dance floor precisely as if she knew where she was going. What she wanted. It was damned sexy. And it was just possible, he decided, that she simply had no idea that every male in her vicinity wanted to unwrap that tight little package.

Or maybe she did know and it was another weapon in her arsenal.

He wasn't sure which he found sexier.

If tonight was his lucky night, she'd be here looking for a little action.

Or not.

She flashed a vid-player and the hunter in him went on the alert. From where he was, he was too far away to see the screen, but clearly she was looking for someone. Asking questions. Questions made his clientele understandably nervous. The bartender was shaking his head, but moments later the little bastard had pocketed a stack of bills and had his face right up close to hers. Brends made a mental note to have a little conversation with his employee later that night. A conversation that was going to include an unexpected severance package, if the cocky little bastard didn't hightail it back to his side of the bar and start doing the job Brends paid him to do.

Maybe Brends would do *his* job.

He'd find out just what his newest guest was up to. And then some.

THREE

Oh, hell. Coming out of the women's restroom, Pell froze. She recognized the slim, elegant figure perched by the bar. Maybe she'd been kidding herself when she'd thought her family—and her cousin—would let her go if she threatened to bond with a fallen angel. She should have known that Mischka wouldn't let her go. Wouldn't let her fall when there was something Mischka thought she could do to stop it. Mischka was like that. She'd spent a lifetime rescuing her baby cousin from herself and usually—usually—Pell had been grateful. You couldn't put a price tag on that kind of love.

She wasn't grateful. Not tonight. Not this time.

Her heart beating hard in her ears, Pell headed back toward the private table. And *him*. Maybe Dathan would have some ideas on what to do next, because she was fresh out of getaway plans. The writhing crowd of dancers would cover her movements for now, but she couldn't count on anonymity for long. Mischka was too logical, too precise.

Too stubborn.

Pell was going to get caught unless she pulled a rabbit out of the hat. Now. She couldn't believe that Mischka hadn't seen through her threat to run away with a Goblin, hadn't recognized the ploy for what it was. Sometimes, Mischka was naive. Sometimes.

Fallen angels were out of Pell's league. Goblins played for keeps. She'd always pegged them for kindred souls since the rumor on the streets was they'd been kicked out of the Heavens for being a tad bit less than perfect. Well, she wasn't perfect, either. And she'd been known to break a few rules. Okay. More than a few. Being friends with Dathan, however, probably violated at least one international treaty. Now she could only hope that her friend would be able to save her from her current mess.

Because Mischka's unexpected presence at the club was only the tip of the iceberg.

Spotting a break in the crowd, she scooted through the opening. It had been a mistake to let Dathan coax her into coming here, a place where she was known. A place Mischka knew she visited.

When she approached the leather banquette where Dathan lounged like a pasha with his harem, he took one look at her face and leaned over, coolly dismissing the hangers-on from his booth. The young blonde shot her a look Pell couldn't quite interpret. Part intoxication, part chagrin. Too bad if the blonde was jealous, because nothing was going to happen. Dathan was her friend. If he wanted to use her to send unwelcome human company packing, that was fine with her. Words were cheap, and she didn't care if the clubbers thought she was Goblin bait. God help her, though, if Mischka saw. Or if word got home to her parents.

Dead wouldn't begin to cover it.

"She's here," she all but babbled, sliding onto the banquette next to him. The heat of his large body was a welcome solace and she fought the urge to tuck herself into the shadow of all that girth and strength. She was going to be a big girl tonight. She really was. Right after she asked him for one last favor.

Dathan's large hand wrapped around hers. She expected him to tug her up from the banquette, but instead he turned her hand over in his, wrapping her in hard, reassuring warmth. Anchoring her.

"Don't panic," was all he said, but his free hand was flipping out a cell and dialing. He spoke a few low, guttural words in an unfamiliar language.

He must have a plan. Thank God. "Didn't anyone tell you it's rude to speak a foreign language in front of others?" She spoke lightly, but her eyes were moving over the seething dance floor, looking for Mischka.

He barked a final word into the phone and snapped it closed. Dark eyes swept up, and for a moment she wondered if she'd accidentally sat down with a stranger. He looked different. Harder.

"No," he drawled. "Really? Maybe you should consider giving me a few lessons in—linguistics." The words sounded almost dirty. Playful. If she hadn't been so worried about Mischka tracking her down, she would have been tempted to play. They'd teased each other, flirted, for months now. It was good having a friend with whom she felt comfortable. And they both knew that the words were only words.

"Don't, Dathan. Not now," she said.

Those dark eyes stared at her and then his face relaxed, the unfamiliar tension melting away. "All right," he agreed. "I won't. Now why don't you tell me what's up?"

The firm pressure of his hand stroking hers was

rubbing away the panicked tension until she wanted to melt into a puddle of bliss. That was Dathan. So uncomplicated. Always there. Really, she didn't understand why Mischka was so prejudiced against the fallen angels. Dathan was her friend. The older brother she'd never had. She'd leave town when the itch got too bad, travel as far as her money would take her, but whenever she came back to M City, he was waiting there for her. Dathan's fingers moved along her hands in sure strokes. When they discovered a sore spot she hadn't realized was there, they pressed knowingly. The ache melted away and she bit back a moan of pleasure. God, Dathan could have made a fortune in a five-star day spa. His hands were pure magic.

"I'm in trouble," she admitted.

"Really," he said dryly, bending his dark head over her hand. "I'm shocked, Pell. How out of character. Tell me about it and we'll see what I can do."

That hair, she thought, was sinful, the color of midnight and lost souls, even though he usually kept it pulled ruthlessly back from his face. Dathan was neither handsome nor beautiful, but she'd always thought the strong lines of his face possessed an animal magnetism. Since other women stared when he entered a room, she figured she was right.

Stalling for time, she let her eyes trace the familiar hard line of his jaw and cheeks. Dathan had the golden eyes of an animal, never unaware of his surroundings. Even relaxed on the leather seat opposite her, his impossibly large body confined in the close space, she recognized the loose fighter's stance. His right hand rarely left his blade, one thumb stroking the sharp edge over and over. *Protector*, her gut sang. *Predator*, her mind supplied.

"Well," she said, and wondered why it felt so awkward to confess this to him. "You know my family. And I've told you about my cousin."

"Mischka." He nodded. "The perfect one."

"Yeah," she said glumly. "Well, she's convinced that I've decided to sell my soul to the fallen angels and—" There was really no way to put this tactfully, she decided. After all, the male holding her hand was one of them, even though she knew he would never take advantage of her. They were friends.

"And you'd like to convince her of the utter untruth of that particular statement?" His head never moved. "Which is why, of course, you've spent the last two weeks in my guest room and are now here in my very public company. Wise move, Pell. Your cousin isn't going to accept a notarized document when she gets wind of this. Which she has." His head snapped up. "If she hadn't, you wouldn't have bothered telling me this."

Bingo. "Mischka just walked in the door of the club."

He shook his head. "Right. I suppose you'd like to slip out the back door?"

"Yes." She looked at him expectantly. "That's my current plan."

"Baby, you have the worst plans I've ever heard. *If*," he added skeptically, "that even counts as a plan. I strongly suspect you're making this up as you go along."

There was nothing wrong with spontaneity, so she stuck her tongue out at him. "Stodgy, that's what you are, Dathan."

The look in his eyes was one that she couldn't quite decipher. "Practical," he countered. "If you're having issues with this cousin of yours, Pell, you need to talk to her. You skip out of here with me, someone will tell her, and that's if she didn't spot you when you spotted her. She'll never believe you then."

This was the awkward part. "Yeah, well, she might have grounds for concern."

"Really." His eyes surveyed her.

She paused. Then again, this was Dathan and they were friends and she could tell *him* the truth. "I might have claimed I was going to find me a fallen angel."

"And?" Lethal force underlay the word.

"And more or less implied that I'd bond with him."

"And why would you want to bond with one of us?" he drawled.

She fought the urge to flee. "Safety," she blurted out. "Protection."

"From?"

She shook her head desperately. "You won't believe me, Dathan. No one does."

She hadn't wanted to turn to him yet again with more evidence of her imperfections. Of the endless series of screw-ups that was her life. Because friendship only went so far, and this time . . . well, this time, she hadn't come home alone. This time, there had been a man coming after her.

"Boyfriend?"

If only. That would have been so much simpler. She shook her head.

"Creditor." Dathan sounded patronizingly amused. "How much do you owe?"

He'd always been carelessly generous, but money wasn't going to fix this particular problem. "I don't owe him anything."

Dathan's eyes narrowed. For a moment, the lazy look vanished from his face as if someone had drawn a curtain over a window. He looked hard. Dangerous. Unfamiliar. "Him? This person following you is a male?"

"Yeah." Why would Dathan care?

"You brought a boyfriend home?"

"He's not my boyfriend, and I'm sick of playing twenty questions, Dathan." She should have found her own place. She shouldn't have come here with him. It was just that Dathan was a habit she couldn't seem to break.

"I should paddle your ass for this." His dark eyes gleamed with an unfamiliar emotion. He was her best friend, but she couldn't stop the forbidden rush of heat at the mental images his threat aroused. He wouldn't. She should *not* be thinking about her best friend like this. But she couldn't banish the images.

Dathan never did anything by half measures once he had committed himself. There would be the delicious exposure as he drew her too-brief dress up and her panties down. The first crack of heat would surge on her backside and send a thrill straight through her.

Had his eyes darkened? Surely, he couldn't smell the arousal dampening her panties. He couldn't know what she fantasized about at night. He was a fallen angel, not a mind reader.

And she hadn't heard that the fallen angels specialized in bringing fantasies to life. *Liar*, the little voice in her mind chirped. *Liar, liar, pants on fire.* With lust. For one of the fallen angels. And here she'd thought her evening couldn't possibly get any worse.

"Try it," she suggested lightly, "and I'll get even, Dathan." Self-consciously, she shifted on the leather seat, the slick material clinging to her bare skin. This was awkward. She knew Dathan had a certain reputation among her human friends, but she'd never seen this side of him. The charming, nonchalant companion had vanished.

He ignored her unease. "If he's not your boyfriend, who is he?"

"Just a guy." A description that didn't begin to cover the man she'd met. "I was traveling in the South Pacific and met him in a beach club. I'd only been on that particular island for a couple of days and I didn't know if I was staying or going. He'd heard of my arrival, so he stopped by to introduce himself." She still couldn't shake the memories of those dark eyes. The man had been cold, so cold. Almost eerie in the tropical heat that surrounded them. Most of the locals were deliciously warm, sun bronzed and laughing, their curiosity about her tempered by respect for the boundaries she'd unconsciously thrown up. Eilor hadn't cared. He'd glided up to her table and sat down across from her. Sure, he'd bought her the obligatory drink, but there had been almost something possessive in his eyes. He'd scared her. And then he'd said he'd been looking for her. Somehow, she didn't think he meant that day. He'd been looking for her, and so he had come to this island to find her. He'd followed her.

She'd listened to her instincts and run.

"And he followed you here."

"He might have." This was the point at which most of her acquaintances would have tried logic, dissuasion or outright disbelief. After all, how likely was it that a random stranger had followed her halfway around the globe?

"When did you realize he'd followed you?"

"When I got to the airport."

"You got to the airport three weeks ago, Pell." Dathan's voice held a stern note. So she'd been in denial. None of it had seemed real.

"I wanted to be sure before I told anyone. It all seems so crazy."

Three weeks of feeling her skin crawl, feeling like there was an unseen watcher tracking her. Worse, knowing that the watcher could have caught her at any time. She hadn't wanted to go back to the flat she sometimes shared with her girlfriends. Going home hadn't worked too well, either. She'd been edgy. Nervous. In the end, she'd picked a fight so that she could storm off.

She eyed the male across from her. Apparently, straight into Dathan's arms.

"You made me wait."

"We're friends," she snapped. "Did you think I wanted to bring this down on you, too?"

"We're friends." He stared at her and she couldn't read the expression on his face. "Yes, darling. And friends should really be honest with one another, don't you think?"

"Sure." After all, it wasn't as if she'd lied to him about this.

"Absolutely." His hand released hers, sliding off the table. With his other hand, he deftly poured champagne from the bottle chilling in the stand attached to the sleek table. He nudged the flute across the table, and she wrapped her fingers around the stem out of habit. "What did he look like?"

He'd been tall. Dark. And the bar where she'd met him had been darker still. Still, he'd seemed almost familiar somehow. Maybe because his rough, brutal features reminded her of the fallen angels. "Like one of you," she said before she could stop herself. Well, no one had ever accused her of diplomacy before. *Way to go, Pell. Next, you can accuse Dathan of stalking you.*

"Like one of us," he mused. "We're interchangeable, then? You can't quite tell us apart?"

That wasn't what she had meant. "No," she argued. "You know I know who you are, Dathan. I always have. I just meant that he had a look about him that reminded me of the fallen angels."

"Be specific."

She couldn't. The man who had stalked her had been like looking at Dathan's face through the shadows. Harder. Darker. Twisted somehow.

"Fine. So he looked like me, like one of my brothers, but you can't describe him. Didn't manage to snap a photo."

He raised an inquiring eyebrow and she had to shake her head, an embarrassed flush creeping over her cheekbones. No, she hadn't thought to take a picture. Or a vid. All she'd wanted to do was run back home.

Scared little baby, her mind taunted her. *Too chicken to stick up for yourself.*

"No," she managed. She hated feeling stupid. Inadequate.

"Did he do *this* to you?" His hand, strong and sure, stroked an unfamiliar path across her bare thigh.

To her eternal embarrassment, she squeaked his name.

His eyes didn't release hers, and that hand—that wicked hand—continued its slow, bold march up her thigh. Her bare thigh. Oh, God. The sexy black cocktail dress that had made her feel so mature, so in charge, also meant that she'd forgone any lingerie besides a miniscule thong.

Why was he doing this and why was she so *interested* in letting him?

"Don't do this." She knew Dathan didn't want her. He'd had plenty of others in the four years she'd known him and he'd never made a move on her. Whatever bizarre reason he had for acting like this, it couldn't be lust.

"Did you let *him* do this?" Was that jealousy she heard in his voice? For a whisper of a moment, back there on the beach, she'd considered letting the stranger have what he wanted. She'd been lonely. And he'd reminded her of someone she couldn't have.

His hand nudged her thighs apart. She knew she should resist. But at the same time she didn't want to. Nothing screwed up a friendship faster than sex, and yet . . .

"Tell me," he demanded, his fingers inching upward to the edge of her thong.

"Someone will see, Dathan." Could he tell she was wet for him?

He shook his head slowly. "This is mine."

His fingers pressed against her core, rubbing the soaked fabric of her panties against her pussy.

She heard herself whimper his name, the dark, needy whisper from her own mouth shocking her.

"You're going to bond with *me*, Pell," he said in the unfamiliar, hard voice. "And in exchange, I'll keep you safe."

From the man on her trail, maybe. She had no doubt he could do that.

But who was going to keep her safe from Dathan?

FOUR

Mischka stood at G2's back door and squared her shoulders. She'd been told the club's owner, Brends Duranov, had stepped out for a moment. Perfect—she wouldn't have to scream over the music to be heard. She just wouldn't think about what he could possibly be doing in the back alley.

The obligatory neon red exit sign glared down at her. Never mind the sign—Mischka didn't care if the Cyrillic curlicues proclaimed THIS WAY TO HELL. Nothing was going to keep her from rescuing Pell.

Nothing.

She shoved the door open.

The alley was as dark as she'd expected. Some things never changed, no matter where you went. Maybe there was a law that required alleys to be dark, too-small slices of space between buildings. Some light from the street reached this far back, but the mazh-lights out in front of the club hadn't been particularly powerful to begin with, and this far back, the light was more like a lessening of the gray. The moon wasn't going to be much help, either. It hung low in the sky, a cold silver sliver half obscured by the haze of mazhyk that wrapped itself around M City. Every six months or so, someone took a space cruiser out and tried to settle a colony on its inhospitable surfaces, but she figured that the would-be settlers took one look at the hard, cold moonscape and hightailed it right back to Earth. Better the devil you knew. Plus, there were the inevitable whispers that the moon had a paranormal population of its own, one that didn't need a space suit to survive. Yeah, she'd stay right where she was.

"Hello? Mr. Duranov?" Deliberately pitching her voice low and comforting, she made sure she spoke loud enough to be clearly audible. Jumpy males sometimes did things they regretted later—and since he was undoubtedly the kind of male who went armed, there was no point in inviting a bullet. When there was no response, she cautiously stepped through the doorway—and stepped onto a murder scene.

Please God, don't let it be Pell. Not tonight.

The door beneath her fingertips was cold and reassuringly solid in a world that was rapidly falling part. If she'd thought coming to a club and known Goblin haunt was surreal, this death was something else entirely. *Look.* She had to look. She had to *know.* But she didn't want to, didn't want to know if she'd been too late. If she hadn't been in time to keep Pell safe.

She'd promised her aunt. She'd promised Pell.

Promises didn't matter if Pell was dead.

She let go of the door and tried to keep panic at bay. The winter air was unmistakably chilly, but she'd left her coat in the club's checkroom because she hadn't planned on being outside.

Don't let me be too late.

The dead woman lay on the ground in a puddle of crimson blood that steamed unpleasantly in the sharp cold. The color made a sharp contrast to the no-nonsense blue jeans and the heavy down jacket. Dressed like that, the woman hadn't come here to do a little dancing and drinking.

Stepping cautiously around the prone form, Mischka eyed the woman.

Not Pell. Not Pell. Not Pell. The blood rushed back to her head. She was suddenly lightheaded, but there was nowhere to sit down and now she didn't know what to do next.

Mischka's parents had been surprised.

The memories rushed at her, the coppery, sticky scent of desperation and death all too familiar. She'd been twelve and she'd overslept, had woken to hear her parents screaming downstairs. She'd known enough not to go in, to peek through the kitchen door and then run like hell to find help. But it had been too late. She'd known that before she cleared the yard. And they hadn't caught the bastard. She'd caught half a glimpse, an out-of-focus mental photograph she'd never managed to clear from her memory. The tall, broad-shouldered male figure had used expensive weapons and an unusual blade, so MVD had concluded he was not your average psychopath. She knew he was cold. Methodical. Ruthless. Some part of her had *wanted* to go into that kitchen right then, so that he could put an end to her life right there and she wouldn't have to spend the rest of it looking over her shoulder. Waiting for him to catch up to her.

His eyes had given her screaming nightmares for years, until she gave in and saw a counselor. Those de-monic eyes glowed until she could have sworn she was looking into a hellish furnace. He hadn't, of course, been human. She'd known that, even before he picked up her burly father and tossed him against the wall like so much dirty laundry. Her parents hadn't stood a chance.

Her aunt and uncle loved her. They'd stepped in and had done their best, never trying to replace the parents she'd lost. She'd loved them and they'd loved her—but part of her never stopped waiting for her parents to come back home.

This dead woman in the alley behind G2's wasn't her parents and she wasn't Pell, but she had been someone else's daughter. Cousin. Friend. Somewhere out there, someone was waiting for her to come home and she never would.

She should call the authorities. That was the right thing to do.

She blindly groped through her bag for her cell phone, her eyes riveted to the scene before her. The woman had been sliced open, throat to sternum. Blood saturated the brown strands of her hair, her face now a frozen mask of terror and resignation.

The woman had seen death coming for her, but she hadn't been surprised.

Shit. The waitress had said that the club's owner had got a page and gone tearing off into the alley. Had he killed this woman? He was a paranormal, after all. She listened, stretching her all-too-human senses, but she heard only the harsh rasp of her own breathing and the faint rattle of her teeth chattering in the alley's bone-chilling temperatures.

Flipping open the phone, she checked the screen.

Weak signal, of course. Reception should be better out front rather than sandwiched between buildings, so she made for the pinprick of light that marked the end of the alleyway, where the narrow space connected with the better-lit street.

And stumbled over the dead Goblin.

Brends hovered in the shadows of the alley, watching his ice princess practically trip over the body of his fallen brother—the dead Goblin she'd passed right over in her righteous concern for the human female.

If he'd been better, quicker, maybe Hushai wouldn't have died just outside the safety of G2's. He had been very, very close to making it inside—mere yards from the door. So close, but so far.

This brutality had all the earmarks of their serial killer. Decapitation was the only way to kill one of the Fallen, and Hushai's head had been torn from his body. Definitely time to take care of this particular rogue.

Silently, he drew a wicked little shortknife, running the blade between his fingers. Hushai would be avenged. But what interested him even more was the human woman he'd died to protect. Hushai's bond mate.

Hushai's body lay in front of her, one arm thrown out as if to ward off whatever had attacked them so unexpectedly. Even in death, the warrior's touch seemed gentle. *Protective.*

Brends had never fought alongside a more brutal or determined warrior than Hushai. Tender was not part of that male's vocabulary, nor was a poetic, moonlight walk through M City's ice-cold streets at midnight. So there had to have been a reason, a compelling reason, for the warrior to have protected his bond mate's life at the cost of his own. If they had been outnumbered, which seemed likely, given how quickly the killings had been accomplished, then the human's death would have bought Hushai the time he needed to make his own escape.

The Goblins were nothing if not practical. Fight with a feral, brutal intensity. Leave no attack unpunished. But if there was no other choice, they fell back to live and fight another day because all of them—*all*—had vowed to the Heavens and to Zer that they would do everything in their power to unseat Michael, no matter what they had to do to accomplish it. Abandoning a fight would have been a high price personally, but one they all would have made in the interests of serving that one greater goal.

So why had Hushai remained?

Brends cursed silently in the ancient tongue as the woman straightened up and shook that long, dark hair away from her face. What was it about her? The primal need to go berserk, to Change and allow his Goblin form free rein, fought with a more basic need to touch the female standing so tantalizingly close to him. Hot desire competed with the metallic tang of blood, the psychic scent of violence and death that had his beast pushing at his skin, clawing for the freedom to drink.

She would run screaming if he let his Goblin free.

Still, the fantasies flooded his mind, and worse yet, he could almost *hear* the hum of his beast half's approval. The beast was as intrigued by the woman as the man was. Pleasurable. That constant temptation was the worst part of the Change. The transformation sliding over his skin would be pure power and it would be so very, very easy to let go. To live for nothing but the basest of pleasures. Food. Drink. Sex. *Blood.* Every part of him yearned for that satisfaction, but he couldn't, wouldn't give in. He was a Dominion, damn it.

He wouldn't give in to the Change.

"You know something about this you want to tell me?" The male voice rumbling out of the darkness behind her was a low, throaty growl. Mischka fought the urge to jump; she had no doubt that whoever—whatever—was waiting in those shadows would feed on her nervousness. Fear, you could master. Had to master, if you wanted to keep on living. Still, it took a long minute for her to win the battle.

She wouldn't let him see he had the upper hand.

"Maybe I should be asking you that same question," she said with deliberate sweetness. "Seeing as how you appear to have been here first. Before me," she added delicately, just in case he was missing her point. And her accusation.

"I followed *you.*"

"Prove it. Prove you got here after me and didn't do this."

"I don't need to." He sounded confident, as if he didn't care about her opinion one way or the other. Under other circumstances—circumstances that did not include being out here in the alley with him and two dead bodies—she'd have admired that kind of brass. This was a man who demanded the world deal with him on *his* terms. A quality she liked.

"Right." Turning away from the shadows where he

lurked, she looked down at the body again and summoned her resolve. She still needed to call someone. Do something, now that she no longer felt that her own life was threatened. Flipping open her phone, she searched for a signal again.

A hard hand reached out of shadows, clamping gently but inexorably around her wrist. Strong masculine fingers, smooth gold skin and at least a half dozen knife scars, the healed skin paler against his natural glow. A dark shirt cuff appeared and then the rest of the man slid out of the darkness with lethal quickness.

"Put the phone away," he ordered, clearly not feeling the need to raise his voice. The hard eyes and sheer size of him would have been enough to convince even the toughest male to defer to his will. He pulled her effortlessly toward his larger body.

And then she got her first full-on eyeful of him. She wasn't alone in the alley with another human at all. She was alone in the alley with a Goblin. A Goblin who had a sword strapped across his back.

She'd heard that the Goblins, the Heavens' Fallen, were monsters of depravity. This male was no twisted beast, hunched over from the weight of his sins against humankind. He was large and dark—and very, very male. There was nothing malformed about him. Just hard planes and, as he moved his free hand away from his blade, the powerful ripple of muscle beneath the thin fabric of his shirt. If this male was evil incarnate, what did the Heavens' angels look like?

He was impossibly broad shouldered and tall, dark as the night, with strange pinpricks of light for pupils. A dark curtain of hair flowed loosely down his back in a decadent mass that she longed to push her hands into. He had sharp, high cheekbones, black pupilless eyes. He looked like a predator who fed on humans, dressed in black leather and shitkicker boots. A long duster flowed around him. This male hunted. Defended. Killed.

"Let me go." Though she suddenly wanted anything but.

This sudden lick of lust had to be suicidal. And yet she missed the warmth of his hand as he released her.

He was too hard and too large and she knew he was bad news. He was every guilty pleasure she'd ever fantasized about, someone strong enough to take charge, to make her come. There was clearly a kink in her brain, she admitted. A kink that wanted to throw itself in the arms of the tallest, strongest, hardest male she could find—and challenge him. See what the guy was made of and if he could take charge of a situation.

She shouldn't want those things.

Not when the other woman in this little scene was dead. Her interest died a sudden death, too. Hooking up with a Goblin was clearly not the smartest thing a girl could do.

Brends had a job to do. He couldn't afford to taste this female until he had the information he needed, and she clearly wasn't interested in playing show-and-tell with him. But he could smell the arousal. She couldn't ignore the sexual tension between them—unwilling but strong on her part—and his hunger demanded he take what he knew he could coax her into offering.

Her soul would taste delicious.

"Why are you here?"

Maybe she'd tell him outright and the game would be over before it had even begun. When she glared at him, though, he knew she wasn't going to give him an inch. She'd make him work for what he wanted.

Her eyes flickered first toward the now-closed door she'd used to enter the alley and the lighter patch of light that marked where alley met street. Yeah, the main drag was a short sprint up the alley, but she didn't know just how fast he could move to cut her off. Or what other creatures might be waiting to trip her up. For one, a banshee lurked by the entrance. Probably waiting for a drunk who needed to take a piss or an employee slinking off to commit some on-the-side illegality, although truth be told, there wasn't much left that was illegal in M City. The banshees weren't lethal, but they fed off emotions, fear being their preferred drink. If one of them sank his teeth into his companion, she wouldn't die—but she wouldn't enjoy the emotional abyss that followed, either.

No, what he didn't know was why she'd come to G2's, why she'd picked a Goblin establishment, but more important was finding out why she'd picked his alley for a rendezvous with a dead woman. She hadn't noticed the dead Goblin at first. No, she'd had eyes only for the human female sprawled near the door, and Brends didn't know why her disinterest in his kind had him growling low and deep in his throat.

Maybe she didn't know how his kind reacted to being ignored.

Passed over.

She shivered and he was reminded that they were

both standing outside in the middle of an M City night and that it was months yet until summer came. Her dress was no protection against the cold. In fact, he could see her nipples puckering under the thin fabric.

Still, he couldn't afford to give her an inch.

She wasn't the killer, but his instincts said she knew something important.

"I'm going inside," she declared, turning toward the closed door. "I still need to find someone. And I'm calling the police. You can't ignore what happened here. That's not right. We have to tell the authorities."

"Don't go," he growled. He *was* the authority—she just hadn't realized it yet. His word was law here, second only to his sire's, and Zer hadn't overruled him in centuries.

"I don't take orders," she said, reaching for the door.

She'd take orders from him, he thought with savage satisfaction. Hell, yeah. He looked forward to having her spread and hot beneath him in bed. He'd make her so wet that she'd beg him to take her. She shouldn't have come here. Shouldn't have stuck her pretty little nose into Goblin business. Since she had, she could take the consequences. Every inch of them.

She eyed him distrustfully. "You want to intimidate me," she said, and her tone was colder than the Siberian plains. Well, he hadn't thought she was stupid, just sexy as hell. "I'm not running from you."

"Good choice," he growled. "You run and I'll be all over that delicious ass of yours. And just in case you don't know my kind, we catch what we hunt. You don't get any farther than I want you to get." And Heavens help her if he Changed and his beast came out. She wouldn't like what he did to her then.

She swallowed and his eyes tracked the delicate movement of her throat. Maybe she was finally speechless, although he figured she'd regroup quickly enough.

"Who was she?" He pushed the advantage she'd handed him.

She shrugged. "I have no idea." Her eyes looked relieved. Why? "Not who I was looking for."

"So why were you here?"

"I don't see what good we can accomplish by standing here chatting. We need to get a forensics team, Mr. Duranov."

She knew his name. She'd done her homework. "Brends," he said, because he had every intention of going to bed with her. "We're not formal here in the heart of the empire."

"Mischka," she said, without extending her hand to him. When his eyes narrowed, she shoved the offending digits toward him. "Mischka Baran, Mr. Duranov. I'm here looking for a friend. And your staff directed me outside to find you."

She wanted information. He'd play. He once again reached out to her, wrapped his larger fingers around hers and held on, savoring the feel of soft, smooth skin against his. He'd take every inch of her that he could get.

"A friend." Deliberately, Brends took another step closer to her, shielding her smaller body with his larger one. It was as if she knew on some visceral level that he was there and that he could—would—look out for her. No one would get to her through him. She smelled so damn good, even standing in the back alley of his club, that he fought the urge to bury his face in the soft spot where her neck and shoulder met and lap at that sweet scent.

Shrugging off his leather duster, he held it out to her. "You look like you're freezing."

To his secret pleasure, she took the coat and shrugged it on. The coat dwarfed her, but he took a primal satisfaction in seeing her in his clothes.

"Can we go inside now?"

He ignored her question. "How did you expect me to help?"

"My cousin came to your club," she admitted. "More than once."

He swung open the club door and held it for her. She shot him a quick look before stepping past him and into the warmth of the club.

"Is it difficult to accept that your cousin might want to strike a deal with a Goblin?" he asked politely. "Many of your kind are quite happy to take what we offer. Sometimes they strike a hard bargain."

"That isn't what Pell wants." She moved across the floor and every male head in the vicinity turned in her direction. Not that she noticed. She was headed for the exit. Well, he wasn't done with her yet.

"You can't know that for certain. Have a drink with me," he suggested. "We'll discuss your cousin." Subtly, Brends angled his body in front of hers. She stopped just in time to avoid him. His libido growled in disappointment. He wanted to know what she would feel like, pressed against him.

Instead, he gestured toward his personal banquette.

Even in the packed club, it was empty now that Zer had made himself scarce. Usually, Brends preferred not to mingle with his guests, but he sensed that Mischka would bolt if he suggested going up to his private rooms. She didn't trust him, which was wise.

Sure enough, she hesitated, tilting her head toward the hired guards. That long hair slid forward again, concealing the side of her face. "Is this an invitation? Or a command performance?"

"I'd prefer to think of it as an invitation. Have a drink with me," Brends coaxed, surprising himself. "We'll swap stories. You'll tell me why you think I can help you retrieve this wayward cousin of yours. Maybe you're right. Maybe I can be of some assistance."

She didn't look convinced, but she did allow him to usher her to his table. When he cupped his hand underneath her elbow, the heat of her skin all but seared him. He wanted to press his lips against the delicate crease of her elbow, lick a path to her wrist. Hell, he wanted to toss her on the table and eat her.

"You'll call MVD?"

"For the dead woman?" His newest guest was an unexpected delight. "Yes, of course. If that's what you want." He deliberately omitted to mention *when* he would be placing that call. Naively, she didn't try to nail him down on a time, just nodded in agreement.

Sliding onto the plush bench, she shrugged his coat from her shoulders, handing over the skin-warmed leather. He accepted the coat back, although he would have preferred her to keep it. Instead, she perched on the edge of the banquette, ready to take flight at the slightest provocation.

A quick gesture had the bartender bringing a bottle of chilled Perrier-Jouët. Opening the bottle with a deft twist of his wrist, Brends poured the straw-colored liquid into a pair of flutes.

"Is he human?" She eyed the departing bartender.

"Does it matter?" Strangely, he found himself on edge, waiting for her answer.

"Maybe." She shrugged. "It depends. Is he merely serving me a drink, or do I need him for something else?"

"And if the answer is 'something else'?"

"Then I'd be concerned." She sipped delicately at the champagne, her tongue darting after the tiny bubbles that cascaded to the surface. "I'll be candid with you, Brends. I don't like your kind. I prefer to stick to humans."

"Narrow-minded of you," he said lightly. She didn't like paranormals. That would make his seduction of her more challenging. More delicious.

"Probably." She didn't look concerned, however. "But that's my choice. I like to know what I'm up against, and paranormals tend to complicate my life in unpleasant ways."

"But your cousin would disagree with that choice?"

A strangely off-balanced look crossed her face. "Yes," she said. "Maybe. Honestly, I don't know. Up until a month ago, I would have told you no. I grew up with her. I knew her, or thought I did. I didn't think she'd sell her soul. I've been told she came here, and I want her back. I want you to find her—and return her to me," she demanded. He wanted to hear her demand another orgasm from him in that same delicious tone.

He shot her a glance. "My trackers don't do search-and-retrieval," he purred. "They kill what they catch. I'm afraid there wouldn't be much left of your Pell when they finished with her."

How could he so casual about people dying? The image of the dead woman in the alley came flooding back, and this time, Mischka couldn't stop the shudders.

"I want Pell back," she argued. "Alive."

"So convince me." He stacked his hands behind his head and stared at her, all sleek satisfaction. He had her right where he wanted her, and he knew it. She just didn't know why he was bothering to play with her. Men didn't. Ever. "Convince me," he repeated, "that I want to bring your cousin back alive."

"I don't do lovers." And she didn't do *convincing* either, although part of her was strangely flattered that he'd considered asking.

Not asking. Demanding. "Not a problem. I don't either." His dark eyes ran down her body and she had to fight back a shiver. A *shiver*, for God's sake. He made her feel like she had her senior year of high school when Rod Black, the captain of the football team, had decided she was girlfriend material. Hot. Bothered. Not sure if she wanted to tackle the challenge of taming a male who made it clear he'd touch her and she'd like it and she'd come back for more. Well, she didn't do *needy*, either, and it was Rod Black who'd come back for more.

Still, she'd heard rumors about the Goblins for years. Where there was that much smoke, there had to be some sort of fire. In his case, a very hot, lustful fire. "I thought that's what your kind wanted."

"Lovers?" A hard smile creased the corner of that strong mouth. "No. Not us. We want more than that, *dushka*. We bond with your kind, females who vow to serve us body and soul."

Dushka. Soul. That's all she was to him and she needed to remember that. His arrogance didn't surprise her. What did surprise was the hot slick of arousal. "Charming. You pick them out like chickens at the market?" The women queued up in front of G2's had been waiting for Brends, she realized. The image of him picking and choosing females like pastry from a case was strangely unsettling.

"Maybe." He shrugged. "You do know that when we got our asses booted out of the Heavens, we gave up more than the key to the Heavens' front door, right? Some of us feel more than others, but we're not the touchy-feely type. We don't care if you don't like us. Hell, all you have to do is let us in."

"Into?"

"Bed." He shrugged. "Or wherever. I'm not particularly picky. You got a yen to do it on the club floor, that can be arranged."

Her body reacted to the sensual images his words suggested, her pussy tightening deliciously. Worse, he knew what his words had done to her. Knew how she had reacted to his suggestion.

"Thought you'd like that." He smiled with feline satisfaction. "You're a watcher, and the watchers always fantasize about what would happen if the tables were turned. You imagine that scene all you want, *dushka*, when you're safely back home tonight.

"I don't have time for this." Setting the flute back on

the table, she slid off the banquette and stood. "I need to find Pell and you need to call the MVD about that body in your alley. Right now, I'm out of here."

Screw him and his alpha attitude. She wasn't in the business of convincing pigheaded Goblins to do the right thing. She bit the inside of her mouth to keep from adding her candid opinion of how he ran his operation around here. So he didn't care that there'd been a double murder right outside his club. She'd heard the Goblins didn't care for much of anything—apparently, he was just running true to type. Why should her cousin be just one more victim in what had to be a long, long list?

She headed for the door.

Brends really liked that long-legged stride, but Mischka Baran wasn't walking away from him. He slid from out behind the table and caught up to her in three swift strides. He grabbed her wrist, swung her around and braced her against the wall

"Don't run. Ever," he gritted out through clenched teeth. He could feel the beast rising inside him, the thirst he'd denied demanding that he feed. On her. She'd taste so damned good.

She eyed him and he swore his cock leapt in response to her defiance. "I'll do what I damn well please. Now let me go."

"Dushka," he warned, because warning her seemed only sporting, "your running brings out the beast in me. You run, and I'll chase. It's my nature."

She opened her mouth to protest, but he cut her off. "You can't deny you would enjoy it." He lowered his head, pressing against her, and buried his nose in the crook of her neck. "I can smell your arousal even now. If you want me deep and hard inside that hot, wet pussy of yours, go ahead—run from me."

He could feel the warmth of her skin through that damn silky dress she was wearing. When she moved, pale skin teased him, peeking out from the too-tame neckline that covered her from throat to hem. Not a hint of a suntan—his Mischka was a gal who covered up. Who hid.

But she wouldn't be hiding from him.

Would she let him kiss her? Or would she pull back, retreat into that perfect shell she'd built around herself?

"Mr. Duranov . . ." she said, and he heard the beginnings of a protest, of worry, in her voice. Maybe she didn't like the public venue, maybe she worried about discovery, but he was making discoveries of his own. When she shifted nervously, he followed her, keeping her pinned. The damn dress shifted again, revealing the pale perfection of her throat.

Blood. Probably from the dead female, the scent was faint but unmistakable, a copper bite he was all too familiar with. He was no vampyr, but he was a predator. The scents and smells of a battlefield were an aphrodisiac for his kind.

"Brends," he said, because he had plans of his own for her and they involved getting on a first-name basis. His face must have warned her, because she went still like an animal, cornered, and then clearly came to a decision of her own. Her face lifted toward his, asking.

His.

* * *

His hair fell about them like a sinful curtain as Brends lowered his head toward her, shutting out a world that had suddenly become strangely unfamiliar. Standing on tiptoe, she anchored herself against his broad shoulders with unsteady hands.

He was hot and solid and all too real. The unfamiliar texture of his black leather duster slid beneath her exploring fingertips as she tangled her fingers in the hair at the nape of his neck. Even that skin was hot, firm, without a hint of vulnerability.

"Tell me to touch you," he said in a low, hard voice. "Demand I pleasure you."

She didn't do those sorts of things. *Pell had, though*, a traitorous voice whispered in the back of her head, quickly silenced. Pell had taken what she wanted and let the consequences be damned.

"Kiss me," she ordered, and he cursed, a low, violent hiss of sound that slipped from his mouth and almost shocked her from the strange waiting silence of her needy body.

Then his mouth came down on hers, tasting her like she was the sweetest of fruit. The lips pressed against hers were deliciously hard and masculine. The sharp sting of his teeth had her gasping, and then his tongue swept inside her mouth, invading, conquering her with the spicy-sweet taste of male. A whimper escaped her. Oh, he was so winning their battle. His mouth moved over hers in a wet tide of heat, spreading her open for his intimate exploration. She found herself clinging to his shoulders. And she *never* clung.

When he pulled back, she had to force herself not to

clutch at him, to hold him to her. What had he done to her? This wasn't *like* her.

"You go think it over," he growled low and hard against her ear. "Call me to you and I'll know you want more of this. More of me."

His teeth were a sharp, erotic sting tugging at her earlobe, applying an exquisite pressure to the tender skin she felt clear down in her creaming, needy sex. Surely she didn't want this, didn't want more of him?

One hard finger traced a blunt path from the wildly beating pulse at the base of her throat down between her breasts, over her waist, right to her center—an erotic line from mouth to the pulsing heat of her clit.

"You want me here," he said, "you call me back. You bond with me and take what I give you and I'll take what I want from you. Make no bones about it. I'll have you however, wherever, *whenever* I want you."

"And what I want doesn't matter? I don't bond with Goblins, Mr. Duranov."

"You'll want this," he said, and that wicked finger stroked a blunt message of its own, squeezing the needy kernel of hot flesh where all of her desires were centered. "You'll want what I can give you. Because I can give you Pelinor."

Five

"Fuck. Off." Judging by the look in Mischka Baran's eyes, she meant it and then some. Her eyes traveled down the length of him and back up again. Whatever she saw, it clearly wasn't her idea of a dream date. Her hands landed in the center of his chest and shoved to underscore her point. "I'm not interested in being your chew toy, Mr. Duranov."

Apparently, his kissing her had them back on a last-name basis.

He removed his hands from her person—because that much of him remembered who he had been before he'd become one of the Fallen, and the former Brends would have behaved himself. Even if he still smelled her hot, wet cream. The Goblin he was now made a mental note and started plotting the next step in his seduction. She might deny it, but she wanted him.

Deliberately, he leaned forward, planting his forearms on either side of her head. Those dark eyes were shooting daggers at him. The soft lips he'd just kissed pressed into a hard, stubborn line.

Her fury was delicious but not unexpected.

"You offer to bond with every woman you meet? 'Cause there's a line outside waiting for you, Mr.

Duranov, and that's where you should be looking. Take your offer outside to them. I'm not buying."

"No." He shifted his large body closer to hers. She didn't budge, wouldn't give in to his masculine crowding of her smaller, feminine body. His beast growled with pleasure. Just to rile her up further, he added, "You're not buying. I am."

"And you think that's what it's going to take to—" Her lip curled and he wanted to bite that haughty snarl, drink in her reaction to the bright bite of pleasure-pain. She was so damned *good*. "To *fuck* me." Hearing the obscenity on her lips shot straight to his cock. The damned thing ripened and lengthened, making it all too clear what his body wanted.

Her.

"Yeah." He leaned in, deliberately invading her space. She shot him a cool glance but didn't shift. She was strong and he liked that. "That's what I think. You want to know why?"

"Do tell." That calm glance dropped slowly down his face, examining him. Did she pause for a moment on his mouth or was that merely his overheated imagination?

His laugh came out as a bark. "You need me. You've seen what this killer can do. You cross his path and he'll gut you like day-old fish, baby, and that's if he's in a good mood. He's bigger, badder and stronger than you are, and he's loonier than your average bedlamite. You're not stupid. We both know that. Letting him come after you wouldn't be wise, so you'll do whatever it takes to keep him off."

"Right." That cool gaze dissected him a second time. "I see no proof that this killer will come after me next, and yet you seem to believe I'll trade my virtue for a little bodyguard action on your part."

Virtue was such a deliciously old-fashioned word. "It will be more than a little action on my part, love. That's a hell of a killer out there. He took down a three-thousand-year-old warrior without alerting any of us to his presence. He's probably a rogue, a Goblin who's slipped over the edge, love, and who isn't worried about the consequences of his actions. A rogue feeds his soul thirst—and he kills. Usually in that order. But yeah, maybe he'll give you a pass. Or just maybe you'll be next on his list." Either could be true.

"Which makes your price seem a tad high, don't you think?" She smiled sweetly. "If he slipped past your defenses this time, how do I know he won't be introducing himself to me at a later, more private date—and after I've undoubtedly got to know you quite a bit better than I want?"

She'd want. He'd see to that.

"You should want to help me," she suggested. "If this killer is truly a rogue, he's your responsibility."

Despite having lived most of her life in M City, his companion clearly knew very little about his kind. That, or she was deliberately delusional. Or baiting him. Any one of the three was a possibility.

"Why should I want to help you?" He shrugged. "There's nothing in it for me."

"Moral obligations aside?" She actually waited for him to nod before she continued. "Well, I should think it was a question of public relations. Word gets around that you don't mind hanging your human clientele out to dry, what happens to your business here?"

"Not much," he said drily.

For the first time, she looked startled. The tiny pucker between her eyebrows was the first hint of an imperfection. She'd have the most delightful crinkle there in another decade or two. He'd help her out, he decided, because the sooner she realized he was a selfish bastard who was in it for himself, the sooner she could reconcile herself to making a deal with him. "I don't care what anybody thinks."

"And so you'll demand this bond from me? There's a killer on the loose and all you want is sex?"

"I'll make all your fantasies come true. Every last one of them, if you give me what I want."

He'd never met a pleasure he didn't like or wouldn't explore. Hell, the only advantage to mingling with the human kind was their rather fertile imaginations. Uptight lot, but damn. The fantasies they nurtured made them ripe for his kind. Ripe for the taking. Repressed bastards. He didn't make excuses. He took what he wanted. He gave them what *they* wanted. For that one, dear price.

"I doubt it. You wouldn't know the first thing about my fantasies."

She hadn't denied having fantasies. Interesting. Too many women seemed to believe there was something shameful about their fantasies.

"What do you know about the bond?" he asked.

"Not much." She shrugged. The jersey of her dress clung to her collarbone; the delicious scent of that fabric-warmed skin teased his senses. "I'm afraid I didn't pay much attention, since I've never been interested in selling my soul. Or"—she pursed her lips—"in renting it out for a little temporary use. I like myself as I am just fine."

"You should have listened. You'd have learned something."

"I'm sure you'll tell me now."

"Yeah, I will."

"You notice the markings on the dead woman's wrists?" Mischka hadn't. There'd been too much blood. "Those markings indicated that she was bonded to one of us. To Hushai, in particular."

"And he would be . . . ?"

"The other dead body in my alley." Brends's tone was light but the look in his eyes promised that someone would be paying for that death. Hushai had mattered to him. A lot.

She understood how he felt; if that had been Pell lying there on the ground, she wasn't sure she could have waited for MVD to bring the culprit to justice. Taking the law into her own hands would have been tempting. "Do you guys bond often?"

He stared at her curiously. "You really don't pay attention, do you?"

"I pay attention. I'm just not interested in this particular lifestyle, Brends. I didn't get close enough to spy a tattoo on your friend."

"Damn." He eyed her. "That's cold."

"You're not human." And she'd seen firsthand what paranormals could do. Animals had feelings of a sort, too, but only a fool got within biting distance.

"Right. Well, those markings tell you who is bonded and who is not. Bare wrists mean the guy is up for grabs."

She could just imagine the line. "So he's free to do this bond business?"

"If he wants to. There's a long, long line of people hoping to convince us, that's for sure. Men and women, although most of us prefer our bond mates to be female."

"How does it work?" She strove to keep her voice light, casually curious. "Who asks whom?"

"It's not a marriage proposal." He eyed her. "There's nothing romantic about it. Anyone can ask, but we rarely agree. We're picky bastards, love, and we have to want *you*. You tell your newfound Goblin friend what you want, he names the length of time you're going to serve and then you seal the deal. We don't come cheap."

Right. She'd recognized that Brends Duranov was out of her league, but this was light-years beyond what she could have imagined. "Great." She shrugged. "So you bastards prefer your sex kinky and your females fresh. What happens when the honeymoon is over?"

Brends smiled. Slowly.

She rephrased. "When you Goblins have had your little hookup, had your fill of a bond mate's soul— what then? You buckle down straightway to taking care of the favor? And then everyone goes on his or her merry way?"

He shook his head and she knew she'd discovered the catch. "That's why we set the terms up front. The human bonded gets to serve us for whatever period of time we've agreed upon. The bigger the favor, the longer the term."

"How long?" She eyed him. "Give me a ballpark."

"It varies. But the most recent bond mates I know of? Anywhere from a couple of weeks to decades. Once, a bond that couldn't ever be broken."

"So what could possibly be worth that sort of price?" She couldn't think of anything.

"Any favor you want, Mischka. Think about it. No-holds-barred. No limits. If you can name it, I can get it for you. Most people don't pass up that kind of opportunity."

Hell, no. Except part of her just couldn't *stop* thinking about Brends's offer. The sexy part. This wasn't something she'd do just to find Pell—and it wasn't something she could justify doing for herself. She shook her head, but she must not have convinced Brends any more than she'd convinced herself.

"Goblins are fallen angels, Brends. You seduce. That's what you do. You come after us because we're human and because it's all about the temptation. So you think you know what we want. What you think we need."

"And we give it to you." Yeah, she was all sorts of stupid for even thinking about it. Erotic attraction wasn't an excuse for stupidity.

"No." Selling her soul to a fallen angel was about as wrong as she could get. Saving her cousin from making that kind of mistake was the right thing to do. Besides, she loved her impish rebel cousin—secretly, she'd wanted to *be* her. Could she ever really let go, though, and enjoy whatever pleasures life threw her way? "It's no gift. There's a price, Brends. There's always a price."

"You be careful if you come near me again, darling, because I'll hook you in before you know it. I can promise you that."

Shortcuts never worked. She knew that. The side trip might turn out to be fascinating, but they never got you where you needed to go. Not in time.

She forced the erotic fantasies out of her mind. Brends was simply a diversion she couldn't afford.

Laying a finger over her mouth, he wondered if she'd bite him. Did she know what her drawing blood would mean to him? Maybe she did—smart girl—because she jerked her head away from his touch.

"Think about it, *dushka*," he growled against her ear. "You think about what I can give you. What you can take from me."

"Right." She shoved again, but this time the hand that came up between them held a snug little semi-automatic. The sleekest little ASP he'd seen in a long time. His bouncers clearly weren't living up to his expectations if they'd overlooked this. He was damned near immortal, but she couldn't miss from this close. Even kill him, if she aimed for the throat and squeezed off enough rounds to take his damned head off. Literally. His beast half was humming with approval. This bonded would be strong—strong enough to survive and strong enough to run. The beast liked that.

"You listen to me, Mr. Duranov," she said, "and listen closely. I'm not here to be your bonded. I'm here to find my cousin and bring her back to the family she ran from. I'm stubborn, I don't give up and I'm damned good at finding people. Maybe you think you're the only one who can track her. Maybe you're right. But I'm going to give it everything I've got, and I believe I'm going to succeed. There's nothing you can do or say that's going to stop me from making that attempt. Pelinor Arden is mine. Not yours. And she's coming back with me."

The unforgiving metal stroked a deadly path up his chest and along his jaw. Did she know what a delicious turn-on her strength was for his kind? Maybe he could be himself with her. Maybe she'd be strong enough to survive.

Her free hand coaxed his head down and he let her, her breath an erotic tickle in his ear that shot straight to his bursting cock. "So you think about that, Mr. Duranov, because that's all the *taking* I'll be doing."

This time when she shoved, he let her go.

He even refrained from having the last word. He could indulge her. He'd planted the seed and the idea would germinate. He'd been seducing human females before she was even born, so Mischka Baran didn't stand a chance. He'd reel her in before she knew what had happened.

He didn't know how much of that self-righteous wrath was genuine and how much was a deliberate performance designed to get her the hell out of his club before he decided to keep her there. Because they both knew he could.

That he would, if he really wanted to.

As he watched her stride out of his club, he signaled

to one of his trackers to follow her. Brends was going to have Mischka Baran's secrets. Every last one.

Brends went back out into the alley—because Mischka Baran had got one thing right.

He couldn't leave the bodies where they were.

Unfortunately for Mischka, she was clearly used to being right. Or self-righteous. Brends wanted to kiss that prim, careful smile from her face, coax those plump lips into relaxing, opening up for him. He couldn't shake the hot, sweet taste of that mouth.

Business. He needed to focus on business. Zer would have questions.

Hell, he had questions. Plenty of questions, but no concrete answers.

The air's bite was already noticeably colder as he stepped outside. The darkness was lightening, the blackness no longer almost impenetrable. The mazhlight at the far end of the alley was a paler blur. Dawn was coming, coming fast.

Zer was crouched beside the dead human female, his large hands methodically going through her pockets. The ID he tossed to Brends claimed she was one Ming John. Pocketing the card, Brends made a mental note to check out the address later.

He examined the dead human. Her injuries reminded him of—but no, that wasn't possible. Heavenly angels didn't come hunting down here. Still, the wounds on the female's body were not defensive. Whatever—whoever—had grabbed the female had done so too swiftly for her to have a chance to fight back. That, or she'd been too scared to do so. Either way, she was stone-cold dead and he was up to his ass in shit. No way were they hushing up this murder. The Goblins might own M City, but he knew only too well that it was a leaky sieve when it came to information. This information would find a way out.

"Security vid you wanted." Standing up, Zer passed the thin data stick to Brends. "Check it out."

Sliding the slim stick into his vid-player, Brends watched the footage play across the small screen. First the crisp outline of the night-shadowed alley. The camera made a methodical pan of the space and turned up nothing out of the ordinary. Not so much as a stray dog.

He skipped ahead several frames until Hushai and his companion began walking rapidly up the alley. The female was tucked into his side and the brother looked grim. His shitkickers beat a heavy rhythm on the pavement. When she said something too low for the security vid to capture, Hushai hesitated.

When Hushai bent his head toward hers to catch the words, the world exploded.

The rogue launched himself from the shadows, dropping straight down out of the sky. Hushai had been watching the shadows around him. He had not been watching the sky. It was a mistake that cost him dearly. None of them would make that mistake again; Brends made a note to brief his team and send out word.

On the small screen, the rogue was a large, hulking shape. His back in the shadows, Brends couldn't tell how the bastard had descended so quickly or from where. He'd send his trackers out to look for a tie off, but he didn't think they'd find one.

He looked again. The bastard had grown a pair of wings.

Freezing the vid, Brends looked at Zer. "We need to make our move on Michael. Now."

"You think the bastard got his wings from Michael? He certainly kills like Michael did." Three thousand years ago, someone had carved a very bloody path through the Heavens, hacking up angels indiscriminately. Michael had accused the Dominions of the murders, but the Dominions had believed Michael himself was responsible. "We were both there. None of us imagined what happened. We didn't do it."

Brends looked at Zer. "Someone did. And Michael was never quick to judge, so whoever, whatever, convinced him of our guilt must have made a damned good case."

If this killer was Heavens-sent, it was the chance to prove with black-and-white certainty that there was, in fact, a killer loose in the Heavens. A chance to prove that Brends's sire and his fellow Dominions had not been guilty of the crime of which they'd been accused— because someone else had committed those crimes. Someone like Michael. "What else could it be?"

Zer stroked his chin, all contemplative like, as if he weren't standing ankle deep in blood in an M City back alley. As if he were still the bloody prince of the Heavens, with a full court of angels kissing his royal ass. The time for thinking was over. It was time to act.

"Play the rest of the vid," he said.

The fight was brutal. Quick. Too quick. Hushai was a mean, street-hardened fighter. Their rogue took off his head with ease.

After making his kill, the rogue turned to face the security cameras. Eilor. Brends hadn't known the former Dominion well, but the bastard was humming under his breath as he wiped the blade clean. The entire scene had taken twenty seconds, tops. Brends almost didn't recognize him, but that wasn't unexpected. There were thousands of Fallen and some had hidden themselves away for millennia. Plus, the soul thirst twisted a male. Distorted his face, his features, burning away the man and replacing it with the beast.

As the lupine face of the killer made all too clear.

The club door cracked open in the vid and Mischka Baran stepped out into the alley.

What the hell?

The rogue melted back into the shadows, paused. The humming stopped abruptly and there was no mistaking the flare of interest in the male's eyes. He palmed a vid-player of his own, images flashing rapidly over the small screen.

"Have security run the vid," Brends said. "Slow the feed stream down. Have them find out what the bastard is looking at." The rogue on his screen froze a frame with a tap of his thumb and Mischka Baran's face stared up out of the small screen in his palm.

That was a connection he hadn't anticipated.

The rogue knew who Mischka Baran was.

In the vid, Mischka Baran moved toward the bodies. The rogue's gaze tracked her, one hand going to his knife. He'd thought about using the blade—hell, yeah, he had.

So why hadn't the rogue killed Mischka Baran?

He had his answer in the next frame. Brends saw himself appear at the far end of the alley. The rogue's glance moved between the two of them and a slow smile, frightening in its ferocity, creased his dark face.

Then the rogue shot upward, and the vid ended.

"Put out the description. I want every Goblin from here to Siberia to have Eilor's mug staring up at him within the hour," Zer ordered.

Brends nodded. Interfering with his territory was a fatal mistake. This rogue would pay for that intrusion.

He'd find a way to deal with the preternatural strength of the rogue later. And with the wings. If he was honest, he didn't know if he *could* stop the rogue. But he'd find a way. He had to. The bastard was hunting on Brends's turf and had killed a brother. No one did that and lived. No one.

"I'll catch him," he vowed.

"And then?" Zer prompted.

Information would be useful. First. "We'll have us a conversation," he acknowledged. "I'd like to learn more about these wings of his. Where they came from, who gave them to him."

Zer nodded a terse acknowledgment. "Keep it quiet."

Brends didn't like taking orders. Hell, he'd never been good at it. Still, he hadn't been planning to make a block party of it. "Because?"

"Because I said so," Zer said with smooth menace.

"And because, last time I checked, *you* were sworn to *me*."

Brends eyed his sire coldly. "So now you're going to tell me how to do my job? You want to hunt this rogue down yourself, *sire*?"

"No." Zer didn't back down. In a hand-to-hand fight, they would have been evenly matched, but they both knew Brends wouldn't raise a hand to Zer. Because he *had* sworn to the male. "You take this one. Fine. But I have a job to do, too. Liaising with humans doesn't get any easier, Brends, when one of my brothers is running around publicly hunting down another. They have rules about violence here."

"Rules we ignore."

"But we don't rub their faces in it. A modicum of discretion, Brends, that's all I'm asking for."

For fuck's sake, he had to handle humans with kid gloves now? Sure, Goblins had never been welcome. Sure, M City, heart of the paranormals' empire, had a nuclear arsenal pointed straight at it and a bunch of trigger-happy human politicians who, when they weren't busy grandstanding for their constituents, just might be willing to punch a button to make their point.

Humans looked in their papers, flipped on their televisions and saw a pack of bloodthirsty monsters. Which was not, Brends reflected, all that far from the truth. Soul thirst did that to a male. Most of them simply managed to control it. Or had it controlled for them. That's what the Preserves were for. Even so, delicacy wasn't exactly in Brends's nature. And yet, no matter how rough he seemed to humans, he could never show them the full extent of the beast living inside him. Because if the humans cottoned on to the truth, they'd be punching buttons left and right, more than ready to blow half their planet to kingdom come if it took the Heavens' outcasts with the blast.

His eyes flickered. "It's quicker to simply hunt down the rogue. I get it. I'll take care of it."

Unfortunately, the soul thirst had reduced more and more of the original Goblin warriors to mindless beasts ruled by the bloodlust and primal instinct. They either killed to satisfy those thirsts or their saner brethren locked them up on the Preserves Brends had created. Brends had bought up great sweeps of land on the Russian steppes where the predators could roam in packs, hunting, howling. Where the beast could roam freely and the man knew that he would not tear apart the innocent. He'd built Preserves in Siberia. Two on the African plains. And more in Greenland and the American desert. Human military patrolled the watchtowers on the perimeters. The high, wire-topped walls were filled with the latest sensor technology and to touch the wall was death. All designed to keep the beasts in.

"No civilian casualties. No obvious property damage. By all means, hunt him. Take him to the Preserves or kill him. I don't care which you choose. But you do it without alerting the entire human world to your actions, Brends. No collateral damage."

He didn't kill indiscriminately—only when the situation warranted killing. "Fine. No collateral damage, but"—he eyed the vid—"I'll need the female."

"The dead one?"

"No. That one." His thumb caressed the frozen image of Mischka Baran. "Our rogue spotted her; he's got her pic on his vid. Unless I miss my guess, he'll be hunting her next."

"You see yourself on protective duty?"

"No." Hell, no. The only thing he protected was his sire. And his brothers. The rest of the world could go to hell. After all, the fallen angels had already been condemned to hell. And it hadn't turned out as badly as Michael had hoped. "She's bait."

Six

Eilor was merely a tool.

A century ago, Cuthah had given the Goblin back his wings—temporarily—and Eilor, in exchange, focused his obsessive need for violence on the females Cuthah identified. A win-win situation.

Eilor's kills didn't interest Cuthah. Those were casualties of war, and while the dead were graphic reminders of certain costs, they were really just a means to the end. Cold, raw power. The power to reshape the Heavens. Four ranks of angel guardians were all that was left between him and the final throne. Having the Fallen cast out had been a masterstroke. Their kind, the Dominions, had been fierce fighters. Now, however, he needed to keep them where they were.

Out of the equation.

Impotent.

Soon, Michael wouldn't question any longer. Three millennia the male had waited, wondering why none of his beloved Dominions had found—or even sought—redemption in the arms of their soul mates. And meanwhile, the number of soul mates dwindled with every passing year. When these two were dead, there might not be more than a dozen left in the world. Cuthah would be safer than he'd ever dreamed of being.

Because Michael never went back on his word. And

he'd vowed that the Fallen would never return to the Heavens until they'd found their soul mates.

Of course, as a tool, Eilor simply didn't understand this larger picture, and that meant that sometimes he got things wrong. Very wrong.

For example, Eilor had had no idea that Cuthah, the archangel Michael's second-in-command, had been identifying potential soul mates almost since the Fall. And wouldn't the Fallen be interested in knowing that little fact? Of course, Cuthah had no intention of sharing. The information was too valuable.

Another interesting little tidbit that Cuthah had learned since the Fall was just how one found these potential mates. Sheer, raw sex would eventually do it, but Cuthah had never been particularly interested in running an M City–sized orgy. Instead, he'd researched bloodlines. Granted, the work was slow and rather tedious. Cuthah had been at it now for centuries. It wasn't the possibility of making a mistake and identifying the wrong females—after all, human females were disposable, and knocking off a couple of extra here and there really didn't make a difference. No, the reason for the painstaking research, tracing the females descended from a particular biblical tribe, was that he couldn't afford to overlook even *one* potential soul mate. Until he eliminated them all, the Fallen still had a chance to return to the Heavens.

That tribe had run almost exclusively to females, birthing girl children one after the other. Fortunately, that kind of genetic inheritance meant the tribe had therefore died out quickly, at least as far as names and birthrights were considered. Less fortunately, some of those females had lived on, intermarrying with other tribes, spreading their contaminated DNA far and wide. A genetic clusterfuck of gigantic proportions.

All of the potential soul mates he had discovered so far had come from these lines. He'd spent years sifting through public records until the unexpected boon of the Internet. The Internet was like stumbling on an all-you-can-eat buffet, what with the genealogy sites and fan clubs. He'd picked the females off as he—or minions like Eilor—found them.

Unfortunately, Eilor would have to try harder, or Cuthah would be in the market for an upgrade. Eilor had killed one soul mate—and lost two. Unacceptable.

"Two," Cuthah repeated, because he'd already had this conversation once. He kept his voice flat and unemotional. The facts were all that mattered right now, and the fact was that Eilor had got it all wrong.

"I got one," Eilor pointed out, clearly not wanting to be shortchanged. "Ming John." He, too, believed facts were facts.

"And lost two. Pelinor Arden and Mischka Baran."

"I'll find them." Eilor would. There weren't too many places a human could hide from the likes of *him*, even in the heart of the Goblin empire. Sooner or later, he'd catch up with them. And he'd kill them. It was all really quite simple.

It was still deliciously ironic, however, that the fallen angels running around on Earth had no clue that Michael really had left them a back door, a chance for redemption. Cuthah was doing all he could to keep it that way—and close the door for good.

There were three more names on Eilor's current list.

One down. Five to go. If the bloodline was in doubt, Cuthah still ordered the killings. If a few innocent females happened to end up on the wrong end of a blade, well, they were martyrs for the greater good. Cuthah had no doubt they'd be rewarded. Just not by him. Not now.

He stared at the bleeding rogue. Unfortunately, punishment just didn't seem to *stick* with Eilor. He seemed to thrive on his punishments and see them as some sign of favor.

Really, it made his job that much more difficult.

Cuthah flicked a finger casually, opening another thin slice in the rogue's skin, watching closer. When he saw the flicker of pain in the other's eye, he decided that might be enough. Finally. Eilor was bleeding from the wounds Cuthah had inflicted. The ribbons of pain that colored the rogue's aura were delicious, but—he looked down—he would need to replace the floor. Things had got rather messy this time.

The little human Eilor had collected earlier seemed horrified by the whole proceeding. She'd started by screaming—too loudly, so Eilor had been forced to hit her sooner than he wanted—and had finally subsided into terrified whimpers. Really, she seemed to think that someone would come to rescue her. Her naivety was delightful.

Still, perhaps it was time to check Eilor's violence. After all, eventually even Michael would notice and might start asking questions.

"Just so we're clear . . . ," Cuthah repeated calmly, because with rogues you couldn't be too clear. They tended to go haring off on their own quests, which was yet another disadvantage of using the insane to do your work. All that delightful brutality was paired with a childlike predictability, when it came to distraction. "You're going to go back to M City and you're going to find these two you lost. Find them, Eilor." He held up a cautionary finger. "Or I'll be very displeased. Again. I've Michael to placate as well, unless you'd like the archangel sticking his unwelcome nose into our little business. What he doesn't know doesn't hurt us, but imagine where his interest would lead."

The human whimpered. Again. Really, she was getting too tiresome. They all lived such protected lives that they caved at the first sign of violence. This one might have been related to one of the Fallen. Or not. Cuthah did not care particularly. She was still young and that meant that Eilor had broken her easily. Plus, she had a most exquisite sense of pain.

As he watched, Eilor picked up her hand, gently twisting her forearm. Blood streaked down the pale skin. "Lovely," Cuthah said absentmindedly. "A pity that I really do have to leave you now. And that I am in such a rush today. Perhaps another time? No?" He chuckled when she flinched, unable to control the tell-tale sign.

Eilor pressed a kiss against the raw flesh.

"Well, we'll finish up here now, then, and you can be on your way." Eilor's poor pet shot him a tremulously grateful look, under the mistaken impression that Cuthah would send her *home*. As if. Eilor had a rather more permanent solution in mind for his newest darling.

Across the room, Eilor practically quivered. The

rogue worshipped his punisher, which made him controllable. Eilor understood punishment—he simply preferred to be the one *doing* the punishing. Eilor's little human was an appetizer. A reminder of what he could have if he pleased Cuthah.

"Soon," Eilor said hungrily. His gaze never left the girl's quivering form. "I will have the last of the females on your list soon."

"Very good." With a soft, painful stroke of his long fingers, Cuthah took hold of the girl's wrist. Eilor understood violence and only violence, so Cuthah needed to make his point in Eilor's language. His tongue flicked out, tasting the blood that dotted his upper lip.

Eilor stared enviously.

When Eilor found the last two females, they would pay for all of these indignities.

"Maybe," Cuthah said thoughtfully, and Eilor knew bone deep that the casual tone was all pretence, "when you find these females, you should save one of them. Bring her here."

Cuthah had been a betrayer for almost all of those years and no one, not even that self-righteous Michael, had discovered the truth of his deception.

"Fine," he said, deliberately injecting a note of sullenness into his voice. Let Cuthah think him angry. Cowed. Submissive and resentful. He was not as stupid as his master seemed to think he was.

The next part of the proceeding was his favorite. His master took the little human with a brutal ferocity that Eilor knew he could never rival. His body tore through hers like a knife through butter. Rough and quick. It was certainly quick, which was Eilor's only regret. The female whimpered and then screamed. Once. Rather more messy than Eilor liked, but then, this wasn't really about Cuthah's pleasure. It was about teaching Eilor a lesson. He knew that. He could either have a female like that or he could take her place. The rules in Cuthah's world were quite simple. Fail. Or succeed. There was no middle ground.

"Both females. Two weeks," Cuthah said, pushing himself off the body. "Bring one here."

"And the other?"

"Kill her. I don't care which one you bring me. Just make sure that you *do* bring me one." His master strode toward the door. "And clean this mess up. Now. Or you'll have the Goblins down on you."

SEVEN

So he was a coldhearted bastard. Make that coldhearted and self-centered. Stepping away from the table, Brends flipped open his cell and punched in the familiar numbers. He'd recognized that face in Mischka's vid.

Mischka's AWOL cousin was Dathan's newest fuck partner.

The familiar voice growled a terse greeting over the line.

"I need your help," Brends snapped into the phone.

"Name it." The male on the other end didn't hesitate.

"You've got a female companion. A human."

"Yeah. Pell." Dathan's tone didn't give anything away, but from what Brends knew, the two had been friends for months now. He didn't know what game the other Goblin was playing, but it was a deep one. He'd smelled the lust rolling off the male and he couldn't understand why Dathan hadn't done something about it yet.

"Pell's cousin just showed up here, looking for her."

"I'm aware of that." Satisfaction filled Dathan's voice. Apparently, Mischka's little maneuver had played straight into Dathan's hands.

"You know where she is?"

"Right here with me." More satisfaction. Masculine

satisfaction. Yeah, Dathan finally had Pell exactly where he wanted her. No more unsatisfied lust for that Goblin. "Is there a problem?"

"Not if you keep your Pell far away from M City," Brends said.

There was a beat, and then Dathan said, "Care to tell me why? Might make my job easier. She's spooked enough that Mischka is on her ass. She'll run without much prodding. And I'll make sure she runs in the right direction. She thinks someone is following her."

Someone probably was. "Get her out of here. Let her know her suspicions are probably right and take her out into the countryside."

"Will do." A pause. "For how long?"

"I'll send you the all clear. But probably a couple of weeks."

"You know who's on her trail?"

"Yeah. Eilor." He gave the other male the truth, because he didn't think that Pell was just another human soul to Dathan. Not anymore. There was trouble brewing there, trouble that he'd sort out later. Hell, he'd never worried about it before. "You remember all those human females someone has been slaughtering in and around M City?" He continued when the other grunted. "That's Eilor, and he got another one. Killed Hushai, too." Quickly, he ran down the details for Dathan. "I'm sending you the vid we got. Take a look and tell me what you think." With a soft ping, his handheld finished the file upload to a secure site.

There was silence for several long moments and then, "None of our kind should make a kill like that."

"Not unless he's gone rogue."

The words hung in the air between them. "Which means I need to track the killer fast. Before he takes out one too many humans. Before he gets to another brother."

"Hell." Dathan cursed viciously. "Why now, Brends? Why target human females for so long and then switch to one of our kind? He has to know we'll come after him. The rogues are insane, Brends, but they're not stupid. That's a death warrant. He'd be lucky to be sent to the Preserves."

"Yeah. It means we've lost two of our number. One to the blade and one to the thirst. Take Pell and get out of town."

"To keep her safe."

"That too."

There was silence on the other end and then, "Right. Give me an hour. Two, tops. We'll be on the road and you can get on with whatever it is you have planned for the cousin."

Perfect. Dathan would spirit Pell away. That trail would distract Mischka, keep her motivated. And she'd have no one to turn to but Brends for help. Carrot. Stick. Simple. She'd be angry if she realized he'd manipulated her. But she'd get what she wanted.

And he'd get what he wanted. A clear shot at the killer. It would be simpler to convince her to help him, but he'd cover his bases. Just in case.

Because he always got what he wanted.

Always.

And he wanted Mischka Baran.

* * *

Get out of town or confront a homicidal maniac.

Not a difficult decision for Pell to make.

Soviet-era relics still dotted the city, half buried beneath the ruined hulks of the too-tall apartment buildings designed to house a human population that had grown too fast. Decaying churches, the paint of their bulb-shaped domes faded to a mere echo of color, poked their aging spires up into the almost perpetual twilight of the sky. A few bolder architects had built tall buildings of glass and steel, buildings that stepped over these lesser, squatter remnants of the past. Tangible reminders, she told herself, that the humans had gone up—and the paranormals had gone down. When the paranormals had first gone public, the newspapers had reported that one of the reasons they'd been able to hide so long was the vast underground network of metro tunnels.

For almost two decades after her kind learned that they were not the only race in this world, they'd refused to accept the paranormals as equals. Some paranormals had continued to hide underfoot, inhabiting the tunnels, becoming the dreaded things that went bump in the night. Others, like the Goblins, had set about acquiring the tools of power. Money. Connections. Real estate. Now, *they* owned the city and humans came to them.

When the Great Wars of the twenty-first century had taken place, the paranormals had watched their human neighbors go at it but hadn't interfered. Smart bastards. Much of the countryside between M City and Petersburg had been destroyed. There were still humans there, still the occasional paranormal holed up on his country estate, but most of the area was now a wild no-man's-land. If you couldn't fly by natural or mechanical means, you got yourself over that not-quite-empty space as fast as possible. Or you died out there. No one—human or paranormal—who lived out there was civilized. And most were barely sane. Worse was the occasional patch of complete wasteland, where one of the nuclear power plants that the Soviets had experimented with had breached its protective walls and spilled a lethal load of toxins out into the countryside. Rumor had it the Goblins used those places as some sort of holding ground for their rogue members.

No, getting out of town wasn't the issue. The issue was her traveling companion.

Pell eyed the Goblin pacing next to her. Dathan was big enough. Strong enough. And he'd made it perfectly clear that he wanted her. That he was going to take every opportunity she handed him to convince her to have sex with him. But he stopped when she said stop.

Part of her wished she could afford to say yes.

He bent his dark head toward her. He was too harsh, too dark to be conventionally handsome, but his face drew her. And his body? Well, she'd managed to restrain herself from running her hands all over that big, muscled frame.

Barely.

"You want to run, Pell," he coaxed in that low voice.

No, what she wanted to do was go to bed with him and stay there for at least a week. Yet she also wanted to stay alive. Which meant outrunning whatever—whoever—was on her trail. The fear that shot through her was a familiar, shaky thrill. "Where will we go?" she whispered.

"Away from here." Her companion's eyes darkened, almost glowing in the near darkness. "We'll head out into the countryside."

Straight into the heart of Goblin territory.

"And I'll be safe there?" She tilted her head back and stared up at her companion.

"I will keep you safe. But I'll expect something in return." His voice rolled out of the darkness, strangely formal.

So much for friendship. "You want me to pay you?"

"No, Pell," he said, his voice low and thick with need. "I want you to trust me. And I want you to give me your soul."

EIGHT

Mischka Baran's flat was a surprise.

A very interesting surprise.

Her neighborhood was precisely what Brends had expected—a handful of human holdouts who, unlike most of their kind, hadn't moved to the suburbs. Some of their kind still preferred to pretend nothing had changed.

With a lot of intimidation and a bit of cash, it was simple enough to get the building manager to let him into Mischka's flat. The Goblins interfered with human business more often than they admitted. A few greased palms here, a little computer voodoo there, and they got what they needed. Mischka Baran's flat was in a dinosaur of a building. Had that aging-dowager air of refinement gone to pieces. He'd bet the heating bills were a bitch and the hot water occasional. So what had drawn her here? He'd already tapped into her bank account. Mischka Baran made ends meet and could have lived in one of the newer, modern skyscrapers. Yet she'd chosen to live here.

As they stepped through the doorway, he reassessed.

Tasteful. Elegant. And unexpectedly sensual.

Her flat occupied one entire floor of the antiquated building, the kind of place you inherited rather than bought. Maybe she came from old money, he thought, although human definitions of *old* were still childishly young by his standards. He made a note to look up her bloodlines.

A bank of windows looked boldly out on the river. Two hours still until actual twilight, but already the light had faded to a soft gray. M City lived in an almost perpetual twilight, but this time of year, the water was even grayer and flatter than usual. Spring was coming, but the air hadn't warmed up yet and M City was still a cold, hostile landscape wherever you looked. They'd be fishing frozen drunks from the river for at least another month. From up here, though, you couldn't spot those unpleasant little details.

From up here, M City was downright pretty. You couldn't even see the club.

At first, there wasn't much for the boys to find. Three minutes confirmed that Mischka was just as tidy, just as disciplined as he'd suspected. There were no dirty dishes in the kitchen sink and even the condiments in the fridge were methodically ordered in neat lines. He didn't bother to check, but he'd have bet none of them was past its expiration date, either.

"Not much to look at," Nael complained. The soothing off-white tones of the flat had Brends agreeing mentally. As he searched, however, he realized that the cream-colored fabric was a sensual feast hidden in plain sight. Lush. Every pillow on the too-white sofa was of a different soft fabric. She was sitting on cashmere and velvet, surrounded by sensual indulgence masked in decorator elegance. There were no pets. Just a tasteful handful of silver-framed photos. Herself. An older couple. The damned cousin who'd started this whole mess. But there were layers here that had his gut clenching in anticipation.

He didn't think Mischka Baran was running a con, but he wanted confirmation. More important, he'd take—and use—any dirt he could dig up on her. Electronic records he'd hacked that morning merely revealed a decent amount of cash socked away in a safe savings account, bills paid on time, and a steady supply of books. Boring, well-reviewed, well-received titles.

Nothing blackmail worthy.

Nothing that gave him a hint of his ice princess's true colors. All he knew was, this white and cream was deceptively tranquil. Ice Princess had depths he had every intention of plumbing.

While Jorah worked through the living room shelf by shelf, Nael moved into the hall closet. The Goblin kept up a running commentary on the unexciting contents of said closet until Brends finally told him to shut the hell up. They'd disengaged her alarm system, but there was no point in drawing attention to what they were doing.

Christ, she probably had nice, normal human neighbors, some of whom were undoubtedly home even at this time of day.

The bathroom held a collection of bubble baths that interested him, but now was not the time to fantasize. Instead, he forced himself to check the drawers and then their undersides. He slid them out one at a time. Nothing.

In the end, he took the bedroom. He didn't want the boys in there. She had a closet full of clothes like the jersey number she'd worn to G2's that first night. All the shoes were neatly lined up on shoe racks. Not an item out of place. Hell, did she actually live here? She was a real-estate agent's wet dream; the place was picture-perfect, just waiting for a walk-through. When he hit the lingerie drawers in her dresser, however, he finally discovered her first vice. Simple, bold and expensive, the exquisite fabrics slid through his fingers. Not a white bra among the lot. Even the palest bra was a luscious peach-colored silk. Tucked under it all was the gun she'd threatened him with, a crisp owner's manual and the damned receipt. He didn't know if he felt better or worse that she went to work unarmed— or that she'd apparently considering returning the weapon and blowing his head off in practically the same breath.

Jorah strolled by the doorway, a laptop cradled in his arms. "You want us to download the hard drive?"

"Yeah." He'd go through it later.

"We could leave her a little present, let her know we were here?"

"Don't," he ordered. No. Mischka Baran had passed the test. He didn't believe she was personally involved with these murders, other than having had the bad luck to draw a killer's attention.

The only way left to get her to come to him was blackmail.

Her luscious cinnamon and cream scent was all over the damned room. There was no way to avoid it and every time he inhaled, his cock got a visceral reminder of the woman. She wasn't a journal keeper, but he hadn't expected that. There was a Post-it collection that would have put the average office building to shame, but again nothing incriminating. Or even vaguely embarrassing, unless being superhumanly well organized was a crime these days.

He finally hit pay dirt in the nightstand beside the cream-colored bed. No condoms. No lube. Mischka Baran either slept alone, took outrageous chances or expected her company to bring his own. She hadn't, however, even tried to hide the books. The stack of well-thumbed paperbacks included some rather esoteric Victorian erotica that you'd find in a collectibles section. If you were lucky. And only if you knew what to look for. He smiled devilishly. How very interesting.

Flipping open the first book he grabbed, he thumbed through the pages until he found a naughty domination and submission fantasy. Slid the book, marked with a particularly decadent scrap of silk lingerie, into his pocket. He'd return the book to her and she'd know that he'd been in her bedroom. That he knew what she'd been reading. And she'd recognize the invitation for what it was.

Eilor watched the team of Goblins leave Mischka Baran's flat. Stupid slut.

She'd chosen *them*.

Maybe, he'd wait to kill her. He'd waited that first meeting. There hadn't been enough time to clean the blade, to gut her. Besides, he didn't want to rush through the kill, liked to enjoy the death. In fact, why rush now? He'd found her scent and he'd never lost a trail yet. How much better if he could kill her and whatever Goblin she'd wrapped around her evil little finger.

Two for the price of one. He liked that.

Yes, he and this Brends Duranov would undoubtedly be having themselves a late-night meet and greet. All he needed to do was catch them alone. Better yet, he could use the girl to draw the male out. After it all, it had worked so beautifully with Hushai.

Slowly, he furled the massive wings until they were once again a black tattoo spanning his back. His wings had been restored to him so that he could play his part in Cuthah's great work.

He couldn't fail. He wouldn't.

Brends Duranov needed a serious ego check. Or a simpler explanation of the word *no*. Clearly, he had interpreted Mischka's words the previous night to mean "try again later."

Her first clue should have been the expensive town car that rolled smoothly to a stop in front of the tearoom where she worked. Usually, her clientele consisted of foreign tourists who arrived by the busload. The sleek car was as out of place here as she'd been at G2's the previous evening.

Nevertheless, the vehicle glided to a stop in front of her building, the driver apparently every bit as arrogant as his employer, since he parked blithely in a no-parking zone. Mischka's eyes narrowed when Brends got out, flanked by two bodyguards.

Hell. It felt good to curse, so she did it again. Out loud. The couple leaving the tearoom eyed her and picked up their pace. Clearly, they wouldn't be repeat guests.

She couldn't bring herself to care.

She slammed the reservations book shut. Oh, no, he didn't.

Looking up with as much nonchalance as she could feign, she eyed him as he strode through the door as if he owned the place. Just as large as she remembered. Just as smoking hot. His broad shoulders stretched the seams of a faded black T-shirt, moving with feline grace beneath a long leather duster. His dark hair brushed the collar, swinging freely in a black, come-fuck-me curtain that made her want to grab his face and hold him still for a kiss.

From the small wave of heated whispers she heard building behind her, there were several other women equally interested in leaving their mark on Brends Duranov. In another minute, he'd be inundated.

She didn't share.

And he wasn't a one-woman kind of guy.

"I said what I had to say last night," she said. He took another step toward her and she threw up a warding hand. "Back off, big guy."

He didn't stop coming, so she slipped back around the podium, hoping the furniture would be enough to hold him off. For now.

Slapping both palms down on the smooth wood, his eyes bored into her. "Nothing, darling," he said in that low, sexy drawl that had her thinking of bedrooms, "will keep me away. I promise you that, *dushka*, and I always keep my promises."

His eyes flickered, reminding her that he wasn't human, even if he was male. He was fighting something, something inside him that wanted out. She wasn't sure she wanted to be around when whatever it was came out.

"Bully for you," she said. "Consider your obligations here met." One slender hand gestured impatiently toward the door. "The door's waiting for you."

"You want me to go."

"He's quick tonight." She rolled her eyes. "Absolutely. Go. I've had a little 'me' time to do some thinking, and, before you entered the picture? I didn't have any concerns about my immortal soul. My previous offer stands. Fuck. Off. I'll find Pell all by my little lonesome."

"Right now, I want tea."

Was he kidding? Out of the corner of her eye, she spied her manager headed in their direction. Time to speed up Wonder Boy's departure. "No, you don't."

"Seat me," he repeated, "and we'll discuss what I want tonight."

"No." She wasn't doing this.

Apparently, whatever had happened in the hours they'd been separated hadn't left him in a charitable frame of mind either. "No," he growled low in his throat, as he moved to block her exit. Six-plus feet of hard, hot male standing between her and her exit.

If she hadn't spent the weeks since Pell's disappearance worrying about her cousin, she'd have considered exploring the possibilities. Too bad for Brends. It was his loss, as far as she was concerned.

"I need to talk to you," he said, clearly trying to

sound reasonable. Even as he leaned back against the door and made it absolutely impossible for her to go anywhere without his say-so.

"You talked. I listened. And then you wanted to buy me, lock, stock and barrel," she hissed. Why had she held back earlier? It felt so *good* to tell him exactly how she felt. And after all, it was his fault. Screw being mature about this. One smoking-hot kiss at his club and he thought he could walk all over her?

"He's looking for you," he said cryptically.

"Who?" she demanded.

"The rogue," he said. "Eilor. The one responsible for the bodies you found. Ming John. My brother, Hushai."

Her boss reached the podium and she considered the merits of quitting. On the spot. Not only did her boss recognize Brends, but he descended to a level of obsequious charm she hadn't believed possible.

"Mr. Duranov," the manager beamed. "It's an honor. We've got a lovely table right in front of the windows. You come right this way and we'll have you set up right away. If Ms. Baran is—" He paused, clearly not sure what was happening between the two of them.

Brends, the bastard, interjected smoothly. "I'd like Ms. Baran to join me."

Happy to have the relationship dilemma solved so easily, the manager bustled them over to the table and abandoned Mischka to her fate.

It was stay or go—and she wasn't naive. If she went, she and her manager would be having a very unpleasant heart-to-heart. Her bank account could handle the sudden unemployment, she reminded herself. So why wasn't she walking out the door right now?

Because you find him interesting, the small, traitorous voice reminded her. *Oh, and you really, really want to fuck him.*

"Sit down, Mischka." Brends patted the seat next to him, and she instantly disliked the expression on his face. Oh, he'd got his way with her boss and now . . . well, now thought he *had* something on her. She could see it on his face.

"I gave you my answer last night, Mr. Duranov."

He shook his head. "Brends," he said. "We settled that yesterday."

"Just because you manhandled me last night doesn't mean we're on a first-name basis now." Hell. Had the waiter heard? His beet red face led her to the obvious conclusion that he had. Quitting looked better and better.

"I need to get you out of here. Before Eilor shows up. You think the club and what happened to Ming John was bad?" One hard shoulder shrugged. "Nothing compared to what's going to happen if he gets his hands on you now."

"Mmm. Right." She looked up at him. "It's been a long day, Brends—a very, very long day. I'm off in twenty minutes and I'm going home. Your killer rogue has no idea who I am and no reason to want me."

"You won't be safe there. Not for long."

She closed her eyes wearily and then opened them. "I'm just not interested in your games tonight."

"Love," he said and his hand slid down along her arm, shackling her wrist lightly in a bracelet of hard fingers. "You need to hear me out."

As he leaned toward her, she caught her breath at

the dark promise in his eyes. Deliberately dominating her with his larger, harder body, crowding her backward away from the table until hard edge of her chair bit into her thighs through the thin wool of her uniform skirt. "This isn't a game," he warned. "Ming John's killer, Pell's stalker." Brends gestured at the windows in illustration. "He's been watching you."

"You can't know that for a fact," she pointed out, even though she could hear her heart racing in her ears.

"Oh, but I do." Brends braced a forearm against the table's white-covered top and stared over at her, fire burning in his eyes. "We got vid of the alley during the killing. Eilor has a vid-player with your picture."

That was impossible. Clearly impatient, Brends read the unspoken denial on her face. "You want to sit here," he continued, "and wait for him to catch up with you, that's a dangerous decision. You know it. I know it. I can keep you safe."

"For a price." A price she'd made it perfectly clear she had no intention of paying.

He shrugged, the heavy weight of his duster flowing around him. "Nothing in this world is free, *dushka*. You stop holding out on me, and I'll start helping."

"Did he have Pell's picture, too?" Just remembering the scene in the alley had Mischka battling to keep her morning bagel in her stomach and not splattered on the floor.

"Yeah, he did," he said, leaning back and crossing his big arms over his chest. "So what do you want to do?"

What could she do? Brends was one scary bastard and he wasn't even *human*. She didn't trust him. Or her libido. He was too used to giving orders—and having them followed. If she gave in to him, what independence would she have left?

"You find this killer if you want him. All I want is Pell," she finally said.

"We find her, and we find the killer. And trust me, love, I'll find her."

"In time? And in one piece?"

"If you'll help me." His eyes promised she'd be giving so much more than help. "Bond with me, and I'll help you. I'll keep you safe."

"I don't need anyone to keep me safe."

"You will. Your Pell is headed straight out of town. I'll tell you that one for free. You wouldn't last a day outside M City, and it would be irresponsible of me to let you try." He gave her a slow, heated smile.

He reached out, slid his hand through her hair, holding her head still for his kiss.

Despite the leashed violence of his body, the visible tension thrumming through him, the kiss was gentle. His lips pressed against hers. Resting. Waiting. Silently demanding entrance.

"Let me in, *dushka*," he growled when she hesitated. His thumb traced the damp seam of her mouth and she parted beneath his touch, the tip of her tongue darting out to lick him. He bit back a curse, his breathing growing rougher as he wrapped an arm around her and slid her up against the heat of his body.

"Give me your bond."

"Bond?" she gasped as her body betrayed her, melting in liquid welcome.

His knee nudged gently at her thighs. Coaxing her to part.

"Bond with me," he promised. "I'll keep you safe." His gaze drilled into hers. "Why not take what you want, baby?"

"Because," she said a little desperately as she put some space between them, searching for the right words. She shouldn't have to convince him that she was right. Because she *was*. You simply couldn't go around *taking* pleasure. Not the way he did. And not even—that secret part of her admitted—if you really wanted to. Convincing a fallen angel to behave was a Sisyphean task that she wasn't sure she was up to. "Because you just can't, Brends. It's not right."

"Why not?" he repeated. This time, when he looked at her, his eyes went all molten gold on her, the thick, rich color of sex. "A little pleasure never hurt anyone. So why deny yourself when you want it?" *Want me* hung between them in the air.

"I have responsibilities." Pelinor was out there some-where and Mischka couldn't afford any distractions. "I need to find my cousin, Brends."

He shook his head. "She's a big girl. Why should you have to go looking for her? Maybe she doesn't want to be found. Maybe she's decided to explore a little pleasure for herself." *Unlike you.* She heard the words even if he didn't speak them. The male sprawled next to her was the picture of sensual decadence. And yet she knew he could pull a weapon faster than any mem-ber of the MVD. He wouldn't hesitate to strike, either.

But she couldn't stop herself from staring at those hands, wondering what they would feel like stroking over her arm. Tracing an erotic path from the bare skin of her forearm along the bone to more private, hidden places.

"You want to," he said confidently. "You're tired of going through life without knowing."

"Knowing what?" She was a healthy woman. So she had fantasies. She was strong enough, disciplined enough, to keep those fantasies in her mind where they belonged. She was *not* going to share them with this fallen angel. Plus, since he'd fallen, he'd clearly made mistakes. Chosen wrongly.

She didn't make those kinds of mistakes.

Ever.

And yet she couldn't stop thinking about the fantasies. About *him*.

"You're a good girl," he said, and that low, hot drawl made her think of bedrooms, damn him. "You've probably always been a good girl—but you want to be bad, Mischka. You want to find out what it's like, even as you want to rescue your Pell more. What if there was a way for you to have both wishes?"

She shook her head. "No."

"No, you're not at bad girl at heart, or no, you no longer care what happens to this cousin of yours?"

He had to ask? Clearly, the Fall had knocked all sense of honor and moral decency out of him. Looking at him, she saw 100 percent bad boy, all hot, sexy and hard.

"Being there for Pell is the right thing to do."

"Right." He nodded sagely. "And you always do what's right. Good girl."

"Yes." He didn't have to make it sound so prissy.

Doing the right thing was, well, *right*. She shouldn't have to defend those kinds of choices. Not from his sort. *He*, on the other hand, clearly reveled in his bad choices.

"Because she's your cousin," he guessed. His hands stroked the fragile stem of the crystal flutes set out on the table.

"She's family."

"And family looks out for family." The dark eyes examined her. "It's a lovely sentiment, baby. Very *right*. I'm sure you'll find it satisfying." His tone said he doubted it.

"Doing the right thing? Yes. I will." She wouldn't let him see her doubts. "Someone has to look out for Pelinor, make sure that she's safe."

"And you've elected yourself. Personally, I'd leave her to make her own choices. Her own mistakes. But ruthlessness is a quality you lack, *dushka*." He made it sound like a character flaw. "You'd have to come out of that pristine ivory tower of yours and be *ruthless*."

"You don't think I can do mean?" She could, couldn't she?

Across the room, a woman's head swiveled, clearly mesmerized by the male before her. Mischka fought an unexpected urge to claw.

"No, *dushka*, not a chance. You like it nice and tidy. Follow the rules, that's what you do. You don't hurt others. You don't chuck them away when they become a liability, when they can't help you get where you need to go."

"You'd like that. One more piece of human fodder

for your fellow Goblins." She didn't like the bitter tone in her voice. She liked doing the right thing. Didn't she?

"No. Not particularly." He smiled, a dark wicked smile that she knew better than to trust. "But we've already established my preferences. I like to make mistakes. Or"—he shrugged—"I'm happy to settle for flat-out sin. Have you considered, though, that you're missing out on a valuable opportunity?"

She fought the urge to hit him. Hitting him would also be a mistake. Then he'd know that she could be an animal just like him. Deliberately, she laced her fingers in her lap. "What I want is to find Pelinor. And I want you to help me."

"You know my price."

"This isn't a personal favor. This is the right thing to do."

"I'm not sure it is." He shrugged. "And it is personal. It's what *you* want. If you want to go riding to the rescue of someone who hasn't asked you to stick your holier-than-thou nose into her business, I'm not going to stop you. But I'm not going to help you, either. Not unless you make it worth my while." His smile, when it came, was slow and hot. "Very worth my while."

"You don't know where she is."

"Do you?" he countered.

"I simply want to pool our information. Share our resources."

"No, what you want is to take advantage of my Fallen status. All those special skills Michael gave my kind. You want to use me like a hunting bitch to track your wayward cousin. I don't mind, baby, but I don't work for free. You pay my price and we'll find that cousin of yours. You refuse and you can be on your way. This is my world. My rules." He dropped his mouth to hers for a searing kiss.

"Games," she said—and nipped lightly at his lower lip. His head didn't move, even when her teeth broke his skin and the bright blood beaded the torn skin. "I'll make the left side match the right," she threatened.

"Promises," he purred. "Does that mean you're coming with me?"

"No."

"You forgot your book at home, baby."

The warm look in his eyes warned her. Whatever he was about to reveal, she wasn't going to want the entire tearoom seeing—and most of the room's female occupants were already craning their heads, trying to see what was happening at their table.

He slid the book across the table to her as her boss came scurrying up with a large tea tray. "Compliments of the house," he said, and beat a hasty retreat.

She wrapped her fingers around the volume. He'd been in her flat. That was *her* book. She steadfastly refused to read the title. She knew what he'd found, what she was holding. "Go away. I don't want you here."

"You will," he said confidently, "but you need to start using logic, baby. Forget about feelings. They're just going to get in the way."

"And aren't you the cool one," she snapped. She did use logic, and logically speaking, trying to bargain with Brends was, well, rather like trying to bargain with the devil. When she tried to rise, his hand snapped out and shackled her wrist.

"Sit down," he said coolly in a voice colder than the choppy waters of the Moskva river. He meant business now.

"You want to get me fired?" Although given the way her boss was kissing up to her unwanted companion, staying seated might not be a bad way to *keep* her job.

"No." He shoved his hand through his hair. "But I do want you to listen to me." He let go of her wrist. "We got off on the wrong foot last night."

"Really." She stared at him. "So you *don't* want to fuck me senseless and/or purchase my soul from me for an as-yet-unspecified favor. That's a relief and I appreciate your making the trek all this way into human turf to tell me so. Now, leave."

He shot her a look. The woman two tables over looked like she was going to come in her seat. Lovely. "That offer still stands. I haven't changed my mind about wanting you and I still think we can help each other out."

"I'm not convinced." She leaned back in her seat and watched him pour out tea with those strong, confident hands. He slid the glass cup into a holder and handed it to her. "You look like you could use it. Look, I know the last few days have come as a shock."

"You think? First my cousin runs off with a Goblin and then you start complicating my life. I'd say that absolutely qualifies as a shocker."

He acknowledged the hit with a wry nod of his

head. "Yeah. So you're pissed. I get it. But I still think you're overlooking what I can do. Look, give me an afternoon. What's the most you have to lose?"

My soul.

NINE

What on earth had possessed her? Two hours later, Mischka still couldn't believe she'd agreed to give him an afternoon. She couldn't seriously be contemplating a working partnership with a fallen angel, could she? Because they both knew he was merely marking time until he either seduced her or moved on to an easier target.

He'd suggested visiting Ming John's flat, a logical idea. If Ming John had been deliberately targeted— and after viewing Brends's security vid and the images his tech team had extracted from the killer's vid-player, she was inclined to agree with him—then they needed to determine why.

Because Pell was on that list as well. Not to mention Mischka herself.

Ming John's flat was guarded by a particularly ferocious, five-foot-tall babushka, who clearly felt letting either of them in before they'd provided character references and a security deposit was bad for business. Not to mention her immortal soul. She kept sneaking glances at Brends and crossing herself, making the rosary that spilled from her buttoned-up sweater chime musically.

"You, maybe," the landlady said, pointing at Mischka. She made another not-so-surreptitious sign of the cross.

"Him, I don't think so. He doesn't look so trustworthy. A nice girl like you can do much better. You should upgrade." She eyed Brends suspiciously.

Upgrade? She eyed Brends to see how he was taking this disparaging dismissal of his charms, but he was grinning.

The cold had Mischka's nipples pebbling against the thin fabric of her dress. Erotic heat swept over him. She was going to taste so good. All he had to do was seduce her.

"You'd never do better than me, and we both know it." He crossed his arms over his chest, shooting another lazy smile in the landlady's direction.

"Stop it," she hissed back.

It was time to end the pleasantries, however, and get on with the afternoon's business. Fortunately, as he'd suspected, Ming John's landlady had the delightfully flexible morals of the perpetually cash-strapped, which quickly outweighed her squeamishness about dealing with Goblins. She cheerfully pocketed the cash Brends offered and made no bones about it. Winter was long and she'd have more heating bills before summer came. Since the girl was dead—God rest her soul—there was no point in being impractical. She'd sell information if it covered the last month's rent. And who would want to rent the room now? The running commentary was enough, Brends decided, to drive a male insane.

"My last tenant, murdered—you don't think that would turn off prospective tenants? I do," she said as she turned the key in the lock. "They'll wonder if they're next. And why not? A perfectly nice girl like that," she added. "American. Didn't bother a soul and such a help. Always wanting to practice, practice, practice with her Russian. You're one of them, aren't you?" She turned her gaze on Brends and he realized that the old woman was neither as batty nor as unobservant as he'd believed. "You tell me, since it appears to have been one of your kind that did her."

Mischka intervened. Maybe she was afraid that he'd tell the old woman the truth.

"It wasn't him," she said decisively. "Do you think I'd bring him here, if I believed he was a killer?"

The old woman nodded understandingly. "Right, dear. He didn't kill this one. Doesn't mean he hasn't killed others, now, does it?"

Since Mischka was clearly at a loss for words after that conversational bombshell, Brends stepped in smoothly because, after all, the old woman was right. He'd done more than his share of killing. "She's got you there, darling," he noted smoothly, stepping past the old woman. When his hand wrapped around the doorknob and the gnarled fingers, he thought for a moment she'd call his bluff. Then her fingers slid away.

"All right," she conceded. "I'll let you get on with it. You ring me when you're done and I'll close up. Oh," she added as an afterthought, "and she'd just started seeing someone new. Big fellow," landlady said, looking curiously from Brends to Mischka. "Big as your fellow here. Didn't know they grew them like that around here."

Brends waited until he'd seen the landlady clear the landing before he snapped the door shut. And locked it for good measure.

Unlike Mischka's flat, Ming John's room was typical. Just another M City flat with nothing out of the ordinary about it.

"The landlady said she was an exchange student." Mischka sorted methodically through the haphazard piles of papers on the counter of the tiny kitchenette. "She gave people English lessons."

The flat had been let furnished. It smelled faintly of mold and old hot plates and books. Tucked in one corner was an iron bedstead that doubled as a sofa. Someone, presumably Ming, had arranged a colorful knitted quilt on top of the lumpy surface and lined up a series of small, hard pillows at right angles. The closet was crammed full of American mall wear. Not to mention more stacks of books and newspapers and magazines, unfamiliar Russian words circled. A dog-eared dictionary sat on the floor in the middle of the room. Ming John had been young. Carefree.

So why had she been targeted? Why Mischka's cousin?

On the surface, the two females had little in common other than a taste for Goblin clubs.

"What made her special?" Impatiently, he tapped a finger against his thigh. "This is a waste of time. It would be quicker to watch for our rogue and bag him when he makes his next move."

"Quicker for whom?" Ignoring him, she opened and closed the drawers of a small dresser, rifling neatly through the contents from top to bottom. Periodically, she stopped and turned over a piece of paper tucked beneath the layers of lingerie and inexpensive cotton. Apparently, Ming John had possessed the usual human traits, including the misplaced belief that there was no safer place for hiding personal secrets than in one's lingerie drawer.

"Me. Us." He gestured impatiently.

"Mmm." She acknowledged his point absentmindedly, carefully unfolding a creased piece of paper and reading its contents. When she bit back a smile and refolded the paper to its original dimensions, Brends frowned.

"Personal," she mouthed. Shit, this whole thing was personal. And then she returned to their original topic of conversation as if she had never abandoned the thread. "Quicker for you maybe, but you leave the rogue out there and he'll be killing while you wait for him to fall into your trap."

Probably. But those would be human casualties and acceptable. He opened his mouth, but she forestalled him. "And yes, it matters. You can't just keep killing humans, Brends, even if you don't think we're worth much on your cosmic Richter scale. We matter, too."

Right. Clearly, it mattered to *her*. "All right," he said, surprising himself. "So what do you expect to find here? A note from the killer explaining his modus operandi and outlining his next steps?"

She shot him a look he had no problem interpreting. "Just keep looking."

Right. If it mattered that much to her, he'd sort through this inconsequential pile of human leftovers. At the very least, someone needed to pack up the personal items to ship back to Ming John's family. That someone might as well be him.

He flipped open the cell. Twenty minutes later,

there was a stack of cardboard boxes lying on the floor of the small room. Mischka stared at him. "What?" He eyed her. "You want to sort out her stuff? Fine. We'll box it, too—someone has to ship it home."

"My God," she said, looking at him as if he'd grown a spare head. "The big bad Goblin finds a heart."

Not really. It would get them out of here faster if Mischka weren't constantly retracing her steps. And it would make things easier if she couldn't argue that they must have overlooked something. If the gesture made Mischka Baran a little more amenable to him, well, that was just an extra bonus, wasn't it?

Two hours and ten boxes later, he was holding a cheap Bible and making a mental note to recruit Mischka Baran for his team of trackers. The Bible was standard issue, straight from a hotel room. Tucked between the tissue-thin pages, however, was a sheaf of printouts from a genealogy website with a few phone numbers scrawled in the margins.

"Genealogy?" Mischka leaned in to read the printouts.

"Yeah. She could have been looking for long-lost relatives. Clearly, though, she had a habit of reading the genealogy forums." The printouts were dated over a six-month period and it appeared that Ming John had been a frequent poster.

"Or not." Mischka chewed thoughtfully on her lower lip. "She came here to practice her Russian, not to look up long-lost aunts and uncles."

"That's what she claimed." He flipped open her passport, examining the picture. The image was barely thumbnail sized, a small, grainy moment in time. When he pressed the picture, a little 3-D revolving image appeared above the passport, rotating sadly in place. Leftover pixels that didn't matter anymore. Ming John was never going home.

Mischka flipped rapidly through the papers. "Look at this."

He leaned in, savoring the scent of her hair. She shot him a look but didn't say anything. Score one for him, he decided. She was pointing to one of the names Ming John had found. Pelinor.

"Pell was related to Ming John," he said.

Mischka shook her head. "Not as far as I knew. Certainly not closely. These charts don't indicate a close connection, just a distant family relationship."

There were other names on the bottom of that family tree. Pell. Mischka. And at least another twenty names. All female. All scattered to the four corners of the globe, if the names were anything to go by. So what connected them?

"You recognize any of them?"

"No." He didn't, although he felt as if he should.

"Any chance they're regulars at your club?"

"You think we're looking for a fanatic, a Goblin hater?"

"It's a possibility." She set the pages down carefully, smoothing the edges. "Lots of people hate Goblins."

"The root of all evil? A blot to be wiped from the face of the Earth?" Hell, he had the same thoughts half the time. He just hadn't gutted anyone based on those convictions. There was something more happening here.

She shook her head, but in this case, he wasn't sure her *no* was actually a denial. "Some people really hate

Goblins, Brends. If Ming John had"—she hesitated—"bonded with one, maybe that's the reason she was targeted."

"Maybe. But I don't think it's that simple. Women aren't the only ones who sell out to us, love. The male of your species is just as interested in what we have to offer. So how come there are no male names on that list?"

"Good point." She tapped a pencil against her teeth until he swatted it lightly out of her hand.

"He had your pic, too. Maybe there's another connection. I think it's time to do a little digging on the Internet."

Of course they ended up back at her place. Mischka was surprised she hadn't seen it coming. Brends was a master seducer, and the delicious sinking sensation in her stomach—and lower—warned her that she was going to be putty in his talented hands once he really got started.

The question was, did she honestly mind?

She certainly hadn't intended to spend the afternoon with him—or make him dinner. But that was what she'd done. When he wanted candles, however, she'd drawn the line and turned the overhead light up. All the way. Now they were dining in the hard blaze of white light. No romantic lighting for him.

She had relented when he wandered over to her small wine collection and ran a knowing finger along the bottles. Since she appreciated a good wine with dinner as much as the next person, she'd caved on that one. There was no point in punishing herself.

"Grab a white." It would pair perfectly with the pasta in clam sauce she'd made.

His lips quirked into a smile as he deliberately withdrew a bottle of red from the rack. She raised an eyebrow at him.

"Everything here"—he waved a hand toward the living room she'd spent months decorating—"is white. Cream. Deceptively colorless."

She liked her flat. It was peaceful. It was the haven where she retreated.

"I like white."

"I know. It's calm." Effortlessly, he popped the cork on the bottle he'd selected. "Very relaxing. But just a tad"—he raised an eyebrow—"predictable, don't you think?"

"So I like white," she repeated. "Save the psycho-analysis for someone who cares."

An hour later, pushing her plate to one side, she curled up on the couch and let her fingers fly over the keyboard of her laptop, pulling up the genealogy sites Ming John had visited. She'd already stacked the printouts neatly in front of her, organized by site and then by date.

"You're going to break your back," he observed. Sprawled on the matching cream-colored sofa, a glass of wine cupped casually in his large hand, that strange, curious warmth lit Brends's eyes. He looked harmlessly sexy, slightly sleepy, but she knew better. Give him an inch and he'd be all over her. For some reason, she was now the challenge of the week.

"I'm comfortable," she argued, although she knew

he was right. Sit this way too long and her back would tell her all about it tomorrow.

"I wouldn't have pegged you for a sloucher." Those warm eyes examined her again.

She shrugged. Too bad for him. "Look at this."

He leaned over, his hand tracing the lines on the page. His body was wonderfully warm. How long had it been since she'd had someone to sit on the couch with?

She cleared her throat. "Seems as though some of these women, far, far back on the family tree, share common ancestors."

The next search made her stomach lurch. There were ten names on the first page. Three of those women were dead. Pics from the newspaper flashed by on her laptop. Murdered.

"He's been doing this for decades," Brends said grimly, eying the dates.

"So we have to find Pell," she said desperately.

His gaze held hers. "Or we wait."

"For what? The next dead body?"

"Yeah." He reached out and tapped a key to replay the search. "Something like that."

"No," she said desperately. "You can't do that, Brends. You're not dangling my cousin in front of some deranged Goblin like a piece of raw chicken on a string."

"We're not piranhas, love."

"No, you're cold bastards," she said bitterly. "Probably the reason why you got kicked out of the Heavens in the first place."

"I don't follow rules," he said, and that cold look in

his eyes stopped her dead. He meant every word. "I break them. Ask Michael."

"Michael?"

"The Heavens' archangel and my pain in the ass. He decided I needed an intervention, a lesson in what happens when the Heavens' guardians don't toe the line. I decided I disagreed." The mean, hard tone of his voice told her more clearly than his words how he'd worded his disagreement. Violently.

The look on her face probably did all the speaking for her. Hell. She couldn't double-park without looking over her shoulder for the traffic cop. So the equivalent of a cosmic "Fuck you"? Way out of her league. Part of her, however, admired that kind of balls. The other part was busy realizing that sharing a sofa with the heavenly equivalent of a convicted felon wasn't her wisest move.

"You walked away." He looked at her, and shit, she remembered. "Fell, I mean." Well, wasn't that the gaffe of the century? He might have parted ways with the Heavens' host, but it hadn't been amicable and he hadn't won that particular battle.

"I got my ass handed to me," he snarled. "Don't you pity me, *dushka*. I'd do it again."

Hell. She didn't pity him. She *envied* him. He'd broken all the rules and then he'd taken the punishment and made that *his* as well. She opened her mouth to say so and then closed it. Why would he believe her?

"Why?" she said instead.

He reached for her hand and she let him take it, enjoying the contrast between his darker skin and her paler coloring. His large, warm fingers wrapped around hers, swallowing her up in heat and masculine strength.

"Maybe I just like breaking the rules." She tugged, but he wouldn't release her. "You came looking for a bad boy, Mischka," he growled. "You shouldn't be surprised that you found one."

He wasn't just a bad boy, was he? *Stupid,* she chided herself. He wasn't a fixer-upper project she was considering and she wasn't in the market. Not really. He'd made it perfectly clear that he wasn't helping her until she paid his price.

"You had a reason," she said, suddenly sure. He was too disciplined, too *something* to have thrown away the Heavens on a whim. And he hadn't been the only angel who fell. Thousands of them had been booted, if she remembered her Sunday-school classes correctly. So there had to have been a damn good reason.

"Anarchy, baby," he said lightly. "We picked a fight and we lost." The hard look in his eyes, however, said that he hadn't taken that loss lightly. "Losers get their asses kicked out of the Heavens. It's in the rule book."

"You have a rule book?"

His fingers slid along hers, finding pressure points she hadn't known existed. Massaged. She could feel herself melting into a boneless puddle of pleasure and she'd sworn she'd resist.

"Not anymore," he said.

Sex, Brends decided virtuously. He was going to give Mischka all the luxurious, self-indulgent sex she could handle. She was wound so tight she was making *him* hurt.

Maybe he'd make her ask for it. For a long, delicious moment his mind veered wildly off course, contemplating the possibility of Mischka Baran naked, wet and spread—just for him. He could lick that pink, creamy skin from the bottom to the top. Could savor all the bits she'd kept so carefully hidden away from the world.

Right.

Not happening.

His companion wrapped her arms around her middle. She was wearing a peach-colored cardigan with buttons that drove him to distraction. As if she thought he'd rip the damn thing off her if she didn't hold on to it. What would it take to make her let go?

"Stop staring," she said. "This is a working dinner. Not an invitation to have sex." That was his female: blunt as a two-by-four.

He was offering her any favor she wanted—what more could she possibly *want?* Because clearly, she wanted more from him than really hot sex and a convenient quid pro quo.

"I don't go to bed with strangers."

That caution might have been warranted. She didn't trust him—and she shouldn't.

"After everything we've been through, love, how could you consider me a stranger? What more do you need to know?" If she wanted details, he could produce details.

Her sigh was not encouraging. "I can't give you a list, Brends. It doesn't work like that. Screw this. You want to be a dildo with legs? No, thanks."

"You want happily ever after?" He growled. This

was a first, he thought. He'd always been enough for the females in his life before. None of them had ever questioned what he could offer.

"No." She shook her head, that wicked hair of hers sliding along her cheek. "Not happily ever after, but something in between, Brends. Sex isn't enough."

"You've never tried it." He pointed out the obvious. She didn't know what she was missing.

"I'm not a virgin."

He'd never understood the virgin fantasies some of his darker brothers enjoyed so much. Now, he did. To be the first, the only. To mark her so indelibly. Yeah, he'd like that.

"Fine." The stab of possessiveness was unexpected, so he ignored it. Or tried. "But you've never had hot, no-strings-attached sex." He eyed her confidently.

"So I'm particular." She shrugged. "I don't hop into bed with the first man I meet when I've got an itch to scratch. I like to know the man I sleep with, Brends, and I don't know you."

"Tell me about your first time." Deliberately, he switched the conversation back to sex. That, he was comfortable with. He didn't understand this need for emotions she kept dragging back into their conversation. Either she wanted him, or she didn't. It was that simple.

She shook her head. Hell, he was tired of her denying him all the time. He wanted her moaning *Yes, yes* and *Give me more.* So why was he sticking around? *Because,* that little voice he couldn't quite shake whispered, *you know the rogue will come after her, sooner or later.* Sometimes when you hunted, you pursued—and sometimes, you hunkered down and waited for the prey to come to you. This was a hunker-down-and-wait moment. He knew it in his bones.

Because she intrigues you, some other, unfamiliar voice whispered.

"This isn't about me, Brends. This is about you. You want me to open up to you, to let you into my head." *In bed,* his head supplied, but this time he kept his mouth shut. "But first, you need to let *me* into *yours.* I don't know who you are."

You don't want to, he thought, but what he said was, "There's nothing to know." Before she could protest, he smoothly added. "Although I think you should consider it. The really hot sex part."

"Really." She eyed him. "Thanks for the update, Captain Obvious."

He smiled slowly. "Of course, that would mean being a *very* bad girl, wouldn't it, Mischka?"

She shook her head. "I told you: Pell comes first. I'm not abandoning her, Brends. I need to know she's safe. That she's not in over her head. She never stops to think."

Thinking was the last thing on Dathan's agenda for Pell tonight, so there was no point in pursuing that avenue. "The problem as I see it," he said, leaning forward, "is that *you* don't know *how* to be bad."

"No." Was that a touch of wistfulness he heard in her voice? "No, I don't."

His ice princess was clearly gaining her second wind. She'd snapped the laptop lid shut with a little more force than was necessary, so he figured she was working up to tossing his ass out her door. Still, she'd just handed him a delicious clue to who she was.

His Mischka wanted desperately to throw caution to the wind and be a bad girl. But she either couldn't or wouldn't.

He was betting on the latter.

His good-night kiss scorched her toes. "Dream of me, *dushka*." Lifting his head, Brends stared down at her for a long, hot moment. She was tempted to drag his head back down to hers.

"You dream of me," she countered.

His slow, hot smile wasn't fair. "Deal," he said. "We can compare notes tomorrow."

Watching the door close behind her Goblin, Mischka had to ask herself just when he'd become *her* Goblin—and why she was tempted to run after him.

Just one night. One night of smoking-hot, irresponsible, impossible pleasure.

Emphasis on *irresponsible*.

She couldn't. Pell was out there, just waiting to be found, and Mischka had a perfectly satisfactory life of her own to live. Alone. Besides, bad boy there was a Goblin. No way was she dating a paranormal, and selling him her soul was definitely off-limits.

He probably hadn't reached the street, was probably still trapped in her antiquated lift, when she remembered the book he'd returned to her earlier. Pulled it to her.

She should have been angry that he'd been in her flat uninvited. Instead, she was curious. He'd found her Victorian erotica, a favorite she kept in the bedside table.

He'd obviously flipped through the book. Clues. He was handing her clues, one after the other. If she wanted to, she could connect the dots. Discover what *he* fantasized about.

The thin silk of her favorite panties marked a page in the book. Almost, she could imagine the silk was still warm. He'd held them. Touched the silk that had touched her skin.

She recognized the message.

Page fifty-three.

If she dared.

TEN

"A bathhouse? You're taking me to a bathhouse?" Pell glared up at Dathan as if he'd just suggested she join him in a puppy slaughter and wiener roast.

Of course, she'd probably never visited a bathhouse before. Had never dared. The rumors flew, fast and furious. Some said bathhouses were entry points to other realms, highways to underworlds, and you never knew what you might encounter. Those rumors were undoubtedly exaggerated, and yet there was still a strange sense of exotic, erotic excitement in the air. The bathhouse was a strange pleasure palace: a hot, damp world whose main trade was sex. Anything went in the steam rooms and soaking pools. For all her bravado, his Pell was strangely naive.

He ran a possessive thumb over her mouth. Fought the urge to back her up against the wall and plunder her mouth with his tongue.

Maybe after their house call on his brothers.

Or, hell, during, if she was up for that. He let himself indulge in the fantasy as he shouldered the door to the sauna open and strode down the narrow hallway that disappeared behind the desk. He shucked his shirt and dropped it on the floor. From the looks of the mess, they were the last to arrive.

"I don't think—" she began and then stopped.

Dead in her tracks.

Without looking around, he reached behind him and wrapped his fingers around the delicate bones of her wrist. She was so small, this human female of his. He had an uncomfortable feeling that this night would make that clearer than he wanted.

"Good," he said, urging her gently toward the bright shadow of the open doorway. Steam billowed out in a thick, wet cloud. "Don't think. Act." If there were only a mental incantation he could use to make her lose her inhibitions—in the approximately three seconds they had before she got a real good eyeful of naked Goblin— he'd have done it.

Instead, he just kept drawing her forward.

"I'm not going in there. Really, Dathan." There were some things that she apparently felt the need to pro-test. At length. Stripping down to her skivvies in mixed company was clearly one of them. He was starting to wonder how many of those stories she'd told about her travels were merely stories. Clearly, most of them couldn't have been autobiographical. He ignored the twinge of pleasure that thought afforded him.

"Suit yourself." His hands went to the waistband of his jeans, pushing the denim down his muscled thighs.

"Lady?" A small, high-pitched voice right behind her ear had her shrieking. Damn, it was going to be a long night.

The voice in her ear belonged to a daemon.

A full-fledged, itsy-bitsy daemon. Who acted for all the world like a housekeeper, twitching Dathan's clothes into proper lines on their hangers. Small and red skinned, the half-vaporous creature seemed to flux into existence and then vanish from sight the next. It was nauseating. Couldn't he stand still? Apparently not.

"May I help you disrobe? Perhaps you would care for a towel?"

Hell, yes, she would. She grabbed the large expanse of expensive cotton from the daemon's tiny hands—it was a wonder that the fabric's weight hadn't dragged him down to the ground—and wrapped it around herself. Beneath the concealing folds, she kicked off her sweats and then looked for a place to put them.

The daemon swooped down, plucking the offending fabric from her.

"What are you?" she asked. Should she be demanding a coat check for her clothes? Or was she in far greater danger than facing a long, wet walk back to her place sans clothes and shoes?

"These are the private rooms," Dathan explained. "If you came to the public rooms, Barq here would use his glamour. Wouldn't he?" He eyed the little daemon sternly, who chirruped with glee. For a moment, the daemon vanished and in its place stood a blandly good-looking but nondescript man in a standard khaki spa uniform. Then the illusion vanished and the little daemon was zinging merrily about the room again. "He prefers his natural form."

"What am I doing here?" She was *so* out of her league.

"It's simple." His dark eyes laughed at her. "Strip. Warm steam. Hot water. Cold water. More steam. I guarantee that you'll end up half cooked and blissfully enervated."

"You're sure none of the Goblins we're meeting eat people?" she asked suspiciously.

"Yes." He rolled his eyes. "We have far better taste."

The bath daemon was twitching at her T-shirt now, so she let the little creature pull the cotton over her head while she kept a death grip on her towel. "Miss," it said, and hummed pleasurably as it folded her poor, abused clothes into a set of perfect right angles that the Marine Corps would have envied.

Dathan was blithely shucking off his boxers.

And he hadn't bothered to do more with his towel than drape it over his arm. He could have posed for a Calvin Klein underwear ad. His abdomen all sexy grooves and ridges. His back, though— She swallowed. Hard, white lines, both thin and thick, some ridged and others smooth, made a cruel road map of his golden skin. As if someone had ripped the skin from his back. His wings had been there once, she realized.

"Get used to it," he said, and turned away from her, striding toward the steam-belching door on the far side of the room. Somehow she knew he was challenging her to do more than just take off her clothes and enter the sauna; no, he was demanding she enter his world completely.

"Trust me," Dathan said, holding out his hand. "Bond with me tonight."

The strange thing was that she did trust him. She was the one who shouldn't be trusted, the one who always ran off. "Yes," she said, and took the outstretched hand.

He pulled open the low door. Steam billowed out in thick, white cloud. Strangely scented, but not unpleasant, she decided. "Deep breath now," Dathan ordered.

His fingers stroked a small, sensuous waltz over her the veins of her wrist. Soothing and arousing. "And in you go, darling."

"You'll be right behind me?"

"Right behind you, love, every step of the way."

She could do this. Inhaling, she stepped through the darkened doorway.

"She's pink." The deep, raspy voice slid out of the steam-filled room like sandpaper over wood. "Did you bring us a new playmate, Dathan?" The fallen angel stretched his arms behind his head, leaning back against the damp walls as he stared at the two newcomers, his hard bark of laughter drowning out her splutter of denial. "A shy one, Dathan. You brought us a shy one. It's going to be a long night."

"What the hell is he talking about?" Pell hissed, driving her elbow into Dathan's side. He grunted but looked unconcerned, merely hitching his towel lower on his hips. *Washboard abs*, she thought. Although she doubted he'd got his from the gym. With a second grunt, he shoveled her onto one of the low benches that lined the room.

"Relax," he said. "Vkhin's a friend."

Right. Easy for him to say. He wasn't the one being eyed up as a potential snack by a damned Goblin. The male on the other side of the room had to be well over six feet tall. She didn't give a rat's ass for her chances if she had to fight. In a space this small, strength would count most.

"Cheerful little thing, isn't she?" Vkhin shifted. She caught a glimpse of saturnine features through the thick blanket of wet steam. A Hollywood producer would have had a field day with the high cheekbones and the dark eyes; the fallen angel would have spent every day of his career cast as the tortured hero. His face said he'd been to hell and back, lined with scars so old they were merely faint silver. His eyes, however, warned that he'd never left the underworld. He'd brought it with him, buried deep inside his psyche.

"Try me," she warned, "and you'll find out how cheerful I am."

"What's with her?" A second voice moved closer.

Her eyes opened wide. "Two of them? I thought you were looking for ambience, Dathan."

A knowing smile curled Dathan's mouth and he picked up her hand, the familiar gesture throwing her off balance. She expected him to touch her as he always had. Instead of the soothing stroke of his palms rubbing the tension from her, he sucked one finger into the hot, wet cavern of his mouth. His sharp nip sent a bright pulse of pleasure straight to her pussy. A boneless lassitude was growing on her in the sensual heat of the bathhouse. She wasn't sure she cared anymore what kinky habits Dathan had.

"Why are they here?" She did still care about that.

"Nael and Vkhin? For us." His dark eyes watched her and this time she finally recognized the slow, heated predator's gaze. He wasn't safe at all, she realized. This wasn't just the friend she'd known for so long. This male was more. More dangerous. More heated. Too much.

"I'm still Dathan," he said, correctly interpreting the panic in her eyes. "You know me, Pell. You trust me. Trust me right now. Nael and Vkhin won't touch you unless you want them to."

"You said *you* wanted to bond with me."

"Yes." His eyes never left hers. "I do. We're going to, right now."

"So why are they here?" She didn't do threesomes, foursomes or moresomes.

"Witnesses," he said reluctantly. Oh, hell no, he didn't. No way. She shoved upward from the polished wooden seat, but a large hand clamped down on her shoulder.

"Oh, no." She didn't do watchers either. "I'm not into exhibition, Dathan."

"How do you know?"

A large drop of sweat rolled down her cheek. She wasn't going to win any beauty prizes here. A dark hand came out of the steam, offering a thick towel. Gratefully, she took it, pressing the fabric against her forehead.

"How do you know?" he repeated when she didn't answer. That voice was sinful, a luscious lure to think about all the forbidden carnal acts she'd ever read about.

Ever fantasized about.

"You think about it, Pell," Dathan promised. "You think about what will give you the most pleasure and I'll provide it. Anything you want. Everything."

Softly, he moved the towel down her throat, tracing the smooth line of her body. Long and sweet and hot. He'd touched her as a friend. Now, for the first time, he touched her as a lover.

"Tell me your fantasies." He made the words a sultry whisper in the lush darkness. Her eyelashes flickered as she considered his offer.

"What makes you think I fantasize?" The tone was drowsy, a sultry question, but she knew the sudden tension in her bare body made her interest clear.

At first, she was uncomfortable. After long moments of the delicious, firm strokes pulling along her skin and nothing more, she relaxed. Nothing was expected of her. She couldn't screw this up. His simple enjoyment of her body was a pleasure she couldn't have imagined, the simple act of opening up to him more intimate than she'd dreamed possible. Where she'd initially felt vulnerable, she now felt cherished, wrapped in a cocoon of shadows and warmth and a delicious lethargy.

The padded bench beneath her was all that anchored her and kept her from floating off into the soft pleasure. The cotton towel was a too-hot weight and she preferred the delicious coolness as he slid the unwanted fabric from her.

His whispered "May I?" promised darker, sweeter pleasures.

Dathan's firm hands slid up to her shoulders, then past them. The erotic scrape of his nails against her scalp found pleasure points she hadn't known existed. Arousal was a slow heartbeat of anticipation centered in her heated core. She didn't understand why he was the one lover who could arouse her so. She'd pushed him away. She'd been afraid that he wouldn't really want her, couldn't want her. She was still terrified that she would lose her friend, that the darkly sensuous lover would replace the male who'd always been there.

"No more choices, baby," he demanded, and she knew her frisson of attraction didn't escape those dark, watching eyes. He knew what she liked. There was no pretending this wasn't happening. So why not embrace the moment? It wasn't her choice any longer. Pleasure was a stealthy march over her body. Yes, why not enjoy this? Why not enjoy what he could offer?

She stretched slowly and luxuriously, her muscles and sinews and skin melting into those talented fingers that pressed along every inch of her back and neck, coaxing her to life.

His hands gently parted her thighs. For a moment, she fought a flash of vulnerability. He could see her, all of her. "Shhh, love." His unbound hair brushed over the vulnerable skin of her neck. The sharp prickle of sensual awareness had her shifting slowly again, feeling every inch of her body come alive.

For him.

Wet.

Flowering.

Dathan finally had Pell spread out before him, and no erotic fantasy could have prepared him for the sweet revelation of her naked body and more naked soul. He'd waited three long years to see her like this. He wasn't going to rush. This was for her. The pleasure would bind her to him and then . . . then he could indulge the darker, sweeter fantasies that had tormented him for so long.

He'd been living in a desert for three years. For three goddamned years, she'd denied him *this*. He fought the urge, his beast, which wanted to plunge her deep into sensual pleasure, so deep she'd howl for him, melt for him. He was going to do this slowly. He wouldn't make her run from him. He wouldn't lose her, not now. He'd draw her to him, coax her with every erotic skill he'd mastered.

All for her.

Nothing could have prepared him for the greed he felt, the shock of pleasure, as she lay naked and pliant before him. He wouldn't forget this first time, so he'd make sure she couldn't forget either.

He could just sense her soul and allowed himself a small, delicious sip, because he couldn't restrain himself completely. He'd waited too long for her, wanted her too much.

He'd tried using other females, but each time, every time, he'd known that the woman in his arms offering her soul wasn't Pell. Once he met her, it had been over for him. Finding her had been like finding the lost half of himself. And losing her might be more painful than losing his wings could ever be.

So he wouldn't fuck this up.

Part of him still couldn't believe he had her here, so close. Stretched out, bare. Wet. All that lush, heated flesh inches from his fingers.

He bent his head, moving his tongue over her damp skin with a soft, heated caress. Exploring. Tasting the skin of her neck. Learning the taste and texture of the woman who would be his lover. He knew the friend intimately; now, it was the lover's turn. His fingers stroked gently against the skin he'd tasted, soothing, anchoring her in his pleasure.

"You're beautiful." He'd never had the gift of words.

For her, though, he would have written poetry if he could have. There were no words to describe the sight of her in his arms.

"Not really. Not—" She gasped as his tongue discovered a particularly sensitive spot beneath her shoulder blade. "Not like the women who chase you at the club."

"More beautiful." God, it was true. "I've never met another female like you."

He welcomed the small flash of jealousy, the small stamp of possession from this woman who had eluded him for so long. He was going to be *hers*, just as every inch of her belonged now to him. Or would. Just as soon as they were bonded.

His cock was thick, harder than it had ever been. Already, fluid wept from the plum-colored tip of him. God, he wanted her.

And she wanted him.

He drank in the tiny moan she gave him as she stretched beneath him, seeking more contact.

"Hold on," he ordered. "Don't let go." Deliberately, he wrapped her hands around the edge of the padded massage bench.

"Or?" The note of sensual challenge in her voice made his cock stiffen further.

"Or you'll get what's coming to you, baby." Deliberately, he made his voice a low growl, watching the delicious flush of arousal pinken her skin further. The small, sharp slap he landed on her ass made a cherry-colored brand that faded even as she moaned. Oh, yeah. She liked that. Liked his possession.

"Remember," he breathed. "You're going to be mine. You're going to do what I tell you to do when we're in bed. You're going to enjoy it. Imagine how many times I'll make you come. First, riding just my fingers, so I can feel every spasm. Then against my mouth. I want to taste you. Eat you up."

"Oh, my God, Dathan." The needy whimper was back in her voice, her body undulating beneath his. Reaching for what he wanted to give her.

"Do you want to come now for me, baby? Do you need to come?"

Her breath was a ragged pant. Her fingers curled around the edge of the bench. Holding on. He wanted those fingers wrapped around his dick, tugging him to her. But her pleasure came first. Always would.

"Yes," she hissed. "Yes, Dathan. Yes to all. Do something. Make me come now."

His fingers slid along her hot, wet sex. Slid forward through the thick juices.

She whimpered.

With one finger, he slipped inside her, feeling the heated flesh clamp desperately around his finger, milking him. Oh, yeah, she was hot for him. He let the other fingers dance wickedly over the flesh surrounding him. Petting. Stroking in a diabolical rhythm.

Deliberately, he slid his heavy cock along the seam of her ass.

"That's it," he groaned. "Ride my fingers. Take me."

When she came, milking his fingers, a piece of him came with her, his soul spasming with the pleasure of her orgasm.

"That's once." Primal satisfaction filled his voice. She was too dazed with pleasure to care. "Let's make it twice."

He slid down her body, and she buried her face in the now-heated leather, muffling the moans that she couldn't hold back.

"I want to hear you, darling. Let the boys here hear you."

God. Their audience. She'd forgotten all about them. Embarrassment was washed away in the next wave of pleasure, however, as his mouth found her ass. A dark spear of unspeakable pleasure twisted through her as those lips traced a wicked path and his fingers followed.

"Don't let go." A sharp, sensual tap on her ass followed his words. She held on tighter, the pleasure coiling deep inside, filling her. "Hold on for me, baby."

Then his mouth covered her sex and rational thought vanished.

The world around her narrowed to a tunnel of heated sensations and textures. The soft grain of the leather. The scent of her arousal and his.

"Wet for me, baby," he groaned against her. "You're so wet."

Male satisfaction filled his voice and then he dragged his tongue through her folds, tasting her as he'd promised. The dark stabs of pleasure had her pussy tightening. His thumbs spread her open. Not enough. Too much. He was eating her like a starving man, whispering his praises in between each delicious, hot drag of his tongue through her saturated core.

The pleasure built uncontrollably.

"Tell me you want me," he growled, his tongue leaving her for a moment so that she wanted to let go of the bench and drag him back to her to finish what he had started. "Say it!"

"Dathan," she panted, writhing against him. "Oh, God, I want you!"

"Now tell me what you want from me," he demanded. "Name your favor, Pell."

She couldn't think past the pleasure he was giving her. Finally, "Safety," she gasped. "You keep me safe, Dathan."

"And?" he prompted, those wicked hands stroking her flesh. Laying her bare.

"I'm all yours," she whispered.

"Body and soul," he promised. "Bond with me, Pelinor Arden."

"Yes," she groaned against his mouth. "God, yes, Dathan."

He drove into her mind as he slid his cock into her body.

Her hot, wet pussy was clamped desperately around him, squeezing his cock in a velvet grip, and the sexy little whimpers she was making in his ear were driving him insane. Driving him over the edge. And God, the sense of welcome. Of homecoming. Nothing had prepared him for this.

Her mind opened before him as he slid inside her thoughts. Now he truly had all of her. Her emotions overwhelmed him, calmed that terrible thirst. Hell, his beast was almost purring at the taste of her lust. Heat. The intimate connection to him. Oh, yeah. She knew who was holding her, whose body was penetrating hers.

Her hips arched up to meet his and he forgot the sensual skills he'd spent centuries mastering. He'd waited so long and now he wanted all of her.

"Pell," he breathed as they came together. Dark pleasure rocketed up from his balls as he shot inside her. He knew the moment she sensed his presence inside her, inside her *mind*. Her eyes snapped open. Wide. Not afraid—she wasn't afraid. Desperate relief poured through him. Maybe, just maybe, she could accept him. All of him. The skin on the back of his neck was twitching with a life of its own, his entire body preparing to turn itself inside out.

All for her. Only for her.

"Dathan?" Her soul whispered to his.

"Yes," he breathed.

The bond snapped into place, the thick bands of dark ink twining around their wrists.

Eleven

M City in the early dawn didn't look that different from the urban centers Pell's travels had taken her to in the United States of North America. The changing light hid the truth.

Hid the upheaval she'd lived through last night. She wasn't the same woman who had gone into the bathhouse. And he wasn't the same male. Dathan. She shot him a sideways glance and decided not to push her luck. *Something* had happened in the dark. Something, she thought, that might not be reversible, no matter what the bond lore claimed.

But she was getting what she wanted. Dathan had sworn to protect her.

Neither the Goblin nor the man would fail her.

Pell knew that in her heart now.

When his cell rang, Brends snapped it open without hesitating. Time to put the next part of the plan into action.

As he'd expected, Dathan's voice was on the other end. "It's done."

"Witnessed?" Without witnesses, there wouldn't be a bond, and he needed the pair bonded.

"Yeah. We're headed out of town now."

Brends couldn't stop himself from imagining for

one brief moment what it would be like if he were the one headed out of town with a new bond mate in tow. The lightheaded ecstasy of finally connecting to a soul. The thirst a sated, lazy beast prowling on the edge of consciousness but its claws sheathed for the moment. He'd had other souls, but none, he suspected, would come close to what having Mischka would be like. The low, warm note in Dathan's voice conveyed more clearly than words that the brother wasn't regretting his most recent choice.

How long had it been since Brends had really tasted a soul? He'd drunk wildly those first decades after the fall—driven by desperation and the unimaginable sensation of being cut off from the Heavens and all that was light and good. A male got used to it, however. Got used to it or went insane—slow or quick— and then made the necessary choices.

Zer's private residence was an old M City palace on an old boulevard with the psychic stink of old crimes. The very stones reeked of vice and misery. Zer might have replaced the century-old plate glass with more bullet-resistant material, but the dark woods and thick carpets were decadent, a deliberate nose-thumbing at the former human owners who had squandered a considerable fortune over the short course of two centuries and been forced to sell long before the Soviets had confiscated worldly goods from their more prudent brethren.

Zer hadn't let the Soviets gain so much as a toehold in his private citadel. Even now, the bar was stocked with antique crystal and imported bottles. Brends caught sight of his own dark face as he crossed the room. Hell.

He needed a drink. He couldn't get Dathan out of his mind and that wasn't like him. Pell. That was the girl's name. Pell had turned Dathan inside out and Dathan didn't seem to mind.

How could one human female change a fallen angel so much?

And why hadn't Dathan fought her influence?

At any rate, as long as Dathan kept himself whole, Pell Arden could look forward to a lengthier life than she had any right to expect, because the bond mate lived as long as her bonder lived.

The soft slide of footsteps on the expensive carpet yanked Brends from his thoughts. Nael preceded their sire into the room, his cold eyes examining the room for potential danger. He'd served the last five centuries as Zer's self-appointed bodyguard. He might have possessed a frat boy's sense of humor—even though there hadn't *been* frat boys that long—but the warrior's honor was solid. As was his loyalty. He'd lay his life down for their sire, and Brends respected that.

Zer entered the room on Nael's heels, not waiting for the other male to finish his inspection, tossing weapons onto a leather club chair. Dark. Dangerous. Brends studied his sire's face, but there were no obvious signs of anger. "No more deaths," Zer confirmed. "Not yet. Has your tracker got a bead on the rogue?"

"A partial." He took a sip of the Armadale he'd lifted from the liquor cabinet, savoring the smooth, ice-cold burn of the liquor. "We've got tracks outside her flat. Tracker spotted movement the first night, but turned up nothing. The killer is out there, Zer—I guarantee it. He'll come out when we find the right draw."

"The girl."

Mischka. Fuck. She had a name, even if Brends himself was reluctant to use it. He didn't want to make this any more personal than it had to be. "Yeah. The rogue wants her, wants her cousin. He'll come for them and we'll be waiting."

Zer nodded, pouring two fingers of vodka into an iced shot glass. Banged back the liquor without so much as a flinch. Tough bastard. "Cousin's out of the picture now?"

"Dathan bonded her last night. He's taking her out of town now. I'll put a tracker on their trail in case the rogue switches targets again, but in my opinion, they should be clear. Our rogue has a real thing for the other one."

Nael chimed in with a lazy assessment. "Dathan bonded her good." The amused arousal in his eyes was obvious. "She said all the right words in all the right places. Hot little piece. Too bad she wasn't in the mood to share."

Sometimes, the newly bonded females were willing to take their witnesses as well as their bonders. Brends had taken part in more than one orgy, but he was al-most certain that Dathan would not have permitted it last night, even if his new bonded *had* been willing. Dathan had it bad.

Something was up with that brother. That was more than some really, really—really, from the look on Nael's face—hot sex.

Zer put it into words. "You think it could be some-thing more? This thing between Dathan and his new bonded?"

"Sex," Brends said. He propped a booted foot up on the table. "You should try it."

"This from the male who's still looking to end a decades-long drought."

He gently swirled the liquid in his glass. "So I'm more particular than Nael here."

Nael cursed lightly and fluently. "Perhaps I'm looking for my soul mate; bet you'd like to find yours. I know I'm doing the best I can to track down mine." His dark eyes fired with lazy sensuality, growing heavy lidded.

"Pass," Brends snorted. "Bedtime fairy tale for younglings. Don't you think that if there were soul mates, someone would have found one of these women by now? We've been down here for what, a little over three millennia? And the soul-mate count? Is still at zero. Although not"—he eyed Nael—"for lack of trying on your part. Last time I checked, you were sliding from bed to bed as if you were *personally* going to check out every female in the city."

He'd ceased believing in the legend of the soul mates more than a millennium ago. He hadn't had a soul mate then and he certainly didn't have one now. Let alone one that could redeem him, hand him the keys to the Heavens and his lost wings.

"Sacrilegious bastard. Just because no one has," Nael muttered, "might just mean it hasn't happened yet. Maybe the others will find soul mates. Maybe you will."

Brends had given up hope a long time ago. There weren't going to be any soul mates in his brothers' futures; the one perfect female was just a myth. Another example of Michael's twisted perversions and why

Brends's only regret now was that he hadn't managed to kill the other male when he'd had a chance.

No, there wasn't a night that went by that Michael's perfect, golden countenance didn't dance in his dreams, taunting Brends as he plunged his shortknife through the thick membranes of Brends's wings as casually as if he were sawing a loaf of day-old bread in half—rather than inflicting a gut-wrenching agony. The screams of his sister followed him in the dreams as he fell, screams that were cut off long before enough distance had separated them from the blessed sensation of sound. Michael had gotten to her. Michael had put his hands on her pale, gold body.

Hell, yeah, he wanted to gut the bastard.

But fucking another human female wouldn't help him win that particular war.

If that made him a cynical bastard, so be it.

"We need to know where Mischka Baran is. At all times." Zer was clearly thinking things through. "It would be best if one of us bonded her—easier to track her with that kind of connection." He set his own empty glass back on the bar top. "You want to do it, Brends, or you want me to do it?"

Brends fought the unexpected swell of instinctive possession. No way in hell was he letting any of his brothers at Mischka Baran. He'd shared any number of females with them over the centuries, but he wasn't sharing Mischka. He wasn't sure why she was different. Hell, maybe it was a family thing, seeing how Dathan had reacted to that damned cousin of hers. Whatever it was, he wasn't going to be sharing. Not in this lifetime.

"She's all mine," he growled, not bothering to conceal the possessiveness he felt.

"What's she into?" Zer sprawled in the leather club chair, arms wide. Imagining that large, hard body covering Mischka, Brends knew his eyes were glowing, could feel his beast stirring as it struggled for release. The beast wanted to stake its claim, to hurt Zer for even thinking *Mischka Baran* and *sex* in the same sentence.

"Not group sex, if that's what you're getting at. Hell, she doesn't like our kind at all. She only came to G2's because her cousin went there first and Mischka's like a dog with a bone. She doesn't give up when she wants something. It's going to take a couple of days to work her over, get her in the mood."

For seduction. The words hung unspoken in the air between them.

"You sure you can do this?"

"Christ, Zer. I'm a damned fallen angel." Emphasis on *damned*. "Of course I can. I'd just prefer to do it right. There's no need to brutalize her. She's interested but fighting the feeling. I'm just giving her a day or two to come to terms with the idea."

"You can't possibly be her first lover." Zer dismissed the idea. "And she came to the club. So I'd say she has some idea of what to expect."

What could a human female really understand about taking a Goblin lover until she'd done it? And once she'd accepted him, it would be far too late for her to change her mind. He should just do it quickly. He shouldn't worry about hurting her damn *feelings*. Hell. He wasn't going to end up like Dathan, all noble and shit for three fucking years while the female he wanted pretended that friendship was more than enough for her, thank you very much.

No way in hell.

Zer sighed. "Fuck her, man, if she's just another female. Take her."

She wasn't. Problem was, Brends didn't know what that made her. And *different* didn't necessarily mean *good* in his book. "I'll take care of it," he snapped. "I'll invite her to the gardens. She won't refuse the next time I ask, I guarantee it."

"Tonight," Zer countered, but Brends was already out the door. "Good hunting," he yelled, laughing at the obscene gesture Brends tossed him.

Zer straightened from his slouch. "Damn. Brother has it bad."

"Yeah." Nael looked uncharacteristically thoughtful. "If I didn't know better, I'd think he *felt* something for this human. Question is, why?"

Zer shrugged. "His human female's a handful. Stubborn and sexy as hell. Why wouldn't he want her?"

"Would you?"

"Sure." Zer shrugged powerful shoulders. "But I don't think Brends is in a sharing mood."

"No," Nael said, leaning back and crossing his arms over his chest. "I don't think so either. So why is he reacting so strongly to this female? Is there any chance she's his soul mate?"

Zer stared. "Those are fairy tales, Nael. Have to be. Three thousand years and you'd think we'd have found at least one female who qualified."

For a long time, there was nothing but the quiet click of ice cubes as both considered the odds.

"Why haven't we found one?" Nael asked

"Maybe they don't exist."

"Michael swore they would."

"And Michael is a lying bastard. We know that, Nael. He booted our asses out of the Heavens for his own shit. He let us take the blame for what he'd done."

"Maybe." Nael was quiet for a minute. "Maybe."

Twelve

Dathan's fingers slid deep into Pell and she rode him, hard. That dark, unfamiliar twist of pleasure unfurled inside him. He could make her happy. He could be *enough* for her. For the first time in millennia, he felt a sense of homecoming.

She had to want to keep him.

"More." His fingers moved as he palmed her sex. "I'll give you more."

Ducking his head, he captured her mouth in a hot, deep kiss. Simple. Direct. He savored the honey-sweet taste of her. This was the Pell he'd craved for so many years. He still couldn't believe the miracle that had brought her to him.

When the brief daylight hours began to fade, they'd stopped for the night at what had once been the summer dacha of a Russian nobleman. Age and neglect had transformed the gravel courtyard into a wilderness where weeds choked out the stones, bursting into a glorious carpet of yellow bedstraw and dark blue prickly thistle. He'd carried her over the threshold to her laughing protests, leaving the black Jeep alone in its floral sea.

They hadn't made it past the first salon. The faded daybed surrounded by moth-eaten draperies was the perfect spot for an afternoon tryst. Although the glass was long gone from the French doors, the expanse of gardens still ran wild, sweeping away from the small summerhouse. Unfamiliar emotions, emotions he hadn't felt in millennia, threatened to sweep through him likewise.

Dathan kept his gun and blades close to hand. There'd been no sign of pursuit, but this close to the Preserves, quiet was not always friendly. Only fools—dead fools—were complacent. There was too much at stake here for carelessness now. He scanned the lengthening late-afternoon shadows around them, but there was nothing to trigger his instincts. Nothing out of the ordinary.

Other than the woman in his arms.

His body moved over hers, sliding smooth and deep inside her. He reveled in her reaction. The soft moan, her nails digging into his shoulders. "Oh, my God, Dathan."

"Tell me, baby," he coaxed. "Show me how you feel."

Stroking deeper, he shifted to find the angle that had her gasping faster, her hips moving. "Just like that, Dathan," she moaned, "but more."

If she wanted more, he'd give her more. His finger slid down the smooth curve of her ass, parting the luscious curves. Watching her face, the dark lashes fluttering shut as she focused on his touch, he stroked a wicked circle around the small opening. "Open up for me, Pell. All the way, baby."

Teasingly, his finger stroked her ass. Sank deep.

With a shriek of pleasure, she convulsed in his arm and he went over the edge with her, losing his soul in hers.

Suddenly his back exploded with a burning itch. As

much as he wanted to hold Pell forever, he was in too much agony to do anything but jump out of bed.

"Dathan?" Her beloved, sleepy voice followed him. She was teetering on the edge of sleep, confused by his sudden withdrawal. He ran to the bathroom, slamming the door behind him. It felt as if something alive was crawling underneath his skin and doing its damnedest to gnaw its way out. The itching was nearly unbearable. What the hell was happening?

He flipped a light switch, pleasantly surprised when the light went on. Someone hadn't bothered to cut power to the summerhouse. The bathroom was a Tuscan fantasy, the walls tiled in a cool terra-cotta. Large pillar candles decorated the rim of a claw-footed tub. He'd have had fantasies about those candles and Pell if the skin on his back weren't threatening to implode.

He stripped off the shirt he hadn't taken the time to remove. He couldn't let Pell touch his skin, not if he'd caught something. Hell. He was near immortal. A little rash shouldn't affect him. Which meant that it would be a really, really big rash. And nothing he wanted near Pell.

Pell. His other half. The woman he loved. He was going to have to find some way to convince her to stay with him when this was over. There was no way he could give her up. Somehow, somewhere, he'd fallen again. This time, in love with her. That was a fall he'd do over any day, because Pell was worth it all.

Sucking in a deep breath, he turned his back toward the mirror. He needed to know. *Chicken*, his mind laughed. *Great big scary three-thousand-year-old warrior, and you're afraid to look at your back?*

But holy hell. His back was a mess of black. As he watched, the lines writhed, sorting themselves out. Into a tattoo of large, feathered wings. What the hell was happening to him?

"Dathan?" Pell's sleepy voice came from bathroom door. She'd wrapped one of the sun-faded drapes around her. The faded fabric slipped, revealing the sweet curve of half-bare breast as he stared, stricken.

"Go back to sleep," he said roughly. Whatever was wrong with him, he was keeping her out of it. Pell stayed safe.

She ignored him. Christ, she always had. "Dathan, are you okay? What's wrong with your back?" Those familiar eyes were full of unfamiliar concern. Her hand reached out, and before he could stop her, she had touched the inflamed skin of his back.

"Christ, don't," he groaned. He couldn't hurt her.

Something tore through his skin at her touch. Not his beast, but the same powerful rush.

Wings. He had wings.

"Oh, my God, Dathan." She stared at him. "You're a bloody angel again."

THIRTEEN

Finding another female on his list had been simple.

Following her through M City's deserted daytime streets had been even simpler. In the end, Mischka Baran had led Eilor straight to her Goblin lover. Hidden beneath an ornately carved stone overhang, Eilor had a perfect view.

"I'm not sure about this." Whatever her doubts, the female touched the male's arm, her hand smoothing the pale silk of his shirtsleeve. The material clung and bunched beneath her fingertips, giving Eilor precisely the information he needed. Bare wrists.

The pair hadn't bonded. Not yet.

The Goblin bent his dark head, his low voice coaxing. Seducer.

Just like Eilor's own Saraiah, this female sighed and turned her face toward the fallen angel who held her in his arms, promising heaven on Earth. This time, however, Eilor would be in time to pluck the female from that insidious embrace. He'd punish her infidelity and get his revenge on the Goblins who'd stolen his female and consigned him to the hell of the Preserves as well.

It was perfect. God had chosen him to be the agent of his revenge.

The female he was watching nodded. "Fine," she said. "I'll come tonight. To the gardens inside G2's."

The Goblin's head came up, scanning the street side where Eilor watched. Sliding farther back into the comforting shadows, Eilor knew the Goblin wouldn't scent him. Wouldn't discover him, hunter that he was. There were advantages to serving Eilor's particular master.

When the pair parted, the female didn't resist the Goblin's quick, hard kiss. Yes, she was just as weak and sinful as Saraiah had been. She deserved the punishment.

And he would see that she received it.

Whoever had designed Mischka's costume had not had M City's winter weather in mind. "You'll be fine," the shop assistant had insisted when Mischka had requested something in syn-fur instead. Something *warmer*. "You do want to stand out, don't you? This is the way to do it. Besides, they heat those Goblin places."

She did want to stand out.

Plus, the shop assistant had had an unbreakable grip on her American Express card, so Mischka gave in. Which left her standing yet again inside G2's, but this time in a white leather corset dress that stopped a good foot above her knees—or mere inches beneath her ass. The lacing on the front of the corset was more than merely decorative—it scooped her breasts up and put them on display. The short dress had a long train that shifted sinuously behind her in a spectacular display of feathers, rhinestones and yards and yards of silk tulle. Fortunately, all that extra fabric kept the backs of her legs warm.

G2's apparently had more levels than a video game.

Two nights ago, she'd seen the main rooms, and while the ambiance had been upscale and vibrant, the glass and steel décor hadn't seemed out of the ordinary. Expensive, yes, even with the liberal wallpapering of orgy-ready club guests, but not atypical. Tonight, however, she was rethinking her perceptions of G2's.

She'd been ushered into a different set of rooms, if the word *rooms* even applied to where she now stood. Someone had recreated an entire garden half inside the cavernous depths of the club and half outside, a darkly scented, lush expanse of exotic greenery surrounding a delicate grouping of pleasure pavilions at its center. Tonight's music was a welcome respite from the shrill, nerve-tingling racket of the previous night, dusky notes that had her body humming with an unfamiliar pleasure, so alien and exotic, she could have listened to the throaty song all night.

Still, even inside the artificial gardens, she could still tell it was M City. And winter. Prancing around half-naked was not a great idea. Although she liked the boots. Sleek, expensive syn-leather and black as sin, the boots cupped her calves and extended over her knees, framing the pale, bare skin of her thighs. Better yet was the wedge heel, not one of those spindly stilettos. She might not be able to stake the Goblin through his nonexistent heart, but she'd be able to run like hell if she needed to do so.

Always have an exit plan.

Surrounded by a bevy of M City beauties, Mischka didn't have to be a rocket scientist to figure out that Brends could have his pick of human females. Any one of those women would have been happy to pair off with him and let him do precisely as he wanted. So why hadn't he chosen one of them?

But he'd invited *her* tonight. She'd given no indication that she was seeking his company, nor had she asked him to bond with her. Hell, the rumor on the street had been that he was one selective bastard, a Goblin who hadn't taken a bonded in decades. Of course, the girls could have been wrong. Maybe he just didn't pick up women from a club line—but there'd been that look in his eyes.

Almost as if he knew what she liked, what her secret guilty pleasure was.

And his eyes had promised he'd deliver.

Information, not orgasms.

He was a lead. Nothing more, she told herself firmly. Accepting his casual invitation to visit the gardens was a smart move on her part. Ming John was very, very dead, and right now it looked like Mischka's only hope of picking up Pelinor's trail was Brends.

None of which explained the hot trickle of awareness in her stomach. Brends wasn't good looking. His features were too dark, too harsh. But he commanded attention and looked like he understood danger. He'd take charge, whether she wanted him to or not. And when he did, all she would be able to do would be to hold on and enjoy one hell of a long, hot ride. Because he'd looked at her like her wanted to eat her up. For breakfast. In bed.

She had a rule, she reminded herself. A good one. No sex with paranormals, no matter how hot the subject seemed.

So the question was, why had she come here when

he'd called? Danger. Logic. Desire. There really wasn't any easy way to balance the three. She still wasn't convinced that she *should* take a chance on Brends. All she knew was that she *wanted* to. She wanted *him*. So she'd come here tonight looking for an opportunity to let go—just a little bit, not too much—and fall.

Page fifty-three.

Why couldn't she save Pell and enjoy her Goblin as well?

Eilor preferred to work at night, preferred slipping in and out of the shadows. The element of surprise made the females' terror that much stronger. They hadn't seen it coming. In the remaining seconds of their lives, he could see the questions in their eyes. *Why me? What did I do? If I stayed inside, would I have been safe?* They had never been safe from him. They never would be. But he loved watching them panic, wondering if there was something, *anything*, that they could have done to prevent their own deaths.

Of course, there wasn't. He needed their fear, though, and playing on that uncertainty only strengthened that emotion. *If you'd only gone home a little later*, he'd breathe into the trembling ear, *you'd have avoided me. Made a mistake, didn't you? Because here I am. Here you are.*

He already knew that this part of G2's offered no hiding places.

He'd selected this place specifically.

Now, in the twilight hours, the shadows had only just begun to bleed into true darkness. This place was narrow enough to be concealed, but not too far from the very heart of the ungodly garden where the Goblins lured humans. *He* was stronger than their temptations. He visited these gardens only to hunt.

The last hunt had been deeply satisfying. Maybe, deep inside his own territory, the Goblin had not expected trouble.

Maybe the Goblin had been too busy planning how best to sink his cock into his companion.

Either way, the element of surprise had been on Eilor's side, of course, as he'd intended. The scent of the female had distracted the other male as well. When Eilor had slipped up behind the pair in the alley behind G2's, the Goblin had one tattooed forearm braced against a wall, leaning down to capture his female's lips in a hard kiss. A quick strike to base of the neck to daze the male and then it had been so simple. Break the male's forearms, snapping the thick wrists like twigs. Two more quick slashes of the blade to hamstring the male and render him immobile, while the blade slid in so, so smoothly through his neck, parting skin and bone effortlessly.

Doing the female, plunging the blade into her body, had been almost anticlimactic. Still, when he stared down at the woman as he drew her into his arms, he'd recognized the moment for what it was.

Loved it.

He'd begun the killing to keep the Goblins from finding their soul mates. But now he lived for the delicious thrill of draining the weak females and then stabbing them in the heart. He'd mimic the sex act with the slow in-and-out thrust of his knife while the body jerked beneath his blade. He never stabbed too deep at first—just deep enough to hurt, for the pain to paralyze the female while he wrapped his arms lover-like around the body.

For now, that he killed on Cuthah's orders was acceptable. Cuthah was not only generous with his money, but his demands that Eilor kill were a delicious treat. Sometimes, though, he wondered what would happen when he no longer needed to hide who or what he was. When he could kill openly and Cuthah made himself known to the Goblins.

God, the memories were delicious. The jerk of the blade in his hands as cartilage tore and he forced the ribs apart, ripping an exit point right in the bitch's chest. The wet crack of a rib. She'd been quiet, too shocked to do anything but whimper as breath and soul fought free from the prison of her body. Dropping the body onto the ground, he'd withdrawn his blade and seen the dark blood that slicked the smooth sur-face, beading on the serrated edge. Ming John's death had satisfied his thirst.

The best ones died slowly. Too quickly spoiled his pleasure.

Because he was thirsty, he wrapped an arm around the waist of a human female strolling through the gar-dens. She wasn't Mischka Baran, but she could take the edge off his hunger. Ignoring her struggles, he slapped a hand over her mouth and dragged her deeper into the shadows. She'd do for now.

Perhaps, then, tonight he could move more slowly. Dreamily, he imagined sliding the blade between Mischka Baran's ribs, tearing upward as he gutted the unknown woman in his arms. Humming softly, he reached down with his left hand and freed his cock, fisting himself to the remembered rhythm of his blade.

The artificial grotto caught Mischka's attention first.

Damned Goblins had some sexy imaginations. They'd transformed the club into an outdoor wonderland. Waiting for Brends here was no hardship.

Mischka didn't even notice the sounds until she stepped under the grotto's overhanging lip and ducked inside. Cool air smacked her in the face and the riotous noise of the gardens was abruptly cut off. At first, she thought she'd interrupted a pair indulging in a little sex. The familiar smell of semen mixed with other, earthier fluids. When she started to back out of the cavern, however, she came to a frozen stop.

This wasn't a lover's tryst. This was a nightmare.

A dark, winged shape crouched over the body of the woman on the ground. There was so much blood. It was worse than the scene behind G2's. There, the cold night air had arrested the spray, frozen it into a gruesome necklace. Here, in the lavish, semiheated interior of the club, the blood spouted freely, staining the woman's expensive black cocktail dress and forming a garish smear against her pale flesh.

As Mischka watched, the rogue pulled the knife free from the woman with a sickening crunch of splitting bone, and before she could stop herself or complete her hasty retreat, she was pausing. She'd seen cuts like those before.

The male's gaze snapped up. Deliberately, he straightened and looked her up and down. "Nice dress," he said in a low, raspy voice, running his cold gaze over her elaborate corset-and-lace number.

She recognized those eyes. That voice. *Eilor.*

She reached slowly for the handgun she'd popped into a thigh holster, hoping the paranormal facing her couldn't tell that her palms were slick with sweat. Deliberately, she raised the muzzle of the ASP until it pointed straight at the paranormal's heart. Kill shot. Had to be. Even for his kind.

"Freeze," she said more calmly than she felt.

"Why?" He took another step toward her. Despite being as tall and broad-shouldered as a male suit model, he smelled rank. Like something unwashed and damp that had festered for a very long time in the dark.

"Because," she said, silently blessing the fact that the ASP had no safety to prevent her from plugging the bastard as soon as she wanted, "if you don't, I'm going to shoot your ass. Right now. Right here in this garden."

"You will not, *bébé.*"

Every instinct she had screeched that he was the paranormal straight from her own worst nightmares. "Last chance," she warned. "Hands up." Maybe he'd be foolish enough to refuse. Maybe she'd get lucky here, because she wanted to pump him full of lead.

She needed to do it.

His gaze flicked up from her thighs and he shook his head. "Don't. I've been waiting for you."

His flat tone bothered her more than anything else. Didn't he care that she'd stumbled onto his act of murder? He was either bona fide crazy or knew something she didn't. Either possibility left her feeling antsy, as if she'd overlooked something. She hated feeling incom-

petent. She was in charge—of her life and her business—
and she liked it that way. Needed it that way.

It was payback time. The paranormal facing her
made the mistake of taking another step toward her.
One more step, and he'd be able to reach her. Right
now, she could take him.

Mischka sighted and pulled the trigger.

The bullet struck the paranormal dead center, but
instead of a crimson blossom of blood, there was—
nothing. The monster just stood there with that same
half smile on his face.

Hell. She hated paranormals, she really did.

She scrambled backward, cursing the boots and the
elaborate fabric skirt of her costume. If she tripped,
he'd be on her in a heartbeat.

"Run, little human," he breathed.

Running seemed like her safest bet, but those dark
eyes glowed at her, the deceptively human gaze ruthlessly examining her face. Recognizing her. The dark
planes of his face lit with unholy interest. God, yes—he
recognized her. He inhaled sharply and then launched
himself at her.

She wasn't going to outrun him.

He struck her fast and low, sending her flying. Tulle
floated around her like snowflakes in a blizzard. All of
her nightmares come to life crouched over her, holding
a bloody knife.

She kicked futilely against his chest. The damn
bastard was built like a brick wall and weighed twice
as much. Panic exploded through her as a fetid odor
washed over her. The smell of death.

She opened her mouth to scream.

His hand around her throat cut off the sound.

"Interesting." His voice still sounded like crushed gravel, as if someone had squeezed his throat, twisted the voice box, and then released him at the very last moment. More disturbing, though, was the new tone. Satisfied. Gloating. God, he knew he'd won this time.

Dark wings rustled and stretched. His legs straddled her waist, pinning her to the ground. Gritting her teeth, she tried again to fight free, but he restrained her effortlessly.

When the lethal point of his blade slid beneath her corset lacings, the cords gave, the sharp pop obscenely loud. Her breasts spilled free.

He leaned forward, forcing more of his weight onto her.

"Mischka Baran." His dark face pressed against her throat as he dragged his tongue along the shrinking skin. God—was he vampyr? The heavy, wet brush of his tongue nauseated her. "I've met your cousin, haven't I, *bébé*? And she ran from me, too." Lifting his head, he licked the last drops of blood from the blade. "I was saving you for last, and yet here you are."

His free hand shot out and pinned her throat. The lethal pressure of his fingers had dots swimming in front of her eyes. He was going to choke her and there was nothing she could do to stop him.

Desperately, she stretched her fingers out to the side, reaching for her dropped gun.

"Should have stayed in hiding, little human."

Hell, he was right, but she'd had enough of being terrified. Of the dark face gloating above hers. She'd do whatever it took to stop him, even if she had to bargain with the devil himself. Desperately, she hooked her fingers into his eyes, tearing at the tender flesh. He outweighed her, but he could still be hurt, right? *Give up now and die.* Swearing viciously, he reared back and she rolled to the side.

With her other hand, she brought up the gun, even though the last shot had done no good. She wasn't going down without a fight.

"Oh, hunting you is going to be fun. I'll be back for you, *bébé.*" He chuckled—and then whirled, shouting something in an unfamiliar language. Guttural and almost Slavic sounding, she decided. There was a harsh clicking sound, like a child's toy winding down, and then he just shot up out of sight.

With a roar of rage, Brends exploded into their little slice of garden. His long black duster coat flowed out around him while his steel-toed boots moved silently along the ground. Legs braced for an attack, he held his weapons ready.

Too late.

Her legs crumpled beneath her, taking her to the ground.

FOURTEEN

Brends launched himself at the disappearing rogue, but the bastard had a head start and a strong instinct for self-preservation. He flew straight up, disappearing into the black cover of M City's sky. The rogue was huge, wrapped in skin-tough leathers that would deflect most of the metal Brends could send his way. Worse, though, were the wings. That gave the rogue a serious advantage.

The rogue still fired off two of his own blades, the heavy steel thrumming ominously close to Mischka's sprawled body. Brends got the message loud and clear. The rogue had targeted Mischka, and this was just the appetizer. The feral rage of his beast had the Change flickering over his face as he fought for control.

His own team would be in pursuit, although he wasn't optimistic. Right now, his job was to keep his little human safe. Whether she wanted him to or not. They both knew she didn't take orders, but she'd made it equally clear that she didn't want to die, either—and Brends had made his own orders explicitly clear.

No one got to Mischka Baran without Brends's say-so.

Crouching swiftly beside Mischka, Brends saw that the rogue might have roughed her up some, but she was essentially unharmed. Brends intended to keep it that way.

"You know," he growled, seizing her arm in his and turning it to inspect a particularly nasty scratch on the soft curve, "you're in over your head here. If he didn't before, that killer has a blade with your name on it now."

"Call the authorities, Brends." Her pale face glared up at him, but she still kept it together. "Call them now. This isn't just about you and me and whatever battle you think we're fighting here."

"We've discussed this."

"Brends—" she warned.

"They can't help us."

She needed to accept the plain, unvarnished truth: her kind was second-class here in M City. The only power they had came from selling their souls. He'd never made the mistake of underestimating Mischka Baran's intelligence. She had to have figured it out by now: she wasn't getting to Pelinor Arden unless she went through him. "I told you once. I'm telling you now. There's no authority here but my kind."

"Your kind." Her gaze dissected his face. He could almost see her doing the math, totaling up the plusses and minuses she kept in that neat little mental ledger of hers. Clearly, his being a paranormal still weighed heavily in her negative column, but what had just happened might be tipping the scale.

In his favor.

Bruises were already purpling on her throat, and he swallowed his anger. Taking her into his arms as he wanted to do would cost him the upper hand here and there was too much at stake. Too much that he could lose.

"My kind," he agreed, leaning closer. She flinched, but held her ground. Good.

And then she scared the hell out of him, the aftershock washing over her. Hell, she was fighting back tears. Would not cry. "Ah, baby." He'd rather have faced Michael again and lost than watched her cry. Instead, he wrapped his arms around her.

"You're used to this," she accused. "In your world, you kill each other all the time." He didn't let her see how much her words hurt. They were the truth, after all. "People don't do that where I come from, Brends." Her voice didn't sound sure.

He gave in to temptation and buried his face in her hair, losing himself in her scent.

Eilor, a cold-blooded killer, knew where she was. Still, she was here and she was alive.

Relief washed over her, a surge of adrenaline that had her panting in small, hard gasps. She was *alive*. She was being chased by *paranormals*. Just like her cousin.

"Breathe," he coaxed. "Just breathe with me, baby."

She gulped in air. She didn't want to live like that again, sunk in paralyzing fear. Jumping at shadows. If she bonded with Brends, she wouldn't have to. She'd only have to worry about what he could do to her.

She'd wanted to fall. Except that it was hard to hear her mind's cool logic over the heavy, no-holds-barred thumping of her heart. Face-to-face with what she'd schemed for, she finally had to accept the truth. She'd spent a lifetime fighting to be bad, but she wasn't stupid. And every instinct she had screamed that the male she'd come to find was a predator. But there was good hiding inside Brends, too. Somewhere.

"Let me in," he coaxed in that dark-chocolate voice of his. It was as though he could sense her wavering.

His teeth nipped at the softer skin of her neck, emphasizing his words. She struggled to fight the pleasure, to remain in control, but the erotic prick of his teeth sent a bright sting of pleasure-pain to her center. She'd never got off on power plays, had shown any lover who tried to dominate her to the door. So why was she still here?

"Because," he said, and she wondered if Goblins could read minds. "Because you've always wanted to do all the things you shouldn't, couldn't do with those other loves. You want to be bad, *dushka*, and I'm strong enough to let you."

She shook her head, but his large hands were threading through her hair, holding her head still for the kiss that tugged at her lower lip. "I don't want a dom, Brends."

"Maybe you do." His eyes darkened. "You let me in," he promised, "and I'll make it good. I'll give you whatever you want, *dushka*. No questions. No explanations. Tell me, if you want, or make me guess." His otherworldly eyes glowed with heated passion. She was surprised they hadn't lit up his damn gardens. "I'm a good guesser, *dushka*."

He trailed the sword-roughened pads of his fingers down the bare skin of her arm and leaned forward. The hair she'd unbound slid around them, sealing them into a dark, decadent world of pleasure. The spicy scent of male and sex surrounded them.

"And Pell, too," he promised. "I'll bring Pell back for you."

"For a price," she said, desperate to shake off his erotic spell. Her core was liquid, greedy for this male.

"Everything has its price, *dushka*," he whispered against her ear. "But I'll tell you what mine is. No surprises. You pay it and we're done. Give me until we find Pell. Until you're face-to-face with her again. One month at the most, I promise you, and nothing more."

Thirty days of taking orders from an alpha male who wouldn't hesitate to tell her what to do. Would give her orders and expect her to follow them. She didn't follow blindly, not anymore. Her clit pulsed with need, reminding her that she needed *this*. She needed him. She wasn't going to find Pelinor on her own, not in time. Brends, on the other hand, could lead her straight to her missing cousin. Before the killer got there first and all she had was a body to bury.

And she was suddenly sure that he wouldn't hurt her. Dominate her, yes. Touch every inch of her intimately, yes.

But he wouldn't hurt her.

Not intentionally.

Surely she could keep herself safe from accidental hurt?

She wished desperately she weren't so attracted to him. If they bonded, he'd have an inside track straight into to her head. He'd be able to connect to her. Communicate with her.

"And?" Her voice sounded dry. As if her throat was closing up.

"If the killer were to come for you"—he eyed her closely—"I'd know. I'd be right there."

"You want to use me as bait."

To give him credit, he didn't hesitate. He gave her the truth, although she supposed it only helped his cause. "Yes."

She might be able to help stop this. And stopping this was the right thing to do. Before she could rethink her decision, she said it. "Yes. Bond with me, Brends." Savage satisfaction lit his eyes and she had no time for second thoughts before his head lowered and blotted out the gardens around them.

FIFTEEN

Lifting her into his arms, Brends moved rapidly. He wasn't doing this on the ground. He wasn't an animal, even if that was what Michael had tried to make him. His thirst for this female did *not* rule him.

Keeping Mischka safe was just good business. And if pursuing the sexual attraction that flared between them kept her off balance, that was just fine with him. He'd protect her because Mischka Baran would lead them straight to the serial killer whose kill had framed the Goblins and stirred dangerous public outrage. She was bait in their trap. Nothing more. The bond would let him best protect her—and he'd have a mental connection with her that he could use to compel her obedience.

The punch her kiss had packed still surprised him, however.

If he spent too long wrapped in her arms, he'd forget all the logical reasons he had for pursuing her and simply lose himself in the sensual delight of her body and soul.

He should have been elated, and he was, he told himself. She'd accepted and that was what he wanted. What he needed. She was just like the other human females lined up outside his club, wanting a Goblin favor. She'd simply resisted longer, better, than most—

but she'd been willing to sell her soul in the end. All he had to do now was get her where he could touch her freely, before she could change her mind.

The desire flooding his body battled with his thirst to taste her. Touch her.

When he shouldered open the door to the club, his security detail didn't move. Their eyes followed him as he deliberately carried her through the crowded club. No one at G2's that evening would doubt that she was his. He pressed his mouth against the pale skin of her wrists, giving her a small, heated kiss. Her pulse jumped, beating a hard tattoo against his mouth.

Zer fell into step behind him. "Does she know?" His sire's eyes held his.

"Does *she* know what?" Mischka pushed at his chest, but he wasn't relinquishing her delicious weight or the feminine warmth cradled in his arms. He wasn't letting go until he had to.

"Bonds require witnesses, *dushka*." Brends reached the elevator bank and keyed in his private code with one hand. She might balk. Sometimes, the humans who came to the clubs weren't ready to accept the earthy nature of the Goblins. Sometimes, when the bargain was spelled out in black and white, they reneged and ran. Until she agreed in front of his chosen witness, she could still walk away.

Never mind that he'd chase her to the ends of the earth.

"And his role in this?" She jerked her chin toward Zer as he followed them into the elevator cage, leaning with boneless indolence against the chrome and glass wall of the elevator.

"He's the witness," Brends growled as the doors slid smoothly open onto his private office. He'd deliberately picked the big teak desk and black leather couches for the impact. Guests in his personal domain wouldn't forget who was dominant here. Couldn't forget that Brends was a sensual master in that domain.

Her eyes widened, her breath catching, as she surveyed the place, her eyes returning to the nearest couch.

"A witness to what?" She phrased her words as a question, but she knew. He could see that. The pink flush spread over her cheeks, down the curve of her throat. Instead of protest, though, there was only shocked interest that made his libido ratchet up another notch.

"Does that make you wet, baby? He's here to watch us. Watch you," he growled against her throat, chasing that delicious flush of color with his mouth. She tasted so good. Through the fragile beginnings of their bond, he could sense *her*. Bright and spicy, the sweet, wet welcome of her body mingled with the cinnamon and chocolate scent of her soul. Warmth. Heat. A welcome he'd forgotten ever existed.

"He's going to watch us," she repeated, but her eyes never left his face. Her thighs pressed together and he swore the scent of cinnamon and chocolate grew stronger. More inviting.

"Yeah." He waited.

She surprised him again, and he should have known by now that Mischka Baran had a gift for surprising him. And that she never, ever backed down from a challenge.

"All right," she said, stepping toward him, sliding her arms up around his neck.

* * *

"Kiss me," Mischka ordered so that she didn't have to think of Ming John or Pelinor or what the rogue out in G2's gardens had tried to do. She was done thinking for tonight. Right now, she was going to do what her body demanded. With a small grin, she tugged his head down to hers. He was going to kiss her, and she was going to enjoy it and enjoy it and enjoy it. He cursed, a low, violent hiss of sound that slipped from his mouth and almost shocked her from the strange waiting silence of her needy body.

He wrapped one hand around the back of her neck, holding her still for his kiss. His tongue plunged between her lips, stroking and licking her mouth as if it fascinated him. As if *she* fascinated him.

She knew the moment Brends stopped holding back.

His kiss was a hot revelation.

He angled his head down and her chin up. His fingers were firm on her jaw, nudging her mouth open so that his tongue could sweep inside. His hands were deliciously warm and reassuringly solid after the shadowy coolness of the cave. Sliding her hands up his arms, she reveled in the feel of all those hard muscles.

He smelled so damn good. Of outdoors and heat and some tangy musk that belonged to Brends and Brends alone. His hand tangled in her hair, using the long mane to angle her head backward for his deeper kiss. His tongue stroked the roof of her mouth, pressed against her own tongue. Deep, slow strokes that made her grow wetter. Fuller.

Told her exactly what he wanted.

With a guttural groan, he lifted her effortlessly to the edge of the massive desk that dominated the room.

She turned the tables on him.

From her perch on his desk, Mischka wrapped her legs around his waist. The wicked slit in her cocktail dress spilled the frothy, delicate fabric back around her waist. The thong she wore sent another heated bolt of desire jolting through him. A *leather* thong. Oh, yeah. His bonded-to-be had a wicked streak.

"Put your leg here." He patted the sleek surface of the desk beside her hip. Without taking her eyes from his, she slid her booted foot up beside her. Heat burned through him as the thick wedge of her boot arched her calf into a delicious bow, opened her up for him. He could almost taste her. The beautiful curve of her thigh had him clenching in anticipation.

Her fingers ran lazily up the leather. Their fingers met, tangled on the zipper. The soft rasp of the metal filled the room. When he pulled off the boot, she arched backward on the desk. Watching him with heated, wary eyes.

Running both large hands up her legs, he savored the delicious quivering of her muscles and the sweet, hot scent of her welcome. "Brends," she groaned, shifting restlessly on his desk.

"Yes?" he growled, wrapping both hands around her hips and dragging her closer to the edge. To him. The second boot followed the first, his hands massaging slow circles across her flesh. She shivered.

Her fingers stroking over the harsh planes of his face, his cheekbones, dragging his face down to hers drove him crazy. Burying his mouth against her pulse, he drew her scent deep inside his lungs. His female.

A delicious dampness moistened her thong.

Deliberately, he stroked the hot, wet core of her through the fabric. She shuddered. He wanted to give her all the hot, messy, luxurious, self-indulgent sex she could handle.

He was going to wake his ice princess up, damned if he wasn't.

Mischka recognized a challenge when it stared her in the face. Zer was here to make damned sure she didn't hurt his boy. Fine. He wanted a show—he wanted guarantees— She'd make sure he couldn't forget tonight.

The wet ache between her thighs guaranteed she wouldn't forget. She'd never been this aroused before, and Zer's hooded gaze only made those flames burn higher. Because every time Zer looked at her, she saw the possessive heat in Brends's dark eyes. Brends wanted her. And he wanted all of her.

So if he wanted to play games, she'd play. And she'd play to win. Slowly, she stroked a hand up her midriff, drawing her fingers between the damp valley of her breasts. Two pairs of dark eyes followed each light touch and the sure knowledge of her power, of their attraction, made her grow wetter.

Brends inhaled slowly and his eyes blazed. Oh, he knew. He knew what he did to her.

She drew her fingertips over her collarbone, savoring the sensation as her body came alive. Sliding closer to the big male, she looked over his shoulder, pinning

Zer with her own gaze. "You want to watch, big guy, you watch. But right now, Brends is all mine."

Deliberately, she reached up and pushed the heavy leather duster down his arms. His broad shoulders flexed as she trailed her fingers over their hard width. She wanted to press her lips to all that smooth, hot skin, but first she wanted him undressed. The leather straps of the longswords, which crossed his chest, stymied her.

"Off." She snagged the offending leather with a finger and pulled. Behind them, Zer inhaled sharply, but she was done caring about his presence. All of her senses were riveted by the male she was slowly revealing. Brends hesitated, but unbuckled the weapons, setting them carefully to one side. Close to hand. Hell, even with Zer to watch his back, he didn't trust that he was safe. She should have been offended. Instead, she was flattered.

Maybe he hadn't underestimated her after all.

She threaded her fingers through the long, sleek weight of his hair, tossing the leather band carelessly to the side.

"You're teasing the beast, baby." His words were a primal promise. His eyes glowed for a minute and she hesitated. He wasn't human. But she'd given her word. And somehow, she didn't think stopping him now would be simple. Some sixth sense warned her that he'd stop his penetration of her body, but the bond they were building between them would remain in place nonetheless.

He'd warned her.

And she'd still wanted him.

He braced his legs and reached for her.

There was no turning back now, for either of them.

Mischka Baran was a gift Brends didn't deserve, but this was one present he was unwrapping. Her confident blue eyes, glazed with passion for him, were the hottest damned sight he'd ever seen and made his cock harden more than he'd thought possible.

The bond was an excuse, he freely admitted, to get his hands on her delectable person. To give her a reason to trust him.

He raised his hands to the front of her wicked cocktail dress, where Eilor's blade had sliced through the laces. She'd dressed for him. Worn what she had to know would appeal to him. The concession to her femininity made him even hotter. The ruined sides parted with a delicious whisper of fragile fabric and he ran his hands up the delicate lines of her ribs, cupping her breasts.

Those nipples that had teased him all night hardened.

"I want to tongue those tight little nipples," he said. Her eyes fluttered shut and the sweetest little whimper escaped her mouth.

"Do it," she panted. Oh, yeah, he would. He was going to do her good. Real good.

"Rough or gentle, Mischka?" For now, until he had her bond, he'd give her the illusion of control. Bending his head, he tongued her nipples, rolling the sweet little fruits into his mouth. She tasted so damn good.

When he shaped the soft skin in his hands, her legs scissored around his waist, all that damn material billowing around them like they were angels on clouds. Which he wasn't. Would never be again.

Ruthlessly, he stripped the material from her, dragging down the wicked scrap that passed for panties. He left the corset.

She wasn't cold now. No, she was all hot, wet cream.

He ran one large hand down the arch of her spine and she pressed up into his caress. Stretched out before him. His beast growled, demanding its freedom. The thirst was an impossible fever, urging him to take more than her body. Already, he could sense *her*, the fiery, sweet soul that was Mischka Baran, the hesitation that had her holding back from him, keeping that little bit of herself disengaged from the pleasure he was pressing on her body.

When they bonded, he'd be able to touch her mind whenever he wanted. She would—could—hide nothing. He'd feel every touch he gave her, would know what made her hot, would know if she held back any inch of herself from him.

Damned if he'd let her hide from him now. She'd show him exactly how she felt.

Dragging his tongue along the velvet bow of her neck, he savored the sweet female taste. Damp skin. The urgent beat of the pulse in the vulnerable hollow. She was nervous. And aroused. His. He tasted her, whispering compliments, praise. The soft texture of her skin, its warm scent, fascinated him.

Brends's spicy male scent teased her, but she couldn't quite block out the hot, dark presence of the other male in the room. Zer was so still. Only his dark burning eyes moved. He wasn't polite. No, he stared at her, making a blunt examination of the scene playing out before him. For him.

When Brends lowered his head to her other breast, Zer leaned back against the walls, arms crossed over his chest with the inborn stillness of a predator. What would happen if her nerve broke and she ran?

He'd stop her.

She knew it bone deep. If Brends decided to have her, Zer would make sure that his brother got what he wanted. When he shifted, the small sound was almost swallowed by the heated whisper of skin against skin, Brends's hands stroking over her bare skin.

Brends froze. Possessive growl. Something unfamiliar, bestial, flickered over his face. Dark. Hard. Feral. Was that the inner beast she'd been warned about?

"Mine," he snarled. There was no mistaking the dark thread of masculine satisfaction. "Does it turn you on," he rasped into her ear, licking a hot, damp path around the fragile curve, "knowing that Zer is watching you?"

"He's watching both of us." Was that her voice that sounded so breathless, so needy?

"No," Brends contradicted. "He's watching you. Watching you open for me. Smelling hot, wet pussy and knowing why."

His fingers stroked down her throat, smoothing into the sweat-slicked valley between her breasts. Circled each, teasing the tips.

"Brends—" The word caught in her throat. She needed this, she needed him.

"Whatever you need, baby," he promised. "I'm here to give you whatever you need."

His fingers circled, moving lower to her slick, aching core. And then those fingers paused wickedly, tracing small, teasing strokes on the soft curve of skin just below her navel.

"Maybe what you need is this," he said. Stepping closer, he sank to his knees. His broad shoulders split her impossibly wide. Exposing her to his gaze. And Zer's. Oh, God. When she hesitated, those large hands continued stroking their sensual pattern on her thighs.

"Open up for me," he urged. "Isn't this what you want, love?"

She looked up, dazed with the pleasure that fired her nerves. Zer's gaze was hard and hot, fierce in its intensity. His eyes held hers and then deliberately dropped.

He was looking at her.

Flushing, she felt herself grow wetter. Brends's thumbs stroked the swollen lips of her pussy, separating her with his thumbs. At the brutal shock of pleasure, she heard her own keening cry. She arched backward, searching for an anchor in the maelstrom of overwhelming pleasure. She was about to brace herself on the surface of the desk when Zer stepped forward.

"Give me your hands," he commanded. He moved behind her, twining his fingers with hers, supporting her. She was practically suspended between the two huge men—utterly at their mercy.

Brends lowered his head and her breath caught. The wicked heat of his tongue pierced her aching core.

Who knew such hard lips could be so wickedly gentle? When his tongue delved through her soaked folds, she came apart, convulsing. Zer's fingers tightened on hers, anchoring her, even as his savage growl echoed in her ear.

The female spread before him was stunningly erotic.

And she was his.

All that fierce desire that his ice princess had concealed behind her perfect facade was *his*. He had a fierce craving to make her lose control again. Brends had never seen anything so sexy in his long lifetime as Mischka Baran coming apart in his arms, those delicious little pants and the catch of her breath as she came.

He was going to make her come again. And this time, he decided, she was going to scream for him. Good and loud. He hadn't had a female in decades, and the lush taste of her on his tongue only made him want more. And he could have more.

She rode the wave of the orgasm, leaning back against Zer. The male was being careful not to touch more of her than her hands. If he lost control of himself, however, he still could snap every one of her fingers. Her head tipped back against the male's dark chest.

Her dazed eyes focused on Brends. Wary but aroused. And the hint of wicked mischief was still in her eyes.

Good.

Deliberately, he opened her. Her flesh was meltingly hot around his fingers. "You feel good, baby." With two fingers, he stroked the small opening, widening her.

He pushed inside her slowly. Deliberately. Her slick pussy gripped him in erotic spasms.

He wasn't anyone's dream lover. He knew that, and so did she. He was a Goblin, a beast who'd been booted out of the Heavens, and three thousand years hadn't been enough time to earn his way back in. Fine. But she didn't fear him and that was hotter than hell itself. He had a feeling that the female in his arms would give as good as she got. Oh, she'd let him push her sexual boundaries and she'd enjoy it. But eventually, she'd push back.

Her pussy clenched on his finger. She was coming. So, hell, why couldn't he enjoy this? He'd keep her safe and Zer would get his killer. Everybody benefited.

Yeah. Before he could change his mind, he stood in one fluid motion and slid his thick cock inside her.

"Choose," he growled, stroking into her with long, slow, wicked thrusts. He could feel himself losing control. Losing the discipline he'd spent three thousand years building. Ice Princess wasn't the only one melting.

Her dazed eyes looked up at him, her lips parting. "Choose what?"

Choose me, he thought. He could feel the fledgling bond connecting them grow stronger, more tensile, snapping into place and coming to vibrant life. "You will bond with me." He made it a statement, not a question.

"Yes," she said. Her fingers tightened on Zer's, her body melting farther around Brends. "Yes to it all. *You* bond with *me*, Brends." She said the words like she was asking him to fuck her. "You do it now."

Her hips twisted against his, her pussy squeezing his cock with a delicious urgency.

Pleasure twisting through him, he lowered his head to her shoulder and bit. The skin broke and he tasted blood. Her blood. He took her essence deep into himself. Savored the wild, unfamiliar taste of his sweet female.

"Mine," he growled. His mouth moved over the small wound, surrounding it in an erotic, wet heat. Marking her. Her erotic intake of breath shot straight to his cock. It hurt, but she'd enjoyed the little sting of pain. Interesting. He made a note for the future. There were other, more exotic games he could show her.

"Name the favor," he said harshly. He dragged his tongue over the small bite. She tasted so damn good on his tongue.

She wet her lips, but didn't hesitate. "Pelinor," she said. "I want you to find Pelinor Arden for me."

"And you swear that you are bound to me, to serve me and do whatever I ask of you."

She hesitated. His arms tightened. His fingers found her throbbing clit. Circled.

Her breath caught. "Yes," she inhaled. His fingers pressed. "Brends," she wailed. "Now, damn it."

"Done." Her scent was all around him. On him.

Zer's hands were stroking over hers, drawing her hands to Brends's chest. "Witnessed." The guttural groan was almost torn from his sire's throat. Unbound hair sliding around their faces, he cupped a hard hand around the smooth skin of their wrists. His kiss burned against Brends's forehead.

Possessively, Brends pushed his thick cock deeper. Intoxicated with the feel of her, he set a demanding rhythm, but her hips were already rising and falling to meet his. When he came, he felt as though he were flying. Flying apart as he desperately poured himself into her. Desperate for her.

The dark marks burned into life around his wrists. A sexy slide, like invisible fingers stroking along the maddened length of his cock. It must have been the same for his new bonded. She shrieked, sliding upward desperately to meet his next thrust. Connected. Came for him in mindless climax, crying out his name.

Sixteen

Mischka checked her watch as Brends hustled her out the door of her flat and down to the waiting cars. Less than twelve hours after she'd sold her soul and he snapped his fingers as if she were a dog trained to heel.

He can damn well rethink his attitude.

After all, it wasn't as if he'd produced her cousin yet. So he had a whole lot of work cut out for him, and she didn't see any need to roll over and play dead until he'd kept his end of the bargain.

This infernal attraction she felt was just sex, nothing more. It didn't *mean* anything that she couldn't stop looking at him.

Liar.

Last night, she'd broken every rule in the book and then some—and she'd loved it.

The car parked by her curb was a sleek black SUV that screamed money. He clearly didn't give a damn about making any ecological statement, although since he was, from what she'd heard, near-immortal, maybe he should have. After all, he'd still be around when her *kind* finished punching a hole in the ozone layer.

So what if she'd foolishly expected things to be different the morning after the hottest sex of her life? She could *sense* the beast in him through that strange, tenuous mental connection that had snapped into place with their bond. The bond that she was still not comfortable with. Although that trickle of emotions made their new relationship seem less soulless, less opportunistic, she had to admit to feeling overwhelmed. The male stalking beside her seemed suddenly unfamiliar. Overwhelmingly sensual. And very, very alien. She was in over her head here and they both knew it. She'd never gone in for casual sex, and in the end, there'd been nothing casual at all about the night she'd spent in Brends's arms. They'd made a connection she'd felt to the bottom of her soul. So where did they go from here? After all was said and done, she didn't know if Brends even had a soul.

Certainly, Brends had old-school, elegant manners when he didn't have her backed against a wall, waging an erotic assault on her nerve endings. Setting her overnight bag down on the sidewalk, he opened the car door for her with a casual snap of his wrist.

"Get in," he said tightly. "We've got a long way to go." He glanced up at the dusky sky. "I want to get as far as possible before it's really dark."

Kicking him would probably dent her toes. It certainly wouldn't teach him any lessons in sensitivity. She slid into the car, the expensive upholstery giving softly beneath her weight. No one could accuse her fallen angel of slumming. Clearly, he'd decided that if he had to live wingless, he'd compensate in other ways.

She wanted information, so she put a hand out, preventing him from shutting the door. Chivalry could take a backseat to her need for information. "You know where we're going? You know where Pell went?"

"Yeah." He nodded curtly, but didn't offer any details. Prying information out of him was downright impossible, she thought, watching him stride around the car to the driver's side.

It was definitely going to be a long drive.

Plenty of time to decide whether Brends was truly a soulless monster—or whether she could take the chance of a lifetime and give him her heart.

Too damn bad if Mischka had buyer's remorse.

It wasn't as if Brends had really expected her to choose him over *them*, the wholesome, middle-aged couple watching disapprovingly as he loaded Mischka's suitcase into the SUV and got ready to drive off with a piece of their family.

He'd pay fair and square for whatever he took—and what he wanted, more than ever, was the damned rogue. The wings. The wings had *Michael* written all over them. And he'd dedicated his near-immortal life span to figuring out how take down Michael. The rogue might be just the in he needed.

He wasn't letting that lead go. He couldn't. So he'd do whatever it took, up to and including strong-arming his bond mate into leaving M City with him.

What he needed was to take off with Mischka clearly in his keeping, make enough of a spectacle to draw the attention of the rogue. Then, if he led, the rogue would follow. That would get him out of city and away from the human civilians Zer didn't want harmed.

This didn't have to be lose-lose. Mischka would learn to take orders, sure, but he was going to keep her safe, no matter what. Even if she was bait, she was still important. She'd bring Hushai's killer to him.

He'd keep her safe.

He moved around the car and slid in. He couldn't stand not to be near her. The tinted windows would shield them.

He slid across the seat and pulled her to him. He should have warned her more, but he was selfish, and even now his inner beast was jealous, because even after last night, he didn't own her. He didn't belong in the too-pristine sanctuary of Mischka's flat. Didn't fit in.

So he'd take what he could.

Sliding his lips over the vulnerable skin of her jaw, he tasted her, every deliberate stroke an intimate, public possession. Dominating her with the sensual promise in the hot tease of his tongue along that stubborn curve.

She wouldn't *give* him anything. Not here. So he'd coax. Make her *want*.

Wrapping a hand around the nape of her neck, he pulled her closer.

"Brends, not—" He didn't want to hear all the reasons for them to move apart. For him to lose the sweet heat of her body pressed up against his. So he angled his head down and her chin up. Tightened his fingers on her jaw, nudging her mouth open so that his tongue could sweep inside.

He needed that contact.

Needed more.

Her hands sliding up his arms were deliciously warm and reassuringly solid, anchoring him in this world.

Those small hands urged him closer, and he knew he was this close to losing himself in her.

God, she tasted good.

So who was holding whom here? He fisted his hand in her ponytail, using the leverage to angle her head backward for his deeper kiss. His tongue stroked the roof of her mouth, tangling against her tongue. Stroking deeper.

His kiss was a mark of possession and they both knew it.

He pulled the fabric of her shirt away from her skin. She hid herself beneath all these layers.

She inhaled. Sharply. "Don't," she whispered, pulling back. "Not here."

Yes. Here. He wasn't going to let her hide, not now. Not ever. Part of him wanted to take her here, lay her bare, but he'd lose her if he did that now.

She wasn't ready for those games and he'd promised only pleasure.

"Open up." His thumb nudged her mouth possessively, sliding over the full lower lip he'd kissed last night. God, he loved the taste of her.

"I'm not in the mood to play games, Brends." Her eyes glared at him. "I want to find my cousin. Now."

Her anger at his orders wasn't unexpected. And there was the sensual thrill of mastering her, of showing her the delicious pleasure submitting could bring. Caressing the luscious curve of her bottom lip with his thumb, he slid inside the wet heat of her mouth.

"Let me in," he demanded, not taking his eyes from hers.

She eyed him speculatively and jerked her chin out of his grasp. "Hands off."

"Hands *on*," he growled, slapping his hands around her waist and hauling her into his lap. The soft heat of her body coming into full body contact with his groin made him nearly come on the spot.

He ignored the foot that came down—*hard*—on his. He didn't wear leather shitkickers for nothing.

"I want you wet," he heard himself growl.

Her head tipped backward, hitting his shoulder and exposing the delicious column of her throat. He slid one finger down the pale line of skin. And she felt just as soft—just as impossibly *sweet*—as she had last night.

"We're not doing this here," she said, swatting him away.

"What? Afraid the neighbors will disapprove? Can't stand the thought of letting one of *us* touch you, taste you?"

"It has nothing to do with what you are."

He didn't believe her for a second. "I get it, babe. In the grand scheme of things, you're a Renoir and I'm sidewalk art. Humor me here."

She looked shocked, and he couldn't tell whether it was because he wanted to get it on in the car with others around or because he'd referred to Renoir. Really, she wasn't the only one with an education, even if their tastes did differ.

"That's not how I think of you. Of us."

"Do tell," he drawled, settling back in the seat.

"We're coming from two completely different places, Brends, and we both need to acknowledge it."

A bit self-helpish for him, but still true. "Baby, you have no idea."

"Then tell me," she snapped. "Don't leave me sitting here in the dark."

"Fine," he growled. "You want to know what I think of when I look at you? I'll tell you. I'd rather *you* told *me*, however, what thoughts are running through that luscious little head of yours when you stare at me and whine that I don't like you, don't like your kind. Don't you presume, princess," making the endearment into the obscenity he felt, "to do my thinking for me. You don't like Goblins. Clearly, you believe we're in the wrong. 'Condemned forever,'" he added mockingly, "and all that jazz. Fine. You're probably entitled to your narrow-minded little views, and frankly, I'm not so interested that I'll bother trying to convince you otherwise. Last night, I was inside you in so many ways, baby. I saw what you're hiding."

"Don't get in my way," she said tightly. "And stay out of my head."

"Try to stop me. You can't, you know. Besides, you liked it." He bent his head toward her again.

"We need to find Pell," she snapped. "This is my business, my family, and I'm in charge here."

"No." He crossed his arms over his chest and stared at her. "No, you're not in charge. You came to the heart of the Goblin empire, to my club. This is my damn town. My brothers will eat you alive for breakfast, and that's *if* the rogue doesn't take you down first. You don't know the first thing about how my city really works and you can't stay alive long enough to learn. Not without me."

She shook her head, then darted in to nip at his lip. Her defiance tasted as good as her submission had the previous night.

"You do what I say, when I say, *dushka*."

They were fighting a war; she just didn't know it yet. He couldn't—wouldn't—lose the delicious tease of her soul, the fiery intelligence, that stubborn streak that had her hung up on the rules. She needed a bad boy and she needed him.

She was lonely, because being the good daughter was lonely.

So she wanted to take his arrogance down a peg. He'd known she was strong. Independent. She never would be—wouldn't want to be—the little woman. And he didn't want that for her either, because then she wouldn't be who she was anymore. But that didn't mean he wasn't going to stop pushing her out of her comfort zone. He wanted that intimacy; she wanted calm, cool discipline. She was collected, and both the beast and the man wanted to undo her mental buttons and get inside her head.

So, fine. He'd play along. For now . . .

He moved to the driver's seat and peeled away from the curb. As they left M City behind them, the too-tall buildings disappearing swiftly into their past, he tossed her the slim volume he'd found in her bedside table.

He'd give her food for thought, damned if he wouldn't.

"I brought your book." He'd grabbed it again from her nightstand when he was inside her flat earlier. A primal pleasure flared in him. She'd reread it after he returned it to her the first time. She'd chosen to keep his "bookmark" at page 53.

"My book?" She blushed.

"Yeah. Marked some more spots as well." He'd bet she'd look before long. That delicious curiosity of hers wouldn't let her hold out. She'd want to see what he'd fantasized about. What he was offering. "Page fifty-three."

Her fingers fanned tentatively over the flotilla of Post-its he'd stolen from her desk. "Among others." Yeah, so he was full of fantasies when it came to the woman sitting next to him, and none of them lived up to the reality of the flesh-and-blood woman. She was better. Simply, perfectly, Mischka. Flaws and all. He frowned as she slid the volume into her bag.

He'd promised he'd make her fantasies come true.

Damn it, he was going to keep his promises. Every last promise, even if he was no longer sure he wanted to. When he'd promised to let her go when they found Pell, he hadn't considered that maybe he wouldn't have had enough of her.

The taste of her was addictive.

And she was going to be pissed as hell at him. Maybe he should have told her the truth about Dathan and Pell, that he knew where they were all along. Not telling was wrong. He recognized that. Maybe, on some level, he'd always recognized that. It didn't erase the bond between them, but he'd cut himself off from something—someone—important when he lied to her.

In her book, that was going to make him a bastard of epic proportions. He didn't like the way that made him feel. He forced his hands to relax on the steering wheel, to keep the SUV moving steadily forward. Feelings shouldn't matter to him.

Shouldn't.

But he was afraid that they did. Well, hell. It was far too late in the day for him to repent. And there was only one way to his female that had worked so far.

So he'd seduce her. Again.

Beside him, she shifted restlessly. "Brends . . ." Here it came. She wanted to get right to work, wanted to take the bit between her teeth.

And he wasn't going to let her.

"You got what you wanted. Now it's my turn." Yeah. She was going to push him right back.

"Did I?" He dissected her face ruthlessly. "Did I get what I wanted, baby?"

"One soul." Even he could hear the slightly bitter note in her voice. "Signed, sealed and delivered."

"Right," he said. "About that."

"You can't change the rules now." Panic made her deliciously breathless.

"I'm not changing them. I'm clarifying them. Now that you're part of my world, you need to understand what that means."

She eyed him cautiously. Wise female. "I thought you explained pretty clearly last night."

No. He'd explained partially. Maybe it would be good to hammer out the rules of their relationship. Then she'd understand where they stood and what her part was going to be.

Yeah, that would work.

"You're my bond mate."

"I was there last night."

"That means that I keep you safe. No matter what. Even from yourself. I'm in charge."

"What's that supposed to mean?" He distinctly heard her mutter something about alpha-male crap under her breath.

"You paid my price. I'm giving you what you want, but I decide when and how. Not you."

"This is a partnership, Brends."

"This is sex," he countered, partly just to rile her up. Hell, he knew this wasn't the right time to be blunt. She hadn't accepted what they'd done. How she'd felt. Not really. "You wanted hot, luscious, no-holds-barred sex. You wanted a chance to be the bad girl. You wanted me for you, Mischka. Not for Pell."

Her body told him more than words. She'd deliberately wrapped herself in feminine armor: no-nonsense blue jeans, a thick sweater. Flat-heeled boots. Nothing too out of the ordinary and nothing intended to seduce. Yeah, she'd spared him the bare-skin, leather-wrapped orgy of G2's, and it made him hotter than he'd ever been. He wouldn't go back to what he'd had before.

Which was precisely nothing. Hell, you didn't have to be a neurosurgeon to know that the best damned thing to happen to him in an eternity was tapping her foot as she leveled a pissed-off glare at him.

Too bad her anger just made him hotter, because it meant he'd got under her skin.

That he *mattered*.

"You're the tempter in this picture," she accused.

No. She had seduced him. With that warmth, the

life of that soul, that piece of her that she kept hidden away. He shrugged nonchalantly, because he couldn't possibly tell her how important this was to him. Hell, he didn't understand it himself. "If the bond makes the sex easier for you, I'm good with that. You do what you need to do. But I'm here for you. To give you what you want."

If she wanted Pell, she'd get Pell. He'd see to it. Hell, he'd sworn it, but it was more than that. It was as if there were emotional threads binding his soul tighter and tighter to hers. For the first time since he'd fallen, he didn't mind. Didn't want to rage against the injustice of it all or move the chess pieces in his complicated game of revenge.

He was goddamned *peaceful*. She'd got to him, done something to him.

So he'd seduce her, if that was what it took to hang on to this feeling. He wasn't letting her go. He couldn't.

This was right.

She'd learn to live with him because she had to. That thought had a heated smile tugging at the corner of his mouth. How far could he push her today? "If I were you"—he raised her bare hand to his mouth so his tongue could taste the sweet skin of her knuckles—"I'd worry that I'd overpaid."

He let the silence fill the SUV until he couldn't resist any longer, and he looked over at his companion again. She had fallen asleep as if their conversation hadn't registered more than a passing blip on her emotional radar. Her breath caught softly, tendrils of dream-thoughts slipping from her to him. She relaxed when she slept. The elegant discipline of her posture vanished completely. She'd curled up in a ball and gone to sleep.

He wasn't in any position to protest. Because, yeah, he'd kept her up last night. There hadn't been a whole lot of sleeping going on in their bed. Still, now he could look at her. Drink in the dark fringe of her lashes resting on the pale skin of her face. He reached for her hand. He wanted to feel her.

Savoring the soft rub of her skin against his, he drove, drinking in the smooth ribbon of road and the softer purr of the motor. Nothing, no one, lived out here. The countryside as you left M City and headed toward the steppes was nothing but thick slices of forest and the occasional ruined town.

And quiet. No sound at all but the softer shush of Mischka's breathing and the whisper of the tires over the pavement.

Just being near her calmed him. The thirst, he realized with some surprise, was more a pleasant ache than a raging hunger.

Peace, he decided, was a strange sensation. And psychoanalysis sucked. Instead, he let himself drive, his fingers stroking softly over the bare skin of her wrist, savoring a moment that couldn't possibly last forever.

SEVENTEEN

The countryside was an education in itself. With the high-speed bullet trains authorized by an ambitious president a few decades back, it now took just one day to reach M City. Since most passengers purchased a private pod, they didn't have to interact with the others. Train staff hooked and unhooked pods as the train pulled into the stations. Your money bought you a four-by-six-foot glass and steel box, two bunk beds and a small glass porthole through which you could watch the passing countryside as it streamed past you.

Convenient. Efficient. Admittedly, a tad bit sterile.

Right now, Mischka would have welcomed sterile. She'd woken from a nap troubled by shockingly sensual dreams. And watching Brends drive wasn't helping cool her blood any. Those large hands handled the wheel of the car with the same sensual efficiency he'd played her body with last night. Male power. A hint of the black markings around his wrist showed as the cuff of his shirt moved when he directed the car around a particularly large pothole in the road. No one maintained these roads anymore.

The GPS unit had fallen silent when they left M City behind six hours ago. It was impossible to lose the road out here, a straight shot away from the city, although she suspected you could lose any number of other things. Starting with your life. Fortunately for her peace of mind, the SUV was built like a tank. The reinforced, bulletproof glass of the windows provided some small comfort. Brends wasn't taking chances.

She was.

Something had been bothering her since they left the city behind them. Something she hadn't thought about too clearly. *You weren't thinking at all*, a little voice nagged her. *You were too busy trying on your bad-girl panties. Or losing them.* How had Brends known which direction to go? He hadn't hesitated. When he slid his large body behind the wheel of the car, he'd punched in a destination for the GPS. Without hesitating. Sure, he could have been taking a stab in the dark, but her instincts screamed that Brends Duranov didn't do a damned thing without having a very good reason.

She sifted through the pictures he'd handed her. Someone, somewhere, had himself access to a particularly well-positioned spy satellite. The images were crisp, full of damning black-and-white details. Pell. An unfamiliar Goblin. Tall and dark like the rest of them, but his body angled protectively between her cousin and the street as he handed her into an SUV. This was no forcible abduction. Unfortunately, she couldn't tell from the photograph whether they'd bonded, but their body language screamed intimacy. This was no one-night stand Pell had picked to piss her family off and make her point. Whoever the male was, he meant something to her.

Damn.

"They knew each other before Pell disappeared." She was suddenly sure of this.

Brends turned his head, his gaze unfathomable before he returned his attention to the silver ribbon of road in front of them. "Yeah." The admission didn't seem to faze him in the slightest. And it sure as hell was no news flash. "Pell came to the club frequently. She and Dathan became friends."

"Friends." She tried the word on for size, but it seemed awkward. And it sure as hell didn't seem to cover the depth of emotion she was sensing from the photographic montage staring up at her. Was friendship possible with a paranormal? Had Pell found something to trust in the unknown male? "She never talked about Dathan." Ever.

His hands tightened almost imperceptibly on the wheel. "Maybe she chose not to tell you. Maybe she didn't know how to tell you." His tone clearly stated that he knew what kind of a reception that sort of revelation would have received. "We've gone over this before. Your cousin is a grown woman, smart enough to know what she's getting herself into and to make her own decisions. She doesn't need you making them for her."

The fear was a familiar companion by now. If Pell didn't need her, Mischka had nothing left to offer. She couldn't bear the thought of losing any more family. She swallowed. "Pell knows I love her."

"And that means you'll welcome her lover with open arms?" His voice was scornful. "Think again, baby. I've heard you talk about paranormals. We're not good enough for you. We're animals, not humans."

She hadn't said that, had she? Although, she admitted, she'd probably thought it. Brends was not an animal. Feral, yes. Wild, absolutely. But she'd never made the mistake since the night she met him of thinking him less than human. He was more. So much more.

"How do you know where to go?" She gestured toward the silent GPS. "You laid in a course. You had a destination in mind."

She hated his damning silence.

"You set me up," she accused.

"I'm taking you to Pell." His eyes never left the road. "You asked me to take you to Pell and that's exactly what I'm doing. Find fault with my methods all you want, but you're getting what you wanted."

The hell she was. "How do you know where she is?"

He didn't answer for a moment. Finally, he said, "Because I sent Dathan out of town with her. I knew you'd want to follow. And our rogue will follow the two of you."

Disbelief warred with betrayal. And anger. She chose the anger, welcoming the hot, familiar slide of emotions. He'd set her up.

"Was it worth it, Brends?"

"No," he said coolly. "Last night had nothing to do with Dathan and Pell. It had to do with *us*, Mischka."

"There isn't an 'us.'" There couldn't possibly be. Not after his betrayal.

"Trust me." His body was deceptively relaxed, but his eyes never left the road.

"Not wise, Brends," she said coolly.

Even she knew she was tense, irritable. He was too close, pushing too hard. Their bond was a dark presence in the back of her mind, a shadow watching her. Too intimate. Too close. He was holding back, trying not to crowd her. Objectively, she knew that, but she still wanted to lash out at him.

When the balloons waved cheerily at them from the roadside gas station, bobbing madly in the car's sharp draft, he slowed the SUV. The balloons were anchored prominently to a clump of bushes. A deliberate attention grab. Brends did a little pedal-to-the-floor action, bringing the SUV to a swift, sudden stop. Two more feet and he'd have missed it.

The human female was petite and slim, with those big, brown eyes that made most males want to go all gruff and protective—until they saw the bite of humor that sparkled in their depths. Unlike most of the females Eilor had spotted in M City, her skin was neither ghostly pale nor overly bronzed—the faint glow of golden color had been rightfully earned playing some sort of outdoor sport. Perhaps she jogged. She'd certainly sprinted through the parking lot where he'd found her fast enough. Pity he didn't have the time to release her and catch her all over again. He enjoyed a good game of chase, particularly when there was no doubt as to the outcome.

Unfortunately, Eilor was behind schedule.

He had no desire to end up like the little human Cuthah had toyed with. That meant he needed to complete his mission. Successfully.

Pelinor Arden and Mischka Baran. Kill one. Bring the other one back.

It was going to be so very simple in the end.

The gleaming black SUV had stood out in the countryside like a neon target. The Fallen inside undoubtedly knew Eilor was on their trail, which meant the warrior had reasons of his own for drawing the pursuit this way. For now, Eilor was willing to oblige. Both his targets were now out in the countryside. They were sitting ducks, just the way he liked his females—and there was nothing the two large warriors who guarded them were going to be able to do to save their female companions.

Just as no one would be able to save the female wrapped up in a few yards of silver duct tape next to him. She was merely an appetizer—and a memo to his pursuers. He hadn't even bothered to search for another one of *them*. His pursuers didn't understand the connection between his targets, and that was best. So this female was merely a happy coincidence.

For him, of course.

Not for her.

"Now, *bébé*," he said as he moved purposefully toward her, "it's just you and me, darling. I believe it's time you served your purpose, don't you?"

The woman whimpered.

Before long, the blade was slicing through the flesh and the female had stopped screaming.

Oil tankers hadn't visited the gas station in at least a decade. The place stank of neglect and something more chemical. Time had done a postapocalyptic decorating number on the unused place. The dirt-streaked windows of the little convenience store prevented Brends from looking inside, but there was a new scent seeping out to greet him. Death. Recent death. The bright, copper tang of blood hit him hard, but there was no whiff of decay yet. The bastard was still here.

Not an ambush, he decided, but a setup nonetheless. There was blood outside on a gas pump. And then he saw the female body sprawled on the cracked asphalt like so much garbage.

The rogue was thumbing his nose at his hunters.

The door of the women's restroom gaped open, a dark cavity of space that invited him in for a look-see. Yeah, as if he'd take the rogue up on that offer.

"Oh, my God," Mischka said beside him, and yeah, she had one hand reaching for the door handle while the other fumbled for her seat belt. He wasn't losing her now.

"Stay here," he barked.

She didn't listen and he wondered when he'd started expecting that miracle. "We have to help her," his bond mate said instead, and the belt clicked free. Christ. He jammed the locks as he got out of the car and headed into the restroom, but he knew locks wouldn't stop Mischka for long. She was going to see the rogue's welcome message and he would have given anything to prevent that. The dead female had probably been a local human holdout. Now she was just dead. The blood splattered across walls was fresh enough; when Brends touched it, his finger came away red. Hell. Bastard wasn't *behind* them at all. He was in front of them.

And not far in front of them.

He heard feet crunching on the gravel. Anger and fear roared through him.

"Get back in the damn car," he bit out. Mentally, he slammed into her. He had to get her to safety. Only after he knew she'd be safe could he do what needed to be done here. He locked her mind down, picked her up and placed her carefully back into the SUV. She wouldn't be able to move a muscle until he permitted it, and now they both knew it.

She blinked once as she lost control of her body to him, and he swore he could see the outrage in those witchy eyes of hers. Yeah, she still didn't like commands. She'd get over it. Or learn to put it up with it. He was keeping her safe, damn it.

"Let me go. Now."

He stared at her, coolly. "No. Not now."

"You bastard!" No sign of his ice princess now. Her eyes flashed delicious fire and for a moment he wanted nothing more than to explore the delicious possibilities of the situation. For all intents and purposes, he had her tied up. Unable to move and at his sensual mercy. Yeah, there were lots of things he'd like to show her.

Too bad duty called. "I'll be back for you, baby," he growled. "Then I'll see to you. You can get as mad as you want." He pressed a hot, hard kiss against her mouth.

He shut the door of the SUV and locked it for good measure, not because those locks would keep anything out, but because it made his point. He wanted her safer, wanted to know that no one—*nothing*—would get to her, but that kind of surety was a luxury he couldn't afford. He needed her here.

He ran the odds in his head and called in his brothers, punching the distress code into the cell and barking quick orders into his earpiece. The rogue knew they were here, so no sense in trying to keep a low profile.

He eyed the gas station, and damn it, he hesitated. He had a job to do here and it didn't matter if he didn't like the balancing act. He couldn't put Mischka first, because that was a luxury he couldn't afford. Mischka alone in the SUV wasn't good, but his brothers were two minutes out. He'd tracked and executed rogues before. This wasn't any different and he had a damned job to do, whether he liked it or not.

Didn't matter that today was a *not* kind of a day.

Muttering a curse, he wrenched open the door of the gas station and stepped inside. Assessed the store, looking for an angle he could work—and came up empty-handed. The store was like any convenience store, although there was nothing convenient at all about the situation he found himself in. A dusty cash register and a plastic-topped counter. Rolls of expired lottery tickets and shelves of stale tobacco. Maybe a dozen aisles with the remnants of prepackaged snacks and long-defunct drink coolers. Whatever had happened here had happened fast. The human owners were long gone, but they'd left their stock behind. Must have been nuclear, he decided. Or maybe they just hadn't given a fuck when the human traffic dried up a few decades back, hadn't felt like hauling a half ton of Twinkies with them when they headed out to wherever it was humans went when they moved out lock, stock and barrel.

He wouldn't have waited around, either.

Palming a blade, Brends drew in a deep breath and centered himself. Fuck, but the scent of blood was worse here. The bastard must have started cutting inside and then moved outside.

The flash of steel coming up the aisle was all the warning Brends got.

Eilor came at him like a steam engine on full throttle. Bastard wasn't waiting for introductions or second thoughts. Christ. Fine with him. It wasn't like Brends had been planning on reading Eilor his rights and hauling his ass back to M City.

Not alive, at any rate.

With a low growl, Brends fended off the attack. Their arms locked, the two of them evenly matched. Then Brends realized his opponent's weapon was no ordinary man-made blade. Hell, no. Bastard had a fyreblade. Power flickered up and down the steel length like a hungry motherfucker. In another minute, Eilor would have enough power to fire the blade and then all hell would break loose.

Strike. Fall back. The familiar rhythm of the fight energized him. God, he'd forgotten how good it felt. Circling his opponent in the tight confines of the store, he assessed the situation. Until Eilor got that damned blade's power up all the way, they were evenly matched. Too evenly matched. Both had been a Dominion, created for the fight.

He hadn't faced an opponent with a fyreblade in millennia. No one who was not angel-blood could draw those blades—let alone pull the power that was needed to send flames flickering down the lethal edge. Hell. If he'd needed any more proof that this rogue was an inside job, he had it.

Eilor flew across the room toward him, hell-bent on taking off Brends's head.

"Not interested, motherfucker," he said, and swung his own blade. He might not have angelfyre at his beck and call, but three millennia of practice came in handy. If he'd connected with his target, he'd have had one fewer rogue to sweat over. Unfortunately, the rogue also had superfast reflexes. He rolled, sliding under the arc of Brends's blade, so that the knife met the plate-glass window of the storefront instead of sinews and skin.

Glass shattered in a deadly rain onto the floor. Too bad a few minor lacerations wouldn't do the job. Instead, Brends went after Eilor, crossing the length of the store in a few quick strides. Their feet were the first marks in the thick carpet of decades-old dust covering the linoleum tiles.

Peeling himself out of the store's new entrance, Eilor made the return trip faster than Brends thought possible. Damn, but the bastard was fast. He barely had time to block with his arm, thrusting his opponent away from him. Eilor landed heavily in a display of soda bottles, sweet liquid spilling all around him.

Maybe he'd finally stay down for the count.

"That the best you can do?" his opponent challenged.

Or not.

Eilor was up and charging back toward him. Brends cursed the difficulty of fighting in the narrow confines of the station, but he couldn't pry the bastard loose and out into the open. If he did get out, his team would take care of business. That was the point of backup. He blocked another punch.

The next punch caught him dead-on, and he heard the crack of his head snapping backward before the blistering pain turned his head into a drum. Shit. Staggering, he caught his hand on the counter. The dark thrum of power from Eilor should have warned him, but the edges of the male's profile were smoking. Hell. This was so not good.

His earpiece crackled. "You got this or you need help?"

"You need help, *bébé*?" the rogue mocked. "Can't take down one nasty on your own?" Yeah, the rogue's edges were definitely smoking, an orange nimbus that lit the room. The sword burst into flames as the first of the backup team came through the front door.

"Fuck." His team was running into a situation he couldn't control. "He's got angelfyre. Fall back, damn it. Fall *back*."

He was already moving, trying to head off the confrontation he saw coming like a bad train wreck. There wasn't any stopping Eilor, however, and his team didn't understand what they were facing.

The fiery edge of Eilor's sword sliced through the first warrior through the door like a knife through butter, making the bad situation clear. Nael staggered backward, cursing. "Guess I'll go get me what I came out here for," Eilor crooned.

Cold rage was pumping through Brends's veins, shutting down all but the most primal instincts. These were his *brothers*. Not livestock to be cut down. Red washed over his vision. Red that matched the color of the blood slicking the fyreblade. There was a copper bite in the air, but the wrong motherfucker was bleeding.

He leaped forward and gave the beast free rein, loosing his rage and the anger. The fear of losing someone else who mattered. He was too late to save his brother, but he wasn't letting the rogue get away. Not again. His body pounded into his opponent, his blade slicing through flesh.

Score one for him. Through an ever-deepening tunnel, as the beast rose up inside him and the man disappeared, he heard the other's low growl of pain and a muttered "Lucky bastard."

Brends's feet were slipping, the ancient black-and-white linoleum slick beneath his boot heels. Blood. Coke. He didn't know and he didn't give a fuck.

His target was eluding him, escaping through the shattered display window, and there wasn't a thing—not one goddamned thing—he could do about it.

Brends watched his team package up the forensic evidence for transport back to M City. As the adrenaline buzz of the fight faded, there was only one answer to the day's fuckup and it wasn't going to be found in the too-careful process of collecting blood and skin samples going on in front of him.

The technicians the Goblins had flown in from M City scraped and bottled industriously, picking through skin and blood like they'd found buried treasure. What the hell did they expect to find?

The dead girl hadn't been on the list. Brends had been so sure he understood the rogue's motivation. That he could predict what Eilor would do next. So how had he fucked this up so badly?

"She was a throwaway." Brends sounded suddenly sure, as if the pieces were falling into place for him, when Mischka was still locked in a fog of confusion. "This kill was a personal tease, a 'fuck you' to all of us. He knows we're tracking him. He *wanted* me to find this body."

"But she doesn't fit the pattern," Nael chimed in. Someone had patched him up, the white bandage a stark reminder against his dark skin.

"It doesn't mean she didn't matter." Mischka's voice sounded sure. However this latest victim had ended up here, she mattered—desperately—to someone, somewhere, even if it was only to his bond mate.

"Yeah." Nael shrugged, uncomfortable but clearly feeling her.

"She's not on the list." Brends slapped the paper down. "Why are these names on this list?"

"Because they're related?" Nael sounded interested now, and even Zer had stopped his pacing.

"Distantly," Brends confirmed. Mischka had never met—or even heard of—any of the women on this list other than Pell. She'd told them that and he'd overlooked the significance of her words.

"So why *this* bloodline?"

"Could be a freak accident." Nael shrugged and winced, but the lazy roll of his shoulders didn't match the keen look in his eyes.

"Or it might matter." Zer nodded slowly.

"Tell me, love," Brends said, turning toward Mischka, "how you'd feel about a small DNA test?"

Mischka opted for the convenience store's bathroom, while Brends's team cleaned up the crime scene out front. Less clean, but more privacy. Would they be able to ID the dead girl, or would the girl's friends and family ever learn what had happened out here? Maybe, the dead girl would just disappear from their lives and that would be that, no many how many times her family wondered out loud about her fate. Or maybe they weren't close at all. Maybe no one would care at all, and that was the saddest scenario she could imagine.

Genetic privacy laws prevented M City's residents from flat-out asking whether or not a person was human. If you weren't sure and it mattered—a lot—there were things you could do.

Like at-home DNA tests.

She balanced the white cardboard box with the DNA test on the edge of the sink. M City had clinics for this. Out here, however, she got a gas-station restroom that hadn't been cleaned in at least two decades.

Possibly three.

She was stalling and she knew it. Swiping the swab tip along her lower lip was simple enough; reading the results on the plastic stick was altogether different. Brends wouldn't have suggested the test if he hadn't believed the suggestion had merit.

"Could be worse," he suggested from the doorway. "You could have had to pee on it."

Right. She shot him a look. "Don't even think it," she warned.

Before she could lose her nerve, she looked down at the slim wand. Two dark bars and a series of smaller dots and swirls—the details. Two bars. She didn't need to unfold the crumpled instructions to interpret Brends's slow smile.

"No," she said, and then said it again, because really, once couldn't possibly be enough. "No. That's impossible."

"Well, hell, baby." His strong hands took the plastic stick from hers. "You've been holding out on me."

Hell no, she hadn't. Maybe she'd done the test wrong. After all, the damn thing was supposed to reassure her that she couldn't possibly have inherited a gene for rheumatoid arthritis or psoriasis. The kit was supposed to tell her who her daddy was. Not that somewhere, somehow, she'd got stuck with a family member who wasn't human.

Explaining this to her aunt and uncle would be impossible.

Unless they knew already. But she really, really doubted that.

She wanted to run out and get another kit. Redo the results. Instead, she settled for crumpling the colorful instructions and cursing.

Ancestry painting was supposed to tell you your ancestors were French. Or Scottish. Or Korean. Anything human. She couldn't explain what she was feeling. No possible way. She'd got up that morning knowing who—*what*—she was, but she wasn't going to go to bed the same way. She recognized the queasy sensation in the pit of her stomach, however. Like missing a step on the stairs or waiting to hear a piece of news the person opposite you had to deliver. Good news. Or bad news. The air had that same heavy feeling, like Brends just knew the storm was about to break but was okay with that.

She needed to get out of here. Go somewhere where she could think. She couldn't be part paranormal. That wasn't who she *was*. Paranormals had killed her parents—surely, they wouldn't have done that if her parents had been one of *them*?

Brends was watching her, of course. "Don't hide from me."

She shook her head. "I'm not hiding."

He eyed her. "Not yet. But you want to. You're thinking about it, baby."

Of course she was. Damn him, he'd just delivered a life-altering detail as if he were asking her what kind of pizza she preferred. How did he think she was going to react? Humans and paranormals weren't supposed to mix. This sort of genetic blending was supposed to be impossible. There were no known cases that she was aware of, so why the hell did she have to be the first?

She'd wanted to be special. She'd wanted to *belong*. Next time, she'd be more specific. Because there was no way in hell she was a paranormal.

"It's defective." It had to be.

Brends folded his arms over his chest and her eyes followed the sexy pull of that cashmere sweater. No. She wasn't noticing that. She was having a genetic crisis, not a hormonal meltdown.

"Get another kit," she ordered.

She focused on the sexy quirk of his mouth as he

shoved off the wall. "Sure," he said. "Whatever you want."

"Don't patronize me." Logically, she knew another kit wasn't going to make a difference. But what if it did? She fought off panic. She was going to hold it together.

He eyed her curiously. "Fine. Then welcome to the club, baby. You're one of us."

"Did you know?"

He shook his head slowly. "No, but it didn't matter to me."

One hand slid into the thick mass of hair at her neck, rubbing away the thick band of tension, while the fingers on his free hand traced down the unintelligible columns of dots as she reached for the kit's instruction booklet. The answer was in here somewhere. She shuffled through the pages and he stared at the marks on the paper. Someone knocked once on the door, a hard tattoo of sound, but Brends sent them away with a muttered "Later."

Fine with her. She wasn't ready to share this news.

"How good's your biblical scholarship?" When he asked the question, she blinked. Not the question she'd been expecting. At all.

When she didn't answer, he kicked open the door and pulled her out.

Mischka's bloodlines followed a direct line of descent back to Jacob. She was related to humans who'd spent decades wandering a desert in exile until they finally came home. He shot her a look, assessing those high patrician cheekbones of hers. Yeah, she had a biblical patriarch in her family tree and that couldn't be an accident. The genetic markers screamed *look at me*, even as her eyes cooled. Ice Princess was back and she didn't like the news he had to deliver.

Too fucking bad.

What biblical scholars didn't know was that there had been thirteen tribes to start with. One tribe had split off from the others, gone AWOL. They'd been wiped from the records, from the face of the earth, as if they'd never existed. And yet they had.

Still did.

If he was right, that lost tribe wasn't lost at all. Just living through one hell of a diaspora. So why would Eilor be hunting her line?

"I'd want to do more tests," he said to Zer, "but the genetic markers are there. Diluted, but there. Her family line traces straight back to the thirteenth tribe."

"The lost tribe? Fuck." Zer swore and punched the wall.

He hadn't lied, Brends told himself.

Brends hadn't known that Mischka Baran wasn't completely—entirely—human. When he'd first spotted her, it hadn't mattered at all. He'd known then that he was going to have her, was going to do everything in his power to make her *his*.

But it sure as hell mattered *now*. Primitive possession warred with dark pleasure. Yeah. She was his, right down to her genetic markers.

He'd had other bond mates, had taken other females. He'd used those females even as he'd pleasured them. Now, however, their faces were pale blurs, unimportant pauses in millennia of memories. This female, this woman pacing and muttering beside him, mattered.

Mischka Baran mattered.

He was a selfish prick, because she was upset but he couldn't stop the feral pleasure that swept through him. *His.* Mischka Baran was his, and the damn cardboard kit she'd put so much faith in had just confirmed it.

Cold, hard facts bound her to him.

"So that's why he's after me," she clarified. "It's not an accident."

"No." He forced his hands to relax by his sides. She didn't need further proof about just how bad the whole situation was. He'd keep her safe. She didn't need to know. "It probably isn't."

She stopped walking and looked up at him then, and he understood what his problem really was. Shit. He was afraid of losing her. That was natural, he told himself. They'd bonded, and it didn't take a rocket scientist to figure out that he was possessive. Always had been. He'd just have to work through this and do what he had to do.

Her next words surprised him, however. "Use me," she said. "Like you said before. As bait." She licked her lips when she said the words, the gesture betraying her nerves. She knew what she was asking him to do. That there was a chance—maybe not even a small chance—that Brends wouldn't be able to come to her rescue fast enough. She'd be alone with the rogue. And he could tell that thought scared the piss out of her.

He ran a hand up her arm, savoring the sweet heat

of her skin. How could he risk her like this? Ask her to take the chance?

Because you don't have another plan.

Not one that would work anyhow. If she followed his rules, she'd be safe enough.

Zer was watching, expressionless as two of the Goblins carefully slid the dead girl's body into a body bag. The black nylon framed the pale skin, threw Eilor's handiwork into stark relief. Eilor hadn't taken his time with this one, just done a quick slice-and-dice that managed to be grislier because of the lack of emotion. The dead girl was just another item on a to-do list, a means to an end.

Every primal instinct Brends possessed growled at the thought of Mischka ending up like that girl.

He filled Zer in on the plan forming in his mind. "We get out in front and Eilor's going to follow. He wants Mischka and he wants her cousin. We hand him an opportunity and he'll take it."

"But we'll control it." Zer nodded.

That was the theory. "Yeah," Brends said. "I can make sure it plays out the way we need it to play out. No one gets hurt."

"Bait." Zer looked at Mischka. "You're discussing this?"

"She should choose," he argued. "This should be her choice."

"She's your bond mate," Zer pointed out, his strong hands zipping up the body bag and hiding away the evidence of Eilor's crime. "That's the only choice she had to make."

She wasn't his puppet, even if he was strong enough

to force her obedience. There would be rules—for her own protection—but the ultimate choice needed to be hers. If she wanted to turn around now, he'd find another way to get her to her cousin.

"Hey, quit talking about me like I'm not here," she snapped.

Zer lifted the body bag effortlessly and turned to face her. "You want to say something?"

"If there's something we can do together to stop Eilor, I want us to do it. No one deserves that sort of pain and fear and horror."

"Do the right thing?" Zer's eyes dipped to the body bag.

"Yeah," she said quietly and then, a little more loudly because for some reason her throat had closed up, "Yeah. That's it."

"Good."

"You don't leave my side," Brends interjected. She could bitch all she wanted, but she wasn't leaving his line of sight again. She was human and that meant fragile.

"Is this typical for a rogue?" she asked. "I want the truth, Brends."

"No, it's not." Why not tell her the truth? Maybe, the next time—and he was certain there would be a next time—she'd listen. She was in over her damn head here, and somehow, he had to get her to recognize that home truth. "I've never seen a rogue quite like this one. He's violent, yeah, but they're all violent."

Her head dipped at that truth, the dark curtain of hair sliding forward and cutting him off. Yeah, she knew what he meant. That a few humans here or there were not the problem. His kind had treated her kind as disposable goods for centuries, so that wasn't really the issue, and she was too smart not to know that.

She was dogged in her pursuit of what she thought was the truth, though. He'd give her that. "So what makes Eilor different?"

"Our rogue has wings. When Michael kicked our asses out of his Heavens, he took those wings," he explained. "This rogue somehow has them back. So how did he get them? They're not standard Wal-Mart issue. I don't know anyone who's been able to get them back. Ever."

They were too close to the Preserves to take any chances of hunting for the rogue now, with night coming on fast; it was best to hunker down and wait for morning. Besides, the longer Brends could keep Mischka at their new base camp, the longer he could guarantee her safety. Camp was all disciplined bustle, with team members coming and going. Enough eyes to do the job and know where his bond mate was at all times. When Brends had suggested sleeping, however, Mischka had settled for a cool shrug. "Whatever. You're the boss."

Yeah, she was pissed about his little mind-freeze trick. Still, he watched her sleep because nothing, no one, was getting through him to her.

Restlessly, she rolled over, grumbling in her sleep and exposing the vulnerable curve of her spine to him as he stood by the side of the bed. All that human fragility and warmth. Hell. Who was he kidding? He was fucked. No way was he walking away from this one—and the most he had was thirty days. Stupid Judas that he was, he'd sold out for days when he should have been holding out for eternity.

He moved away from the bed. He'd protect her. No matter what. And the best way to do it was through the bond. Hell, wasn't he noble? Michael should throw the doors of Heaven wide open, because he was a candidate for sainthood. Never mind that his cock had a life of its own when he was around her.

This bond wasn't about sex.

Wasn't *just* about sex, he admitted to himself.

He'd watched humans come and go for centuries, scurrying about their business, but letting this one go just wasn't possible. Not anymore. She'd let him have his taste and now he would have sold his soul for a second. Hell.

So he'd tried to forget his new emotional connection. Even Zer had noticed his new preoccupation. He couldn't get Mischka out of his head—or his heart. He tried the thought on for size. Not just the sex, but something more.

Sex was simpler.

Brends took what he wanted, gave his partners what they fantasized about. Human females were delightfully straightforward, warm and vocal about what they desired. All that hot, heated skin, the breathless moans, the sweet, wet cream—these were good. These, he understood. This was what he'd been created for, condemned to do. He teased. He seduced. He dominated.

Moving aside the ancient curtain, he stared out into the night. This far out into the countryside, the no-man's-land that stretched between cities was dark.

Here, there was just the faint mazhykical haze surrounding the slim crescent of the moon. The stars were eerily bright without artificial lights of any kind, just a thick, black blanket of darkness.

Yeah, that was a new sensation as well. He'd never thought of the darkness as more than a convenient tool, another weapon in his arsenal because there were many ways to kill another under the cover of darkness.

There was a rustle behind him, almost inaudible, but he knew.

"Go to bed." He didn't turn around. Hell, he always knew when she was near and the instant, sensual knowledge had his blood heating, his cock thickening. Her soul called to his own damned soul, a siren's call of welcoming light and warmth. He didn't want to feel this way.

Like sex, darkness was simpler.

He had others watching the perimeter he'd established earlier that evening. She was safe enough for the moment, he decided, resisting the urge to turn around and wrap her in his arms. She was angry, he reminded himself. She wouldn't welcome intimacy, not now, when he'd held out on her.

"Are you coming to bed?" So she'd reached out to him, despite their fight. He'd done what was right—he'd kept her *safe*—so why did he feel as if he was pushing her away? So what if he'd never felt this way before—hell, he hadn't *felt* for millennia. He'd been living on borrowed emotions and none of them, *none* of them, had prepared him for this. He was on the edge of an unfamiliar precipice and he never—never—lost control. He wasn't going to start now.

"No," he growled. "You go back." He should check that perimeter one more time. Nothing, no one, was getting to Mischka Baran.

"Right." Still, she didn't leave, standing there with her bare feet on the wooden floor. It was too cold for her to be barefoot. He should have swept her up and brought her back inside to the bed's cozy warmth. But he didn't. "Brends." Her voice was hesitant. "Is everything okay?"

No. Things were distinctly *not* okay. She'd stood his world on end and now believed words would make everything all right again. Instead, he swiped irritably at the back of his neck. Damn itch. It felt like something was burrowing beneath his skin. Damn out-of-doors.

"Go to bed, love." He could hear the dark promise of his own voice. They both knew what would happen when he finally gave in to his desires and went to her.

He liked the dark. There were fewer mirrors, fewer lights—fewer reflections. His face was a living reflection of his Fall, as if he needed the visual reminder. He'd gambled—and lost. Fuck Michael. He'd carved out his own path, and thanks to Mischka Baran and the killer on her trail, he was one step closer to regaining what he'd lost.

Hours later, when he couldn't fight his need to be near her any longer and stood over the bed, the soft rhythm of her breathing greeted him. She was asleep.

Silently, he stripped off his clothes, sliding the heavy weight of the duster and his boots down onto the ground. The cloud of dust he kicked up spoke clearer than words about the abandoned nature of the summer-house in which they'd set up base camp. No one, human or otherwise, had been here in years. They were the first.

Nevertheless, he left his weapons close at hand; the countryside around them seemed still, but he hadn't survived this long without caution. When he slid in next to his bond mate, his weight made hers slide softly against him. He adjusted her, tucking her into his side. One arm over her, free to go for the gun if necessary. The last thing he did was slide the blade beneath the pillow.

He dreamed of the Fall.

The battle was over.

Brends flew through the sky and oh, God, every inch of him hurt. Pain was his new best friend, a sharp, red burn that didn't ease when he closed his eyes. The air bent and folded around him, rippled as he flew, but he knew that the world hadn't changed.

He had.

If he was lucky, he'd reach the hidden base camp in the mountains, but the steady drip of the blood down his side was a warning. Pick up the pace. Time was a luxury he no longer possessed.

How could you lose when you were right? Zer hadn't lied; Brends knew that for a fact. His brother was straight up. Fight Michael and what Michael stands for and take a stand for a better way of life for your family, for your brothers' wives and children. He couldn't ignore that call, not after what had happened to his sister. Last time he'd seen her, before he'd sent her off with that monster, she'd looked up at him with those amber eyes she'd inherited from their mother, and she'd made him swear that he would take no unnecessary chances. Maybe she'd been prescient, or maybe that was just what sisters said to brothers when they went out on a date, but the sword he'd taken through his side made a mockery of that vow now.

To hell with being careful, he'd decided, when their entire way of life was on the line. There was a traitor in their ranks and so he defended. It was that simple.

The too-distant mountain dipped sharply in his field of vision and gravity did its thing, jerking his body abruptly downward.

Bleeding out, he recognized on some dim level, because even his near-immortal body couldn't halt that remorseless spread of red forever.

One final wing beat and he was tumbling heavily from the skies, plummeting toward the unfamiliar, foreign ground below. Earth. No. He lived in the Heavens. He lived in that golden landscape, but the dramatic mountains and clouds of his homeland rapidly faded above him and fear rose in the secret place in his soul that coveted peace, not bloody, death-dealing battles. The part that wanted only to return to the mountains and the other angels hidden there for safekeeping while Brends and Zer and the others marched out to rid their world of Michael, because there were some monsters and some crimes that had to be paid for.

Brends's stomach cartwheeled. Flying was impossible. His wings were useless, leaden weights on his bare back. He felt them, but couldn't raise them.

When the agonizing pain finally tore through him, he screamed. All around him, other falling angels screamed, howling out their own horror.

His wings were gone. Ripped off as if by some unseen, giant hand. Like an amputation, the pain burned through his body. In every direction the landscape was washed in blood from the thousands of angels who were falling. Others tumbled as helplessly as he through the skies. Thousands and thousands of them. He had never been helpless before and didn't welcome the sensation now. Dragging up the last dregs of his control, he fought to slow the descent, to regain command of his suddenly heavy, unwieldy body. How did the humans do it? How did they live with their awkward, wingless bodies?

There were thousands of angels, some small specks in the air, others closer and large enough that Brends could see the despair, the rage and anger written on their faces as well. They really had lost. The news shattered him.

Michael's voice filled the air. The ground rushed up faster. "You fought the Heavens. You lost, and now you pay. None of you may return here to the Heavens. You are cast out. Your faces darken and your forms expand, marking you as Goblin, the Fallen, so that humankind can tell which of us are Angels and which are not. You shall be the Goblins, condemned to an immortal lifetime of penance until you find your soul mates, your missing halves. Your lost souls."

He could think only, But I've done nothing wrong.

It was *you*.

The dream Zer caught his eye. "Remember," he whispered hoarsely. "Remember what we fight for." Brends watched helplessly as his bold, brave, fierce leader, the angel who rallied them against Michael's tyranny when they discovered Brends's sister raped and callously gutted by Michael, hit the ground.

Helpless.

But not forever. Half Changed—half golden and glorious and half dark and swarthy—Brends fought the transformation and his Fall until he landed—hard—and the Heavens disappeared above him, closed off from his sight as the light faded.

Eighteen

Unfamiliar beds were a bitch. After a restless hour of watching Brends pace in front of her window, sleep had finally won. He could work through his issues or not, but waiting up all night for him to decide what he wanted was foolish. Maybe tomorrow would be better.

Maybe tomorrow Mischka wouldn't feel so raw.

Too bad the nightmare paying her a visit hadn't gotten the memo.

Her dream body was large and strong. She flew and the air vibrated with each powerful wing beat. A silver-winged angel, its face almost unholy in the sheer perfection of its symmetry, shrieked silently as the unfamiliar blade in her right hand rose and then fell. A crimson band appeared around its neck and then its head toppled, horrifyingly, to the ground, leaving behind a bloody stump, glaring reproaches.

And then she fell, her body a deadweight that sank through the air. Why was she falling? Why did it feel as if her body had been pulled apart? She'd never dreamed of falling before, but now she couldn't stop. And she knew it was bad. She was so strong, but the blood choked her and the ground rushed rapidly up. She knew that hard surface.

She'd fallen before.

She'd fallen this way before.

She fought the sticky webs of sleep, but the ground kept on rising to meet her, and avoiding the inevitable impact wasn't going to be possible. Could you die in your sleep? Fractured images flashed past the eyes she squeezed shut, because really, she didn't need to see the impact. Dark images of violence and taunting faces. An upraised sword that burst into flame. The harsh melody of an unfamiliar language.

Sorting out what was going on was important. The images were dark, taunting. Someone had killed someone she cared for a great deal. Michael. The rage was sudden, sure. Her dream self believed the accusation. Michael was guilty.

Not her dream. With a great effort, she wrenched herself awake and sat up in the bed.

Beside her, Brends slept.

Dreaming.

His body twitched, the rapid movement of his eyelids and the sharp rise and fall of chest betraying him.

She couldn't shake that dream. Mischka was sure Brends hadn't meant for her to watch his dreams. Maybe he didn't know what the bond was capable of. And maybe he was watching her dreams. That thought made her uncomfortable. Privacy was important. Privacy was *good*.

Still, lying here next to Brends, watching him sleep, felt pretty good. She thought about it for a minute. Being here felt more than good. His breathing was evening out now, becoming deep and steady. Maybe he was dreaming about something better.

She shouldn't care so much.

Pushing herself up on one elbow, she stared down at Brends. He was her lover. Somehow, that seemed more surreal than anything. A flash of amusement had her smiling. Apparently, when she decided to spend the night with someone, she did it with style. One gorgeous, six-foot-plus fallen angel in a luxury lakeside summerhouse. No seedy motels for her.

Brends's dark hair spilled over the pillows and his bare shoulders. Part of her wanted to sift the silky strands through her fingers and then explore the intriguing shadow of his collarbone. Taste the dark skin and see if sin indeed had a flavor.

Sex on the brain. Not good. Apparently, one night wrapped in the male's decadent five-hundred-thread-count Egyptian cotton sheets and she was willing to take their relationship to a whole new level. They'd bonded, but they had a thirty-day future. Not a forever future.

Brends had made it pretty clear that he wasn't a happily-ever-after kind of a guy. So it was beyond stupid to read anything into what had happened between them.

Maybe this was just a bonding thing. Maybe it happened to everyone.

Yeah, who was she kidding?

Eventually, he was going to trample all over her heart on his way to the door. Those wicked dark lashes lifted sensually, his fingers stroking softly along her bare skin as his eyes opened. "Come here, baby," he whispered as if he had known all along that she was watching, trying to unravel the puzzle that was Brends Duranov. As if he could see straight through to her soul. His hunger beat at her in waves, and she wanted nothing more than to ease that terrible hunger.

NINETEEN

Brends came awake and he was in heaven. Or as close to it as one of the Fallen could ever get. Mischka leaned over him in a sheer white chemise. God, yeah. The dark shadows of her nipple had his mouth watering. His cock was harder than it had ever been.

She was perfect.

"Show me," she whispered.

He cupped a hand behind her neck, urging her face down to his. She smelled so good. Warm and feminine. "I'll show you whatever you want, baby." He meant it, too. Whatever she wanted, he'd provide.

Then she said the last thing he'd expected her to say. "Show me your beast," she demanded. "That side of you that"—she hesitated—"came out when we found that last girl."

Yeah, he'd lost it there, had utterly lost it. He'd transformed and let the beast out to play. And he'd been far too close to losing control completely. He wasn't sure that his brothers would have been able to talk him down if Mischka hadn't been there. She'd done what they couldn't do, had calmed the beast and the man until he was able to regain control.

So why the hell would she want a repeat? "No," he said.

Her eyes narrowed. "What happened to fulfilling my every desire, Brends?"

This wasn't about sex, was it? She couldn't possibly want his beast in her body. On top of her. So this request had to be about something else.

He just had to figure it out.

Besides, he was the one in charge here, wasn't he? No chance in hell was he letting her see that side of him again if he could prevent it.

Her dark eyes stared at him quietly for a moment and then she rolled over on top of him, straddling him. Her thighs parted and, God, she was wickedly bare beneath that chemise. He froze. Hot, damp female flesh pressed against him.

"I want to see you," she said again. "That beast, he's part of you. So I want to see him."

He hated the beast. That was not a part of him that he wanted to acknowledge. Maybe his brothers could come to terms with that darker side of their warrior instincts, but that part of him didn't belong here, not in this bed. Not with her. She mattered, so he was keeping her free and clear of that dark violence. She couldn't know what she was asking him to do, or she'd change her mind fast enough.

He'd seen the look on her face earlier that afternoon. If the man didn't remember, the beast was more than aware. The image was probably burned onto his retinas. Horror. Antipathy. But no shock. That violence hadn't surprised her. She'd expected it from him. And that just made it worse, really, that she'd suspected what he was capable of and all he'd done was prove her point.

In living Technicolor.

He shuddered, but all that flesh, all that *Mischka*, was getting to him.

"Do it," she said in a hard, mean voice that made his cock jump traitorously. So she thought she knew what she wanted. Fine. He'd give it to her and she'd realize just how wrong she'd been. Then he'd Change back, tuck the beast away, and she'd never ask again.

It would be over. Yeah, the memory would always be between them, but she wouldn't make this mistake of requesting show-and-tell again. All he had to do was prove that he was the evil beast the rest of world knew he was.

"Fine," he growled against her throat. "You want to see me, Mischka, you see me. Just remember that this was your idea."

When she nodded, not hesitating, he couldn't see her eyes, and God, he wanted to. It was better to get this over with. The sooner he let the beast out to play, the sooner this was done. He was in control.

He Changed.

This was the darkness that had condemned Brends Duranov. Looking into his eyes, however, all Mischka saw was the man.

He'd scared the hell out of her before because she hadn't been prepared. Now, she could concentrate. See him for who and what he was.

The man was gone, so consumed by the beast into which he'd Shifted, it was as if Brends had never existed. The silver eyes burned with a lust and raw heat. Lust. For violence. For the dark. For *her*.

His alter ego, his Shifted form, was larger, harder. Darker. The sheer power of his broad shoulders as he punched his way up from the bed overwhelmed her, the sheets tangling around his arms, tearing as the muscles bunched powerfully. His skin continued to darken as he sat up. Drew her toward him purposefully. Nowhere to run, she reminded herself. Nowhere to hide.

You asked for this.

The bloodlust destroyed the civilized facade. The raw power remained, but the veneer of civilization had vanished with his human form. Fully transformed, he was seven-plus feet of lethal power with vicious, silver-tipped nails that elongated as she stared helplessly.

Not helplessly. Her Brends was still in there. He'd sworn he'd never hurt her.

His silver eyes glowed as they focused on her body and a feral howl tore from his throat.

The Goblin fell on her, licking at her lips, pushing her backward and pinning her as he demanded entry. He'd warned her that his kind couldn't feel, but they wanted to. Desperately. Now he was drinking from her soul as though he had an unquenchable thirst, sucking her into an emotional maelstrom.

She was caged in all that heat and strength, but it wasn't frightening. It was hot. Dark. She could hear the harsh rasp of his breath as he fought for control, still struggling not to give in to his hunger. Not to take her soul as completely as he'd taken her body. His beast was afraid of hurting her.

She ran a hand down his back. The muscles jumped

beneath her touch, and Brends buried his face against her throat, licking a hot, wicked path across her skin.

"I like it. I liked what you do to me, Brends." God, when had her voice grown so husky?

His jaw clenched, but his cock was *there*, thrusting between them. Hard. Needy. But he wasn't forcing himself on her. Just dragging her scent into his lungs, over and over. She could have done the same for hours. He smelled so damn good.

"Let's do it again," she offered, running her hands over his shoulders, and scraping gently at the sensitized skin with her nails. He growled. Good. He liked her touch. Coveted it.

"Yes," he rasped. "We're doing all of it, baby. I can't hold out."

He was warning her and she didn't care. He wouldn't hurt her. She slid her hands over his body, down his back and along the smooth curve of his ribs. Cupped the cheeks of his ass in her damp palms. God, he had a great ass.

He lifted his head, watching her. His beast watched her. "Be sure, baby. Damn sure."

She was. "God, Brends." She was impossibly wet. He was alien, exotic. Sexy as hell. He was holding himself in check and part of her wanted to make him lose control. "You're gorgeous."

Her beast's only answer was a low, guttural sound that sounded as if it had been torn from his throat. Brends was still in there, still with her. She was sure of it.

She shimmied beneath him, awkwardly pulling the chemise up and over her head. When she had him in the cradle of her hips, she paused to savor the hot weight of him. Wrapping her legs around his waist, she opened herself. With a hoarse sound, he nudged the tip of that massive cock inside her. And hesitated.

Maybe he was trying to kill her.

"Now," she demanded. "I want you, Brends. This is you, too."

Tilting her hips, she slid down the thick, hot length of him. Oh, God. Thick, sweet pleasure had her flesh melting around his, the covetous spasms of her pussy connecting them in the most basic of ways.

She rocked against him once. Twice. Teasing.

"Give it to me, Brends." Staring up at him, she speared her hands through his hair. "I want this. I want you."

"No going back," he said, and surged forward. He stroked deep and thick into her core, driving the pleasure through her body with each thrust. His immense body shuddered once, twice, suspended above hers.

Her orgasm caught her unaware, rolling uncontrollably through her, jerking her body against his. "Oh, God, Brends—" She couldn't take any more. There was simply too much pleasure. Too much heat. Emotions, pleasure, heat, awe spilling out of her in a tidal wave.

She could *feel* him drinking in those emotions, his body still shuddering against hers as a hoarse sound of pleasure tore from his throat. *Mine.* Buried to the hilt, moving deep inside her, he was all hers. He belonged to no one but her.

All her worries about Pell, the rogue, the fear of the unknown—she let it all go. She wrapped her arms around him and she let go, living in the moment and refusing to worry about the future. She'd savor what she had.

The beast receded slowly, allowing the man to regain control. He hadn't hurt her, Brends told himself. *I didn't hurt her.*

His first reaction was fierce loyalty and then fiercer pleasure. He didn't have to hide from her. She'd accepted both sides of him and the wild, fierce taste of her soul reflected that acceptance.

"Dushka," he breathed. "My soul."

He could dominate her, show her exactly what she needed and how. He could give her pleasure until she screamed with it. He was still hard deep inside her, but more important he was still aware of her mind. He knew that she was aroused by the simple fact that he was larger, stronger. Harder. Deliberately, he gave her the weight of his large body pressing hers into the mattress. God, she loved the dominant side of him, the part that insisted she enjoy every single touch. Every wicked taste of pleasure. His blunt demand for sexual honesty. She couldn't hide from him and she loved every wicked moment.

His wicked girl.

He was bred to dominate. Had spent millennia honing his fighting skills and becoming the warrior he had to be. Now, however, feeling her pleasure through their bond, drinking in her delight and feline satisfaction, he knew that it was all for her. His world telescoped until she was the sun and the stars, the necessary center of his universe.

"You're going to come again for me, baby. I'm not

done with you," he promised against the salt-slicked skin of her throat. "Touch yourself," he ordered. "Page fifty-three, just like you fantasized." He knew what she needed, what she wanted. Tonight, he was going to give his bond mate exactly what she craved. Sensual domination. Pleasure. As if she knew what he was thinking, her breath caught and her nipples tightened into greedy little nubs beneath the thin silk of her bra.

Christ, he loved her lingerie.

"Breasts first," he said when she hesitated. She wanted to. She craved the small brush of skin against skin like a sensual cat. Her flesh pinkened and he inhaled sharply, drawing the sweet scent of her arousal deep into his lungs. She hesitated, but then she did as he'd demanded. Her own hands stroked along the satiny curves cupped in the wicked little demi-bra. The fragile silk was deceptively blush colored. Almost innocent, but not quite. Lacy cutouts framed her nipples in an erotic display. Her hands paused when they reached the tight little peaks of her nipples.

"Oh, yeah, baby." With one finger, he drew a sensual pattern against her bare skin. He opened his senses, tasting the heated, slow ache through their bond. Delicious. His fingers followed the path hers had taken. A harder, wickedly masculine echo of her own touch. Her fingers grazed her nipples again and she sighed.

"Harder," he ordered.

"Like this." His fingers plucked at her nipples and the bright burst of pleasure-pain shot straight to her core. Made her weep with greedy need for him. For the hard heat of him driving her over the edge.

"Now you do it," he said.

No. She wanted him, not games.

His fingers curved around her ass, fingertips dipping wickedly into the shadowy crease. "Do it," he repeated.

He was stronger. He was the one in control, and that thought only made her wetter. Oh, God. Pleasure. He'd promised her pleasure and there was no doubt at all in her mind that he was delivering. Tonight. Right now.

He didn't stop the small, wicked stroke of his fingers against her other opening. "I can take you however I want." Those fingers pressed gently and a dark thrill sizzled along her nerve ends, drenching her pussy. "But I wanna know," he murmured. "What do you want? What do you fantasize about when you're alone at night, baby?"

This, she thought. *I fantasize about this.* God. He was big and hard and there was nothing she could do to stop him or prevent the pleasure from happening.

That finger pressed, teased. Her whole world telescoped, focused on that one small bundle of nerves and his wicked finger. So close. Orgasm trembled just out of reach.

"Tell me," he growled. "Tell me exactly what you want and I'll give it to you. All you have to do is tell me."

His large shoulders blocked the light, plunging her into a world of primitive sensation ruled by the liquid glide of the sheets against her body. The spicy scent of him and the naughty whisper of skin against skin. Her world was shattering in pleasure around her, but she couldn't say the damn words. Still couldn't bring herself to admit that she wanted more. Needed more.

His fingers reaming her ass. Her pussy. Him. She needed *him*.

"Or do you want me to do it?" She could feel his mind pushing against hers, sliding through her mental barriers and deep inside. Taking control. His slow, hard smile was all the warning he gave.

He touched her ass first, stroking wickedly down and in. Teasing the edge of her pussy. Tracing a blunt pattern over the needy flesh. She wanted to move, to open her legs and demand he touch her, all of her, but he wouldn't allow her to move. He was playing follow-the-leader, and the bright throb in her aching pussy told her all too clearly how much she was enjoying that thought.

His dark chuckle made her wetter. God, he was dominant and that turned her on. "You like this," he said. "Do you like this?"

That hard fingertip stroked her pussy from bottom to top. "Me? Touching you, here?" He circled around her straining clit.

God, she was going to burst, was going to come all over his fingertips. She had no control. Was so damned greedy for his touch.

She whimpered helplessly.

"Yeah," he said. "You like that, Mischka." Satisfaction filled his voice. "Let's see if you like this more. I'm going to sink my fingers into you," he warned. "Right now. And make you ride them until you come. And there's nothing you can do to stop me. Nothing you can do but enjoy the ride."

God, would she. Her breath caught in her throat, wrapped in the sensual web he was weaving.

No finesse. Just raw heat and sex, the juicy sound of her sex as he stroked her. She'd invited a fallen angel to be her lover—and he could be nothing other than what he was.

"Spread your legs wider." Deliciously helpless beneath his control, her body did as he demanded, her legs parting.

One more sensual stroke over her outer folds and then his fingers slid into her slick center. "Yeah," he said. "You want this."

So close. She was so close. He didn't stop, sliding his fingers deeper. "Just like this?"

Her body was reacting on a visceral level, reveling in his domination, his sensual promise to take care of her. To take care of all her needs.

"You want more, baby? You want me to spread you wide and tongue your clit like this?" His voice was a low, raspy promise.

"Do it," she gasped, and let go.

He growled his approval.

"Open up," he demanded. "You're getting exactly what you need tonight, my Mischka."

Sliding down, he pushed her legs apart with his shoulders, slipping between her thighs from behind so that his tongue snaked up and down her outer labia, dipping between her creamy lips to explore the sweetness. His index and middle fingers created a delicious friction, moving deep inside her heated flesh.

She rode him helplessly, the pleasure tearing through her.

"You're not coming yet," he growled. But God, she couldn't stop it. Couldn't hold back. The short, hard slap on her ass jolted her deliciously forward, riding her clit against his thumb. Oh, God, she was *bad*. The thought made her wetter. And he knew it.

Fine. She'd be as bad as she could be. As wicked as he was. Sliding her fingers into her own wet sex and separating herself. "Kiss me," she shocked herself. "Kiss me here." His growl of pleasure was all the warning she got.

Mischka opened for him like a sweet, wet flower until Brends was drunk with the taste of her. Not too much, he cautioned himself. But he sensed no alarm, no caution, when he finally moved up her body, sliding his cock deep inside her. Mischka gave herself without holding back.

Before he could stop himself, he growled the words against the sweat-slicked skin of her throat as he came. "I love you."

She stared up at him in shock, her soul in her eyes. No resistance. Just warmth and love and acceptance.

His body exploded with pleasure and pain as the climax ripped through him, his balls tightening as he drove deep and she took him all the way inside her. He couldn't possibly get any closer and the emotions burning through him spilled out. At first, he thought the painful ripple of skin across his back was a psychic echo of the emotions tearing his heart and soul apart. Then his shoulders flexed.

"Brends." Her eyes said something was definitely wrong with him. "Are you all right?"

Another convulsion tore through him. God, something was wrong. He rolled onto his side. Reached out a hand to reassure her. To his surprise, his hand trembled.

"Fuck." He doubled over. Her hand stroked his jaw, but he was lost in the pain, as if some unseen being was skinning him alive. He'd been there, done that three millennia ago. Didn't need or want a repeat.

Shoving off the bed, he stumbled over to window and ripped aside the curtain, fumbling for the door. His hand slid down the wall as another, harder convulsion had the blood roaring in his ears.

He heard her voice behind him again. He couldn't protect her. Needed Nael to do it. He couldn't leave her alone.

Skin shredded off his back and the pain flared again.

Something powerful was tearing slowly through his skin.

Mischka's voice came from somewhere behind him, but he was lost in the red haze. "Fuck," he groaned. "Get out of here, Mischka." This wasn't his beast. This was something else.

Clenching his jaw, he curled his fingers around the windowsill as if hanging on to the wood would anchor his slipping grasp on sanity.

Stubborn as always, she kept on moving toward him. Her cool hand on his arm was a small slice of heaven, but he swung round, crowding her toward the door and safety. The next convulsion took him to his knees. Christ, he was helpless, and despite his determination to keep her safe, there was nothing he could do here but moan deep and low in his throat.

That hand stroked along the edge of his back and then shot back. Wings tore through his skin. Emerging large. Powerful. Black.

The wings unfurled. Deliberately, he moved muscles and tendons. The wings beat once. Twice.

He opened his mouth and nothing came out.

So he settled for stumbling into the bathroom and staring. Wings. He had his goddamned wings back.

The shock of recognition and pleasure was yet another emotion he'd never expected to feel.

"I'm whole again." He stroked a hand along the soft feathers and there was that unfamiliar tremble again. He'd thought his wings were gone forever. But they were back. He could go home. *Home.*

Closing his eyes, he rested his forehead against the cold, smooth surface of the mirror. That meant Mischka was his soul mate.

She moved behind him, her hand touching his shoulder. Avoiding the wings. "Brends—"

Yeah, what could she say?

Then she said the one thing he hadn't expected. "Your wings are beautiful." He couldn't mistake the fierce pleasure on her face. "You're beautiful. I hadn't—" She gestured with a hand, at a loss for words but never helpless. "I hadn't realized what was missing." A smile lit her face and it was the sunrise for his whole universe.

He hadn't known what he was missing, either.

He stretched and his wingspan filled the small room, extending beyond both of them. As perfect as if his wings had never gone at all. Instinctively, he knew he was whole. Finally. His reflection stared back at him as he wrapped his arms around the woman he loved, burying his face in her neck, breathing in and out. With her, he was whole again.

* * *

Brends was larger than before. Harder. His broad shoulders filling up empty space she hadn't known existed. Desire rippled through her. Yeah, he was strong. And he could hold her down with one hand.

But man, he smelled good. The air was thick with the rich, creamy scent of his skin and she didn't know whether she wanted to sit back and stare at those wings or lick him from head to toe. Wings first, she decided. Dark and feathered, the wings jutted from his back as if they'd always been there.

His hands wrapped around her wrists, holding her in place. "Don't go," he said. "Stay with me."

When she tugged, he let go. Instead of getting up, however, she slid a hand down his back, sinking her fingers into the thick feathers. "They're so soft."

The feathers surged against her exploring fingers, bathing her with a sensual heat. *This is part of him.* Wrapping her other hand around his neck, she tugged his face toward hers.

"Kiss me," she demanded. He obliged, bending his head to cover her mouth with his. His teeth nipped at her lower lip, demanding and finding an entrance. His tongue stroked delicately over the damp flesh of her inner lip, sucking at her skin with slick, wet heat. God, he was wicked.

Pulling away from her, he ignored her whimper of protest. She hadn't had *enough* of him yet. "You'll like this," he promised. His lips slid over the skin of her throat and she watched that familiar hard face and the muscle-roped body. The wings were different, but they weren't alien. They were part of him.

"You want me to stop?" Dark eyes burned up at her. "Or you want me to touch you more?" She curled her fingers in his wings. Tentatively, she stroked a finger over them. He groaned, a liquid sound of pleasure.

He wasn't a beast, but something—someone— otherworldly. A warrior made to protect. She found herself wanting to touch him, taste him. Learn this part of him as intimately as he'd learned her body. Her gaze jerked back to his and he froze, predator-still, as if he knew that one unexpected move from him would send her bolting from their bed and fuck the bond that held them together.

The look of dark concentration on his face made her hesitate. Could she handle this?

"I'm still the same, baby." His eyes quartered her face and she didn't know what he was looking for. "I haven't changed."

Was she ready to do this? He had wings. Large, strong, luscious wings. Those wings were unexpectedly alien but also, equally unexpectedly, beautiful. He didn't look like any picture of an angel she'd seen. So it didn't really matter, did it? If she could handle his beast, she could handle this side of him as well. She was done running from what she wanted.

She wanted Brends Duranov, and right now, he was hers.

All hers.

"You're dark," she said, and this time she reached out to touch, because she had to know what those wings felt like.

He hesitated, his wings vibrating with tension. "This

can't be a game, baby. If you don't want this"—*if you don't want* ME hung in the air between them—"you tell me now, straight up."

She slid a hand along the hot, hard skin of his shoulder. That skin burned with heat beneath her exploring fingertips.

"And you'll leave me." Her fingers slid slow and curious into those wings, finding a sensual revelation. She couldn't get enough of touching him. Her sexual reaction to this side of him was a surprise. A very, very good surprise.

"Yeah." He groaned. "Oh, damn, baby, that feels good."

It did. Better yet, she new that he was aware that it was *her* touching him. *Her* acceptance mattered to him.

"You like it when I touch your wings." What if she kissed him? she wondered as she traced an erotic path from shoulder blade to neck, curling her legs around his waist.

His hands wrapped around her waist, lifting her. "I'm coming in," he warned, and a jolt of liquid heat shot through her. The heavy weight of his cock arched toward her, as greedy for her as she was for him.

When the blunt head separated her slick folds, she was lost in the luscious pleasure as he slid, slow and thick, inside her.

Whatever, whoever, he was, she still wanted him.

Afterward, with the sheets tangled up around them, Brends slowly let his wings fold back into a dark tattoo that covered the golden skin of his back, and she lay on his chest drinking in the quiet enjoyment. The steady beat of his heart beneath her cheek was rock solid. Like him. For a moment, she let her lashes flutter against the heat-slicked skin. "Butterfly kisses."

She felt rather than saw his smile at the small silliness.

Outside was waiting to come in and she didn't want it to.

"I have to leave, baby," he said, and she rolled off his chest before he could move her. She'd wanted longer.

The muscles of his abdomen rippled as he stretched, pulling the cotton T-shirt over his head and locating the boots half kicked under the bed. His duster was a dark pool of formless leather, but there was no overlooking the glint of weapons. He hadn't had the patience to remove his clothing in his usual disciplined fashion and that pleased her on a primitive level.

She'd taken him every bit as much as he'd taken her.

"Don't go," she said. She didn't want him to go, didn't want to let him leave their bed, knowing he'd be after that rogue and that there was every chance he wouldn't be coming back.

"I have to." He ran a possessive hand down her arm. "This—the wings—changes things. I can't *not* go, baby. If I can Shift, if I have half the power I used to have, that rebalances the whole equation and we both know it."

"Let someone else go," she begged. "Why does it matter so much?" Because it *did*. And he wouldn't let someone else do what he could do so well. She knew it. But she had to ask, because things had shifted in the last hour and she hadn't realized what she'd be risking when he went off to fight.

When he didn't reach for his weapons, however, she knew their time wasn't up.

Not yet.

The daggers mocked her, reminding her that she was the one who'd decided to take on a trained warrior. She'd known who and what he was, and nothing could change him.

She didn't want to change him, however, just keep him safe.

If he left, he was going into battle. She had no illusions about that. He was a warrior. It was what he did. The hard kiss he planted on her mouth dismissed her concerns faster than his words did.

"I found her on a night like this."

"Who? Who did you find?"

"My pairling," he said, reaching for the stack of clothing. "My sire got two of us on my birth mother. It wasn't unusual." He shrugged. "But we were always close. She mattered to me." His shuttered face said this unknown angel had more than mattered.

"And she died."

"No," he said fiercely. "She was murdered. By *Michael*."

Maybe it had been his fault. Esrene had wanted to make her own choices, but he was firstborn and those few seconds made him the protector. Esrene knew that, accepted that. When Michael had indicated his interest in her, Brends had let her know that the pairing was more than acceptable to him.

He'd entrusted his girl to a monster and hadn't recognized that truth until he found Michael standing there, over *her*.

He would never forget those memories.

"You killed her." His hand had gone to his fyreblade, but the gesture had been pure habit. Dominions were forbidden to raise their weapons against the archangels. Michael's weary, infinitely wise eyes had mocked him, mocked his trust.

"Yes." Michael hadn't sounded anguished or tortured or even satisfied. He had sounded cold. Just very, very cold and distant. "I have, Brends."

Brends had never expected betrayal from this source. When the first deaths had happened, ripping apart the tranquility of the Heavens, Brends hadn't known what to think. Dominions protected. They were the Heavens' cowboys, guarding their first frontiers. He was a fucking protector—and yet he'd failed to spot this danger.

"How could you do this?" he asked. Michael was their leader. Their very best.

"I don't know." For the first time, Michael's icy facade had wavered. Cracked. He had looked briefly confused, staring down at the knife in his hand.

"Figure it out," Brends had snarled as the need for revenge beat in his blood. "And let me know, because you've just signed your own death warrant."

Michael had sighed, shaken his head. "Brends—" he'd begun, but Brends was done listening.

"She was my pairling," he'd shouted, "and I trusted you with her. How could you do this?"

To me.

Drawing the blade, he'd launched himself at the older angel.

"Brends," Michael had tried again, sidestepping the first blow. "Don't do this. Listen to me."

"Did you kill her?" He'd stared at his mentor, feeling the cold hatred sweep over him, freezing his heart. If Michael was a cold-blooded killer, what did that make *him*?

"Yes," Michael had sighed, "I suppose you could say that I did. Or," Michael had added sadly, looking at Brends with those too-familiar eyes, "you did."

"Michael killed her."

"*I* killed her," he said. "I sent her out there with him. To die. I paired her with a monster and she went."

"No," she argued. "It wasn't your fault."

"No worries." He slid into the leather duster. "Everything's going to be fine, baby." She hated the dismissive tone in his voice. She didn't want platitudes, she decided. No, what she wanted was *truth*.

"Brends, tell me what we're dealing with here."

"Rogues aren't as complicated as you're making them out to be." He shrugged, a lazy roll of his shoulders. "They don't have higher cognitive reasoning skills, Mischka," he said patiently. "They're beasts. Nothing more."

She'd seen cornered animals. And she'd been face-to-face with Eilor. The male might have gone rogue, but he wasn't stupid. This wasn't like trapping a rabid dog, and she said so.

"But it is." Brends shook his head. "Trust me, baby."

Because he was confident that nothing could go

wrong, her fear escalated irrationally. It was just the threat of violence, wasn't it? She couldn't possibly care if her fallen angel got his wings singed?

"Stay here," she said. "Stay with me. There must be another way to stop Eilor. We could find it together."

He sighed, took a step toward her and wrapped her in a hard embrace. When he pressed the hot, lean length of him against her, she wanted to curl into him like a cat in a sunny spot. She liked it too much, she realized. She adored the heat of him, the reassuring weight.

"I'll come back, *dushka*," he promised. "I'll always come back for you."

His lips found hers in the darkness. Delicately, his mouth nipped at hers, making wordless promises of pleasure. Flames licked at her skin, and her sex was suddenly all creamy.

Well, hell.

She was sure that he meant his words, or believed that he meant them. That was the problem, after all. How could he guarantee anything, particularly if this damn psycho killer was waiting for him out in the dark?

He couldn't.

He stepped away from her, swiping the duster from the floor and moving to the door. "Looks like rain," he said finally, staring out at the plum-colored sky. "Storm's coming."

TWENTY

He didn't leave, despite his words, but the rain came, sweeping through the thick carpet of green that shrouded the burned-out lake house. The stinging drops were cool but exhilarating. Perhaps it was the elemental nature of the angel-kind: they had an intimate connection with nature, with the shifting weather and winds. The rain started out at first with small droplets; even before he moved outside the shell of the house, Brends could hear the pounding sheets of water moving closer and closer.

Through their bond, Mischka sensed images from Brends, flashes of memory, fragmented moments from long-gone decades. A summer folly. Aristocratic tea parties in the luxurious, sleep-making heat of summer. Pages of old novels and older operas dancing through his head. He'd enjoyed those decades, even though he'd concealed who and what he was. Here on the veranda, the delicate lattice prevented the heaviest of the rain from reaching them until it was rather like standing beneath a gigantic waterfall. The water poured and trickled, wending its way down from the sky. With the water came the scents: crushed grass, the earthy scent of wet dirt, and the faintest whiff of some animal spoor. No roads, no buildings, no human stench. He'd forgotten how much more at home he felt out here, even in the open, away from the artificial lights and colors of M City.

She enjoyed remembering with him, adding that little piece of him to her own memories.

Pulling off the heavy leather duster he'd just donned, he stashed it beneath a bench. He wouldn't need its warmth until much later. His heavy shitkickers were next, until he stood there clad only in a cotton T-shirt and pants. Wind lashed his hair around his face.

He hesitated and then unbuckled the leather holster for his two longblades. Steel throwing knives. Lethally sharp, the curved edges of the blades caught the light. He didn't hesitate, his hands moving competently over the collection. The tools of his trade. She'd known the weapons were there. Had understood the reason why. But seeing them was different. She ran a finger over one sharp edge, ignoring the bright prick of pain. He fought. He defended.

He was going to keep her safe.

So many weapons. So many ways to hurt.

And to defend.

While she hesitated, undecided, he stepped off the veranda. Instinctively, she knew he preferred this, the wild, untamed weather of the countryside, because rain in the city lacked the raw passion of this untamed assault. When he was newly fallen, it had seemed almost as if he could fly up into the face of the storm pounding across the mountains, that the howling air would suck him upward, launch him back into the skies where he could no longer fly. When the wind pulled the damp fabric against his frame, he threw back his head.

No one would tame him. Not Michael. Not her.

She fed him her awe and, yes, her arousal, through their bond. Let him know how he made her feel. What the sight of drenched fabric clinging to taut male nipples did to her, how she wanted to touch those strong legs and arms. Raindrops disappeared in a tantalizing procession beneath the collar of his shirt, tracing damp paths against his golden skin.

Pagan. Untamed.

Hers.

"Come out and join me," he said without opening his eyes. "Dance with me." He extended one large hand to her and she took it, letting him pull her out of the porch's shelter and into the wet.

"You feel this?" His face tightened, tilting up. "This is what we're living for, Mischka. Moments like these."

The dark outline of the new ink on his back was a powerful reminder as he turned away from her. He was alien but not. Hard. Powerful. And yeah, she wanted him. Muscles of his back rippled as if her gaze were a physical touch he could feel. Maybe he could. She could live a thousand years and not fully understand this bond they had between them.

Maybe understanding didn't matter as much as feeling it.

The cold bite of the rain *was* invigorating. Her nipples tightened into needy puckers against her shirt. Delighted, she let him pull her up against his body, swaying softly in place to imagined music. The rain kept falling around them, her clothes slowly plastering themselves to her legs as she moved with him.

"It's beautiful," she whispered. Anything louder seemed like blasphemy.

"Yes," he agreed. He drew her up against him until she rested quietly in the drumming rain. The sting of the drops over their shoulders and heads, sliding between their bodies, was strangely soporific. She inhaled and drew the warm earthy scent of him deep into her lungs.

She was not surprised when he lowered his face slowly to hers, pressing his lips softly against hers. The simple press of his lips warmed her, a hot contrast to the chill rainwater washing over them both. Thunder sounded in the distance and rain swept in a steady susurration across the exposed rock. Lips moved against hers, softly, slowly. *Yes*, she thought. *How perfect.* She reveled in her own stillness, sinking into the moment, into him. The unaccustomed passivity was like the greeting from a beloved friend after a long absence. Slow, sweet, intimate. His lips wandered over hers, exploring with small kisses like soft bee stings, firm and gentle. Alone in a cocoon of wetness.

When she shivered, her spine arched until she was pressing her breasts against him. His hands rested loosely on her shoulders, his thumbs rubbing small circles against the delicate skin of her collarbone, a heavy, welcome pressure that kept her anchored to the ground. He felt good. Like curling up in front of a warm fire on a wet day, or a cup of steaming, sugar-sweet cocoa. Guilty pleasures. They should be doing something practical with their time; they should be figuring out the killer's next move, reconnoitering the countryside for unusual paranormal activity, preparing for tomorrow. Instead, they were stealing moments.

"Yes," he said, as if he read her mind. "Time for us. Just for us."

How many generations of M City teenagers had stolen away up here, making love in the drenching rain while they looked back toward the muted glow of the city lights, with the trees and the summer pavilion at their backs? When she let her back rest against his chest, pressing her hips backward, the thick weight of his erection bumped against her.

"I want you now." Her hands reached behind her, pulling at the wet folds of his clothes. "I want you to fill me now."

"Yes." He helped her strip off her clothes. It felt more intimate to pull and tug awkwardly at the sodden material, laughing together at the unexpected heaviness of the cloth and their combined awkwardness.

He pressed a series of kisses from the tender skin behind her ear to her breastbone, chasing the chilled flesh with his tongue, laving the blue map of veins with his tongue until she wriggled impatiently.

Sliding down, he pushed her legs apart with his shoulders, slipping between her thighs so that his tongue stroked her outer labia, dipping between the creamy lips to explore the drenched sweetness. His index and middle fingers created a delicious friction, moving over and over her heated flesh.

"Now," she demanded. "Come inside me now." His bond with her was a sweet hum in the back of his mind, a hypersensitive awareness of the maelstrom of feelings rushing through her body.

Yes, he thought. *Want me as I want you.*

His penis nudged at the seam of her thighs, begging for entrance and then sliding in shallow strokes in and out of that soft cradle of skin until her legs parted. Sweet cream slicked her labia.

"Now," she demanded again.

"Yes," he breathed, pushing inside her. She squeezed him tightly, a hot, slick fisting that milked the pleasure from him. Sweet pressure built deep inside him. He slipped his hand down her stomach, stroking through the damp cloth of her panties. The shock of wet fabric against her heated clitoris elated him. Right now, right here, she did want him, if only like this. He pressed his advantage, tracing small circles in her hot flesh that echoed his steady thrusting.

"Give you pleasure," he muttered against her neck. His hair fell about her face in long waves, tangling with her own. She pushed back against him, seeking that same end. The thick, endless spurts of his semen filled her wet sex and ran down her thighs.

His voice broke as the orgasm rolled over them both, breathing small unfamiliar words of pleasure and praise against her skin.

If only the world weren't waiting for them.

"Hide here," he groaned, and heard her silent agreement.

She didn't want to leave, either. Didn't want the real world, real responsibilities to intrude. These were stolen moments, and yeah, they both knew it.

Twenty-one

Zer flipped open his cell. He hated to interrupt Brends, but they had an emergency and duty came first. Angrily, he punched the speed-dial button, already striding toward the caravan of SUVs waiting to roll out. As he'd expected, Brends answered before Zer had his ass firmly planted in the driver's seat.

"We've got a situation." With one hand, he steered the SUV, which had been reinforced with enough heavy plating to resist a small mortar strike. His team fell in around him.

"We've spotted our rogue." On the other end of the line, Brends swore. "Get your ass in gear," he continued. "He's got Dathan pinned down."

He snapped the cell shut and tossed it onto the empty passenger seat. Behind him, Nael was loading a small arsenal of black-market weapons.

A cold smile spread across his face.

Showtime.

Far below Eilor, the SUV barreled along the abandoned highway.

The Fallen had taken the bait. That was clearly the problem with being so chivalrous. It got you royally fucked. If he took the bastard down now, he'd achieve half his goal. Because Mischka Baran would be a dead woman if her bond mate croaked it. That was how the bond worked. On the other hand, she got handed immortality on the proverbial platter if her mate kept on breathing.

Not really such a bad deal, all things considered.

Unfortunately for her, he was going to kill that mate.

First, though, he had to let Brends spot him.

Draw the beast out of its lair. Away from his beloved.

Better safe than sorry. That was Dathan's motto. A long-range rifle with a good scope was best in a pinch, but you had to be a damned good shot. Not to mention fast. Squeeze off enough rounds quickly enough, and you could get the rogue down long enough for the killing blow.

He was going to need all the skills he possessed if he was going to get out of this alive. Sometime during the night, he and Pell had been found. And now they were surrounded by a pack of soul-thirsty beasts from the Preserves.

He threw his first dagger at the creature. The blade bounced off the rogue's tough hide, leaving a small scratch, but the beast kept coming. Close up, the smell was overwhelming, the rancid stench of a body that had been dipped in bloody gore and then left to bake dry in the hot sun. Bastard made a charnel house smell like pine-tree air freshener in comparison, but he didn't stop coming.

"Second blade's the charm, right?" Dathan took aim.

Pell was still blessedly right where he'd left her in the Jeep. He only hoped she'd taken the rest of his instructions to heart. If he didn't make it back, she was to peel rubber all the way back to M City, not stopping for anything.

A black SUV came tearing up the road toward his position. The cavalry was riding to the rescue.

As the next rogue climbed through the wall, Dathan greeted him with a quick slash of his blade. The sharp edge cut smoothly through the throat, lodging the blade against a vertebra of spine. One twist. One fewer rogue. Unfortunately, there were more. Lots more.

Dathan was putting up one hell of a fight—but the odds were not in his favor.

It was evac time for their ladies, and pronto. No way was Brends letting Mischka walk into the middle of this firefight. As much as he wanted her to stay, he also wanted to keep her safe. And staying with him was not safe.

He took a last moment to savor their bond, to savor the taste of her. Adrenaline and concern. For him. Christ.

He didn't hesitate. He wanted her desperately—and the right thing to do was to give her up. To keep her safe. To do that, he had to fulfill the terms of their bond, and that meant bringing her to Pell.

Brends brought the SUV to a teeth-jarring stop.

Brends was out of the SUV before the vehicle had stopped rolling. "Move over." He indicated the driver's seat with a flick of his wrist. The look on his face didn't invite discussion, so Mischka slid over.

Dathan and Pell were hunkered down behind a vehicle of their own, and Dathan was squeezing off rounds of ammo from a gun while Pell reloaded an empty clip. They'd pulled halfway off the road, but then life had apparently interfered in the form of a steady trickle of dark shadows sliding from a fissure in the wall. She didn't need to be one of the Fallen to know that the breach was bad. Very bad.

"Get in." Dathan practically shoved Pell into the interior of the SUV. Without so much as a hey-how-are-you, he strode off, pulling knives from his leather duster.

Oh, my God. Pell. Her eyes met her cousin's and she *felt* the impact of that gaze. Something snapped and she saw Brends swaying on his feet. For a moment, he looked as if he'd been struck, and then that hard, cold look was back in his eyes. "I've kept my end of our bargain. You've kept yours. You can go now."

He was done with her. Just like that.

She had her cousin back, she'd paid her price, and now her business here with Brends was done. Over. She could leave.

So why was she still hesitating? He'd never indicated that he wanted their relationship to last longer than their bond. Sticking around would only, she admitted, end in hot sex and a broken heart.

And Brends didn't look particularly sentimental.

"Go," he snapped. "Drive like hell and don't stop. Backup team is two miles and closing. They'll hold the perimeter until you're through."

The sounds of battle were getting closer and the flash of fire from her right was a serious heads-up. A tall, broad-shouldered, dark-featured male strode through the gathering shadows. Not one of theirs, Mischka decided. A wave of dark menace rolled off him and those shoulders flexed as he drew a blade. Hell, no. She wasn't stupid enough to tangle with the likes of that.

"I'm going," she said, but Brends was already gone, on an intercept course for that unfamiliar male. Yeah, part of her wanted to scream and run like hell, but another part of her—that part wanted to stay to watch his back.

"Fasten your seat belt." She didn't wait for Pell to comply, just threw the SUV into reverse as Dathan slammed the door and strode off after the unknown male who had just disappeared into the shadows. There was a moment to appreciate the smooth purr of the motor, the slick glide of the clutch as it engaged reverse and then slid into first. Then, her world narrowed to the mercifully empty sliver of road and the shimmering wall in front of her.

"Wait." Pell reached for the door handle and Mischka punched the lock button on her side. Her cousin wasn't going anywhere for the moment. "Where the hell does he get off handing me off like some package?" When the handle didn't give, she turned and glared at Mischka. "Unlock the door, Mischka. You're not keeping me here."

She was until they got the hell away from these Preserves. "Be logical, Pell."

Her cousin snorted inelegantly. "You're the logical one. You're the one who plays by all the rules. And look where it got you—knee-deep in the sort of paranormal shit you swore you'd avoid at all costs."

True. And she was dealing with it, wasn't she? Why did everyone think she was so rigid, so incapable of change? Brends hadn't thought that and just the quick memory of his inelegant teasing and wicked touches had her flushing with delicious heat. He made her want to be different, to reach.

Still, there was breaking out of the old—and then there was getting yourself killed. Logic said it was suicide to get involved with the firefight going on behind them. The smart lived to fight another day. "There's nothing we can do. Not back *there*." Would Pell listen to her at all now? "Go back, and our only option is to be cannon fodder."

Giving up on the door handle, Pell slouched down in her seat. "I'm not helpless, Mischka. There has to be something I can do."

"You've already done it."

Pell shot her a quick glance. "Excuse me?"

"You've already done it," she repeated. "You've been the bait *they* needed. Why did you come out here?"

Pell glared at her, disbelief painted all over her familiar face. "I *asked* to come out here. I asked Dathan to take me somewhere safe."

"Because our rogue was hot on your ass." And yeah, all of their asses were now on the line, so her cousin could stop being such a whiny ass, shut up, and *listen* for a change. "So why not hole up in M City? Or one of a dozen other well-guarded, strategic locations? That damn club of theirs, G2's?"

"You're swearing." Pell eyed her as if she'd sprouted a second head.

"Hell, yes, I am." And it felt good. She understood now why Brends did it so often. Blunt and to the point. "Your Fallen is playing you. Did you really suggest driving all the way out here, just the two of you, like a giant target? Because that's not really the easiest—or the best—way to keep you *safe*, now, is it, Pell?"

Beside her, Pell's eyes narrowed. "Well." She folded her arms over her chest. "This is just like old times. I fuck up and you come galloping to the rescue."

"You didn't fuck up. You made a choice," she admitted. "And I made a choice, when I decided that you were worth coming after."

"Well." Pell eyed her cousin. "This is awkward. You came out here with Brends. They don't do anything for free."

"Preaching to the choir." But paying Brends's price hadn't been bad. His price hadn't been bad at all.

"I didn't think you'd do it."

"Bond with one of the Fallen?"

"Yeah." There was a brief silence and then a familiar sideways glance. "So spill. What's he like?"

Mischka shook her head. "We're running for our lives and you want to discuss love lives?"

That familiar mischievous grin spread across Pell's face. Oh, yeah, she'd kill any one of the Fallen—any male—who decided to rip out that spirit and trample on it. "You want to discuss the scenery? Trade recipes? I figure, forewarned is forearmed, right? There's a whole lot they don't bother to tell us, just leave us to figure out on our own. If we gang up on them, I figure our odds are better."

"Odds are better for what? Wrapping them around our little fingers?"

"That too." Pell raised an eyebrow. "But I was thinking about playing for keeps. How about you?"

How about her? Because, yeah, her game plan was just as ambitious as Pell's. She was looking for a confession of undying love from a near-immortal male who was sexy as sin and just as stubborn. Were the odds favorable? She didn't know and all she could do was take a scary-as-hell leap of faith here.

"Me too." Saying the words out loud, admitting what she wanted, felt good. It felt right.

"Are Mom and Dad okay? Do they know?"

How did you put into words that you'd not only had hot, fabulous sex, but oh, yeah, you'd met the missing half of your soul and run like hell because there was a homicidal maniac tracking your ass?

Mischka shook her head. "They know. They don't like it."

"But they'll still let you bring him home to dinner," Pell guessed. "So what's he like?"

Talking was beyond awkward, but they were both trying. Too much water had gone under the bridge to just pick up where they'd left off. Besides, Mischka wasn't sure she really wanted to go there anyhow. Still, she needed to hear that Pell was okay, that even if bonding with Dathan had been an impulse, her cousin didn't regret that choice. No buyer's remorse, because really, why not fuck the rules? She savored the obscenity. Maybe she didn't have to lose Brends. Not now, not ever.

Pell was staring, which meant Mischka hadn't responded to some question. Hell. She dragged a hand through her hair and clamped the other down more firmly on the steering wheel.

"Are you okay?" Pell repeated, and Mischka took her eyes off the road long enough to shoot her cousin a look. She was four hundred miles from home, bonded to a fallen angel, with a rogue angel on their heels. There wasn't a remote chance in hell that she was okay.

"You tell me," she said instead. "Are you okay?"

"Yeah. Stupid question. Strike that." Pell leaned back in her seat, crossing her legs. "Polite chitchat isn't helping here. Do you know what's going on back there?"

Pell hadn't asked? Hadn't *demanded* to know? Brends was no longer visible in the rearview mirror. His large body had disappeared, but the sense of loss was greater than that. Every second took her farther from him, and if she was this tense now, how would she feel when they got back to M City? He'd said their bond would end when he brought her to Pell, so presumably these emotions would fade, but it was hard to believe. How could things be over just like that? How could he just let her walk away?

"You really want to leave?" she said, pulling the SUV over to the edge of the road. "I mean, since you're playing for keeps and all?"

Pell eyed her. Maybe she wasn't as relaxed as she appeared. Her fingers smoothed the silky fabric of the seat belt, petting the man-made fibers gently. "No," she said finally. "Of course not."

"So why are you going?" Maybe Pell's answer would help her make sense of her own internal conflict. Maybe there was a really *good* reason why she wanted to flip the SUV around and head right back into the thick of a paranormal battle that would kick her ass.

Pell gave the belt her full attention now. "Dathan wanted me to go," she said, as if that explained it. Since when had Pell started taking orders from a Goblin? Hell, since when had *she*? The SUV was slowing down, the countryside on the other side of the bulletproof glass no longer a featureless blur.

"Back?" Mischka asked, and Pell met her eyes. Nodded.

"Back," she agreed. "Maybe I'm making a mistake, but the bond feels right. He feels right. Dathan is the first man I've met who makes me feel this way."

"Hot sex?" Mischka asked lightly, but she needed to be sure that Dathan was more than just a lover. Her eyes scanned the road for a convenient turnout. Then they could head back and help out with the fight going on by the wall. Or observe, she decided. Sometimes, jumping in hurt more than it helped.

"More than that." Pell shook her head, her hair bouncing on her shoulders. "He's not one of my mistakes, Mischka. My mistake was not realizing who he was before now. He's always been there, but I just didn't see it. Although," she continued, shooting her cousin a look, "that's a whole lot of mistake to be living with. I'm not sure he's housebroken."

Maybe her cousin was right. She hoped so, because

the look on Pell's face said she'd fallen hard for Da-than, mistake or no mistake. The idea of a relationship between the two didn't seem so foreign now, however. Maybe it was because she'd done a little dabbling in the paranormal herself. Or because she wasn't quite human herself. Quickly, she filled her cousin in on the details of the DNA test, enjoying the shock that Pell couldn't quite hide.

"You're not human," Pell repeated, as if processing the idea. "Not one hundred percent," she amended. "Wow. But you hate paranormals, Mischka. You always have."

"People change," she said simply, as if she could sum up in two words what had happened since she walked into Brends's club looking for Pell. But she had changed. "And chances are really good, Pell, that you're not one hundred percent human, either."

"And that's why the rogue is hunting me." Pell nodded. "Well, that makes sense."

Did it? Mischka wasn't so sure, but nothing had been the same since Brends had deposited Pell in the SUV and that connection between them—the bond—had snapped like a too-tight rubber band. "You tell me what this means." She shoved the sleeve of her sweater up her arm, where the black marks were fading right before her eyes. *Don't look.* She jerked her gaze back to the road.

"Oh, wow." Curiosity sparkled in Pell's eyes. "What did you do, Mischka?"

"Nothing you haven't done," she pointed out. Time to see how fast the SUV could fly.

"Well, yeah, but you're not me, are you? I mean—" Clearly, Pell had a fairly good idea of how that last statement had sounded and was considering a strategic verbal retreat. "You're the good daughter. If you'd wanted to go in for a little role reversal, I could have used a heads-up."

"Forgot to send that memo." A slow smile crossed her face. "Besides, I'm not sure you're constitutionally capable of it."

"Dathan would agree with you," Pell said. She blew an errant lock of hair out of her face. "So." She sprawled in her seat. "How'd the two of you hook up?"

"At the club. Just like you and Dathan."

"Hey, I knew him before," Pell said virtuously. "That was no one-night stand. Dathan and I have known each other for years. And he waited all that time . . ." She still sounded incredulous about the whole thing. If he was anything like Brends, Mischka figured he'd be stubborn enough not to give up on Pell.

"You should have told me, Pell. About your stalker."

"Maybe." Her gaze swiveled out the window. "But there wasn't anything you could have done and it would have just made you nervous."

"Wondering if I was going to be next," she pointed out. "That would have been good information to have."

"I didn't know."

"But you do now."

"So do you. But it makes sense. We're family, Mischka."

Mischka reached out a hand. Not the sort of touch

she usually initiated, but tonight she needed—wanted—the contact. "Friends?" Fingers tightened around hers.

"I had no idea," said the voice from the window, "how sentimental you were, *bébé.*"

Twenty-two

Between the devil and the deep blue sea.

Or in this particular case, between a rogue Goblin who wanted to kill them and the wall of the Preserves. Floor it quick enough, Mischka's panicked brain begged, and she'd drive them all into the wall. Problem was, even if she killed herself and Pell, she didn't know if a simple car crash would take out a near immortal. Not to mention, she didn't want to die.

Gun, gun, gun, her mind chanted, and her fingers left the wheel, diving for the weapon on the seat beside her.

Pell wrenched at the door handle, shrieking curses. "Unlock the damned door, Mischka!"

The safety locks. She'd locked them in with a monster.

Too late. Eilor's large fist clubbed Pell in the head. Her skull bounced off the safety glass, and she crumpled sideways in her seat.

Mischka tried to bring the gun up toward her nemesis, awkwardly twisting in the seat while trying to keep one hand on the wheel.

"No, no, little rabbit," he crooned. Too little. Too late. His dark hands found a nerve point in the side of her neck. He hadn't even bothered hitting her. The gun slid uselessly from her fingers and her foot eased off the gas pedal as the bright burst of pain blossomed behind her eyes.

Too little. Too late.

The fading marks on her wrists mocked her. She couldn't even summon up her fallen angel, because he'd set her free. To keep her safe.

Stupid, useless plan. Primitive instinct she hadn't known she possessed warned her that fate had no intention of handing out second chances. She was alone with her cousin and an insane daemon. She could find a way out—or she could die.

The SUV crunched to a halt.

Wrapping his hands around the female's neck was deeply satisfying. Plus, Eilor knew he'd left her mate two miles behind him, firing bullets at a few stray rogues he'd lured out of the Preserves. Just a little break in their precious wall, a thin sliver of free space that the thirst-maddened rogues had been quick to use. They could smell the two females Eilor had all to himself.

Fresh meat.

He was tempted himself to kill them both. He might have time.

But Cuthah was waiting for him in the Heavens. Not to mention Cuthah's threats. And his promises. Eilor wanted that redemption and he definitely wanted to keep his wings. So that meant he had to behave himself for the moment and keep the deal he'd made with Cuthah. Kill one. Save one.

He flexed those wings in the small space of the SUV, the dark tattoo rippling on his back. Transforming now would still be a mistake. He had to wait.

Dropping his prey onto the front seat, Eilor punched open the locks she hadn't been able to reach, savoring the sweet heat of the female pinned in the driver's seat. The metallic click spelled victory.

Did the Goblins know that he'd got their females?

Jerking open his door, he strode around the car and freed the other passenger door. The brown-haired female spilled out onto the ground. He let her fall, because even though she didn't notice her landing, he did. He liked the way the gravel bit into that tender flesh, the cruel indentations going white then red as her blood rushed to fill the lacerations.

Humans were so delightfully fragile.

He got to work then with the nylon cords he'd brought with him, tying her wrists and feet together. When he was done, she was limp and warm, breathing shallowly. The shadow of a purple bruise crept over her temple. He smoothed her hair over the mark, wondering whether he regretted hitting her, but really, she'd left him with no choice. She wouldn't have come with him, had run from him for months. She belonged now to one of the Fallen. He could smell the male all over her and—he shoved up the thin cotton of her sleeves—she'd been marked by the male as well. Too bad for her.

He'd kill her, he decided, because he had to kill one of them now. But not yet.

Dumping her onto the backseat, he went for his other prize, easing her out from behind the steering wheel. Moving swiftly now, because he was exposed, standing here on the empty road, he reached for more cord. Eventually, the Fallen would know they'd been tricked and they'd backtrack. Of course, he'd be gone by then. Back in the Heavens where he belonged.

And *they* weren't ever going to get back into the Heavens, were they?

Cradling the black-haired female in his arms, he made short work of her wrists and ankles. He put her back in the passenger's seat, fastening the seat belt over her. She wouldn't get away from him now.

He slid into the driver's seat and put the car into gear. They were both his, and as soon as he'd summoned Cuthah, so were the Heavens.

The dull stab of pain cutting across Mischka's forehead was worse than any Monday-morning alarm clock. The bastard's pinch hold had done a number on her.

A quick test of the cords only proved that his knot-tying skills far exceeded hers. She wasn't going anywhere fast, but the SUV was. The road hummed beneath the tires, and with each passing second, she felt the bond fade further. Brends had decided to keep her safe by cutting her off, but instead he'd cut off the one lifeline she had. Ironic that she'd spent days fighting to get him to acknowledge that she was *human*, denying that she had any sort of paranormal blood in her—but now, she'd have embraced that unholy side of her DNA if it bought her an advantage.

Yeah, maybe she should have made it clearer to Brends that she didn't blame him anymore for his ancestors. Because clearly, actions made the man—and the evil incarnate sitting beside her, humming a slightly off-key rendition of "Battle Hymn of the Republic," was clearly the paranormal she should have been worried about.

Without opening her eyes, she slid her fingers over the knots, looking for a loose end. A way out.

"You can't undo them." Eilor didn't take his eyes off the road, but he clearly knew that she was awake. Okay. She didn't want to know how he knew that, but she opened her eyes, wincing against the muted afternoon sunlight that streamed through the windshield. They were headed westward, the dark shadow of the wall sliding by the passenger-side window. "And you should know, *bébé*, that I only need one of you. Give me any trouble and I'll slit your throat."

That was convincing.

Giving up seemed wrong, so she pulled at the knots one more time, but yeah, those cords weren't budging. Eilor had made a smooth mass of twists and turns that would have defeated a Boy Scout.

That ruled out a dramatic escape, but leaving Pell here was out of the question anyhow. So what were her options? A half twist of her head made her headache come back with a vengeance and revealed Pell trussed in the backseat. The shallow in and out of her breathing was reassuring, but it also meant Mischka could rule out a rescue from that quarter.

"You son of a bitch," she said, because the only weapon she had left was words. "You lured us out here and sprang a leak in this wall of theirs to distract us."

"Pretty much." He shrugged those massive shoulders. "Not too glamorous, *bébé*, but effective."

"Why?" Her mind raced. She was stuck here in the

SUV, but maybe she could still contact Brends. She wasn't going to have much time, however. The bond was slipping away from her, fading with every ink mark around her wrists.

"I thought you had it all figured out." He took the SUV off-road with a hard twist of his wrists, rolling to a crunching halt right before doing a fender-plant in the Preserve wall. "End of the line, *bébé*. There's someone who'd like to meet you."

"You're a rogue," she said. "I know that."

"Sticks and stones." He eyed her coldly. "You call me rogue. I call me smart."

He got out before she could think up a response and strode around the car. When he pulled Pell out and dumped her on the ground, Mischka winced. And hoped. Was that a flicker of eyelids? Could Pell be coming around? She didn't know what good it would do, but maybe Pell could reach Dathan. They were still bonded, after all. She, on the other hand, wanted to curl up and cry because Brends had walked away from her, hadn't spared her so much as a backward glance, but that was a luxury she couldn't afford.

"Weak," she argued, because he was coming back for her now. *Way to go Mischka,* she chided herself. *Let's rile up the homicidal maniac.* Why not? He already had all the advantages.

"No." He reached for her door handle and there was nothing she could do to stop him. He smelled wrong. As if he were already dead and rotting from the inside out. "In just a few minutes, I'll be back in the Heavens where I belong. You're the ticket and I'm cashing in."

Brends's wings had reappeared when they'd made

love. God, she hoped Eilor didn't think she was his ticket to wings. *You can survive rape,* she reminded herself. *It's his knife you've got to watch out for.* "You think I can give you wings?"

"No." Disgust twisted his features briefly. "Nothing like that, *bébé.* As soon as I decided that there was no point in holding out against this damned thirst for souls, as soon as I drank my first soul dry, there was a price on my head. Those Goblins of yours would have sent me to the Preserves decades ago, but I found a different employer instead."

"One who didn't mind a little murder and mayhem."

His smile was slow and chilling. "One who insisted on it, *bébé.* You humans are such babes in the wood when it comes to your politics. The Heavens are where the real power is. There's a faction of angels who"—he shrugged—"let's just say, aren't interested in maintaining the status quo long term. They'd like to see a little shake-up occur and they recognized my skills."

"You killed those other women!"

"Yeah." He didn't look bothered by the accusation. No, he looked delighted. Done chatting her up, he hauled her out of the SUV and dumped her on the ground next to Pell. Sexist bastard. Unfortunately, his move put her on eye level with the blade he wore at his waist.

He hadn't bothered cleaning it after his last victim.

"I'll give my boss a little call now, *bébé.* He's been waiting to meet you."

His body radiated confidence as he strode over to the shimmering wall of the Preserves, wiping away a top layer of dust. Who knew evil incarnate needed a clean slate? One hand traced a symbol across the wall's surface.

"No telepathy?" As if she knew how you summoned your evil overlord.

"Shut up." Aiming a kick in her direction, he went back to drawing sigils on the rock face of the wall.

Please, God, let Brends find us. Quickly. She felt only a crawling sense of awareness as she looked at the signs Eilor was scrawling across the glowing surface of the Preserve wall. "No cell phone?"

The surface flickered, faded. Hell, that couldn't be good, could it? Shield was down, that much was clear. Worse, she suspected that Eilor was close to finishing his "E.T. phone home" act, because something clicked and hummed darkly, and then the shield simply went out and she was staring at a stone arch.

The doorway was still closed, but she could feel the power radiating off it. It wouldn't have surprised her to learn that her hair was standing on end, or that if she'd touched the rock where Eilor had traced his sigils, the air would sizzle. His signs had just sent a hell of a current through the rock.

"Welcome," Eilor said with a sarcastic bow, "to the end of the road, *bébé*."

It looked like an ancient tomb straight from a Bible story and cut straight into the living rock of the soaring cliffside. The original builders had sealed the space off with a heavy sliding door made of stone, which slipped sideways along a narrow groove. She didn't know whether they'd wanted to keep something out—or something in.

Either way, Mischka knew she wasn't going to like whatever came next.

When Eilor finished drawing his sigil, there was a moment of ominous silence, and then the seams glowed Day-Glo blue and slipped gently apart. Almost anti-climactic, she decided—until the dark, still air that had been waiting thousands of years for an exit swirled around her legs.

At first, the figure emerging from the midnight black tunnel was no more than a whisper of sound and light, like nails grating on chalk but much, much worse. Mischka had never met anything like that and never wanted to. The fiery pillar of light hurt to look at directly, forcing her to avert her gaze or risk being blinded. Still, there was no missing Eilor's fierce look. Or the hunger and desire painted across his face. Not to mention the faintest hint of fear. That hint of fear was the worst: anything that scared Eilor had to be more evil than she wanted to contemplate.

"I've brought you both females," Eilor growled. His knife hand twitched and she couldn't take her eyes from it. She might be able to throw herself over Pell. She might be able to hook an ankle around Eilor's knees. Maybe. But she'd only get one chance.

"Did I not tell you to kill one and to bring one?" The pillar halted its advance, a form coalescing and pulling a male body from the fiery molecules.

"Yes." Eilor's eyes never left the fire angel. Because it *was* an angel standing there. Mischka could see the wings now, the tips brushing against the top of the passageway. "You did." For the first time, he sounded almost unsure. "But they are both evil. They both have lain with the Fallen."

Lovely. Not only was Eilor working for the bad guys, but he was on a moral vendetta as well. The fire angel took another step toward the threshold. Mischka wasn't sure what would happen if—when—the fire angel stepped over that line. She was going to pull Pell backward, she decided. That was about the only plan open to her.

"Kill one," the fire angel repeated. "And bring one to me alive. Very simple instructions, Eilor. I believe I was quite clear. You do not get to keep those wings of yours, my Eilor," Fire Angel continued in a cold, hard voice, "until you've finished the work I gave you."

Eilor started to protest, but there was a note of uncertainty in his voice.

"Are you faithful to me, my Eilor?" Fire Angel pressed his point.

"I am," Eilor muttered.

"Not particularly willingly," the other said, and that cool, amused voice made goose bumps rise on Mischka's skin. Eilor's new companion didn't *care* that Eilor was less than pleased. Didn't care at all and wasn't worried.

Hell, what kind of power did *he* have?

That fire-lit face turned toward her. "Bring me that one. Kill the other. Now."

Eilor's nonchalant shrug accompanied the blade's coming free. Rising. Beginning its wicked downward arc.

Now, now, now, her mind screamed, and she lunged, locking her fingers around Pell's ankles. She pulled her cousin's body out from under the blade just in time. Finally Pell's eyes blinked open. Mischka could see the scream forming.

Eilor growled, a low, bestial sound that left her in no doubt. She'd pissed off the beast.

A sharp pain exploded in her ribs as his kick met her body. Suddenly she was fighting for every breath. God, that hurt. Had he cracked a rib?

Behind her, tires crunched on gravel and a door slammed.

The fire angel stepped back into the shadows, raising an arm. The arm glowed and living skin reshaped, forming a lethal blade that glowed with heat.

Twenty-three

Brends hit the ground running, palming his weapons before he'd cleared the SUV. Mischka Baran wasn't dead, not yet, and he was determined to keep it that way. As their bond had faded and the threads binding his soul to hers snapped one by one, her emotions had overwhelmed him. Fear. Rage. A primitive instinct to protect. And regret. He was going to kill the male who'd made his soul mate feel all that.

He sprinted toward what had once been the well-shielded wall of the Preserves. Now there was a bloody hole in the shield, and it didn't lead inside the Preserves at all. No, it led up. Straight to the Heavens. Eilor had called a doorway between the realms and was about to cross over. If he got both feet over the threshold—and if he managed to take either or both of his captives with him—it was over. The return of Brends's wings might mean he'd received a full pardon or the return might mean absolutely nothing, but stepping over that line would be a pretty damn fatal way to find out.

If he wasn't redeemed, he'd be dead.

And Mischka would be lost.

So yeah, he wasn't chancing it unless the bastard made it through. And the chances of that were looking higher and higher.

Brends spotted a flicker of hot, bright light as something—no, someone—withdrew up the passageway. Fine. He'd deal with the company later, because Eilor clearly didn't work alone, and he was willing to bet that their unseen watcher was also the mastermind.

Eilor turned and Brends got his first good look at the massive body and raw power the rogue was just waiting to unleash. Eilor's face was a feral mask.

"Why, Brends," he hissed. "How nice of you to join us. We were just about to take a little trip."

"To the Heavens?" Someone in the Heavens was on Eilor's side. Really, really on Eilor's side. Brends considered his options.

"Why, yes. That was precisely where we were headed. Too bad you cannot join us."

The rogue's booted foot deliberately pressed down on Mischka's chest. She clawed at his ankle, but the bastard had tied her hands. The shallow rise and fall of her chest bought Brends some breathing room of his own. Yeah, she and her cousin were hanging in there, but his instincts roared for him to get them out of there. Now.

"What do you want?"

"From you?" Eilor's taunting smile mocked him. "Nothing, now. I've got what I came for, thanks to you. You thought you'd use them as bait, but now the fish has the worm and all you have is the story about the one that got away." He ran one hand over the smooth skin of Mischka's face with mock concern. "And I appreciate your help, Brends Duranov. Most considerate of you. Unfortunately, I only require one female today. Alive, that is." His face was a travesty of regret. "That forces me to choose, you see. Which one to keep and which one to kill?"

Options. There weren't any that Brends could see. He had to get their mates away from the rogue. Dathan and the other Fallen were two minutes behind him, but those two minutes were two minutes too long. The bastard was too close. One blow and the rogue finished them. Pell's face was too pale. How hard had the bastard hit her? Finding the SUV empty was a nightmare he couldn't shake.

"Any suggestions for me, warrior? Do you want to choose? Your brother's mate—or yours."

The rogue wasn't offering to let either woman live. Brends knew that. No, what Eilor proposed was merely a stay of execution—and undoubtedly a living sentence of hell. Brends knew Mischka's choice without asking. Yeah, she would trade her life in a heartbeat for her cousin's. So that just made Brends's choices more complicated. No way was he telling Mischka that he'd left her cousin to die.

So how the hell did he get his hands on their mates? Or force the rogue to step away from them?

"I don't have all day," the rogue drawled. "Really, Brends, I have a schedule to keep to, and it's been a terribly busy day for me so far. Choose or I'll choose for you." Lifting Mischka's hair, he inhaled the scent. "She's really far too pretty to die, don't you think? Wouldn't you like to rescue her from me?"

Neither blades nor guns would be fast enough to take Eilor's head right now, so he had to get Eilor to put down his burdens and fight.

"Brends," Eilor purred. "Always charging to the rescue. Never stopping to think." Eilor shook his head mockingly. "That white-knight mentality is going to get you killed."

Brends had accepted the risks long ago. Unfortunately, Eilor's owner had set the angel up with some serious mojo. Not only did the bastard have a pair of wings that had to stretch ten feet from tip to tip, but he was seriously ripped.

"You like this form?" Eilor indicated his body with a taunting gesture. "Because I can do other ones. Better ones." He paused. "More powerful ones."

He Shifted smoothly, the wings ripping out his back as his body grew as if he were amped up on steroids.

Brends drew a blade, knowing talk time was over. He couldn't afford to listen. Or to be caught off guard. Eilor's form shimmied, Shifted into prime-grade weaponry. His new body was eight feet plus of saliva-spitting menace that rocked backward on two legs while it considered the best angle for attack. Lethal claws flexed, the powerful wings pulsing slowly up and down. The beast had a mouthful of razor-sharp teeth that made a barracuda look like a fuzzy bunny.

Brends's right hand took a tighter grip on the hilt of his blade. With his left hand, he palmed a second blade. Throat. Groin. Face. He needed to get the bastard down and out for the count just long enough to snag the fyreblade and decapitate the bastard.

Pushing off his left leg, he lunged forward from the ball of his foot. His blade shot with deadly accuracy toward Eilor.

Shit. Eilor blocked and the blade slid harmlessly from the heavy wings. Fuck. The bastard's skin was next-best thing to a flak jacket.

"That the best you got for me?" Eilor licked his lips and palmed his own blade.

Brends pulled the next blade, knowing that an entire arsenal wasn't going to be enough to kill this particular rogue. Eilor had preternatural strength and hostages. Brends could take care of one—or the other. But not both, and that knowledge was ripping him apart. He was so fucked. Crunch time, but he wouldn't sacrifice. Couldn't bring himself to let Mischka Baran go.

And if he let her go, if he let the rogue slit her throat, he'd gain enough time to gut the bastard. A no-brainer, right? This was the opportunity he'd been waiting three thousand years for: the chance to prove with black-and-white certainty that the killer Michael had been trying to punish was from the Heavens, not the Fallen.

Mischka . . . or his brothers?

He was going to have to choose. Either way, he figured he came out the loser.

To hell with it. He was saving his woman. He figured she had to be worth more than all of them anyhow. She was certainly worth more than he was. Maybe the boys would understand or maybe they wouldn't.

The primitive need to protect his mate wakened long-dormant nerve endings. And his beast, the fallen half of him he'd been condemned to live with for so many millennia? The beast approved.

The tattoo on his back rippled, the skin itching with a life of its own.

"Do it," Mischka said, and he could tell she meant it. "You do what you have to do, Brends." Her eyes flickered to her cousin and he could tell she knew *exactly* what she was giving him permission to do. "We'll be okay."

"You will be." It didn't matter how much it cost, he decided. Mischka and her cousin were walking away when this was all over. They'd have choices. And they'd be able to make those choices. But, Christ, first he had to kill this bastard who threatened his female.

He wasn't letting another woman he cared for die. Not on his watch. Not again. Even if she was no longer his bond mate, he loved her too damn much to lose her like that. He'd let her walk away from him even if it killed him, but she'd walk because it was her choice and not because the crazy bastard facing off against him had decided to use her as a pawn.

His earpiece barked orders and curses. Zer. No time for his sire to reach them and nothing his sire could do that he couldn't do better. All he had to do was find those damned wings again. He bared his teeth and moved in.

"Don't fuck with me," he said. "Or mine. Ever again. Got that?"

Exploding into action, he unleashed the terrifying rush of raw, primal power eating him up inside. The edges of his body blurred as he charged Eilor. Grabbing Eilor's forearms, he drove the other male backward. Slammed him up against the stony entrance of the cave. Stone broke off in a sharp shower and a flurry of curses. Eilor cursed once and engaged, the fyreblade flashing toward Brends with deadly intent.

"Get out of here, Mischka," he roared. He managed to move between her and Eilor.

Bringing his blade up again, he turned the edge toward Eilor's neck and slashed with deadly force. The edge slammed into Eilor and skin broke, but he knew he'd merely sliced the bastard. He wasn't close to incapacitating his opponent.

"Change," Mischka demanded behind him. "Change now, Brends."

He didn't want to. Didn't know if he could hold on to his humanity, his feelings. He wanted to. And he wanted to protect her, he reminded himself. No matter what. Mischka Baran came first. Always. Shoving the unwelcome emotions to one side, he reached inside for that power she'd tapped into the night before.

Fuck. For a moment, he had it, the Change shimmering across his skin, plucking at his nerve endings. Then, nothing.

Eilor slammed into him, shoving him backward, and he landed heavily against the stone side of the barrier. A muffled yelp told him he'd taken Mischka with him. Eilor drew that damned fyreblade again and advanced. Shoving himself to his feet, Brends knew he wouldn't go out on the ground.

"I can't Change," he growled.

"Yes," she demanded. "You can. Fucking do it *now*, Brends." His favorite obscenity was a delicious shock on her lips. He had two, maybe three seconds before Eilor reached them. Might as well die happy, he figured.

Planting a hard, hot kiss on her lips, he made up his mind. "When I engage, you run," he growled. "And,

Mischka? Run real fast. Zer is almost here. You and Pell get to him and he'll get you out of here." He could see the SUV now, cresting the top of the road. The sounds of fighting had lit a fire under his sire's ass all right.

"I'm not leaving."

"The hell you're not." Eilor was coming toward them now like the freight train from hell.

"No. Change, Brends. I know you can. Fuck this. I'm not losing. Not now." He had a moment to wonder what she wanted so damned badly, and then she shocked the hell out him. She dropped all her mental barriers, opening her mind to him. All sweet trust and feminine strength. Holy shit. She was wide open and he froze. Drank her in.

But he couldn't stop the Change, couldn't fight the wings tearing through the raw skin of his back. With a guttural groan, he gave in to the power rolling through his body, shoving up from his steel-toed boots like some sort of freakish paranormal orgasm. Hell. It hurt and it felt right and he embraced it.

There was no time to worry.

Mischka ducked and covered as power blasted from him, throwing her arms over her head.

Fyre shot down his arms.

Hell, yeah.

Gravel crunched. The cavalry had arrived. Maybe, just maybe, he had a fucking chance now.

Dathan came tearing out of the lead SUV like the brother had a fire under his ass. That wasn't surprising—

Brends figured Dathan had promised Pell protection and she sure as hell wasn't safe at the moment. No, what shocked the shit out of him were the wings.

As soon as his brother was clear of the SUV, he Shifted and wings tore from his back.

Pell was his soul mate. Of course. But Brends didn't have too much time to contemplate the ramifications before Dathan launched himself at Eilor. All he knew was that Dathan was fucking huge, and together they might have a chance.

He raised his blade and leaped into the fray.

His first slice laid open Eilor's face. Red droplets sprayed the ground. Bastard wouldn't be so pretty, and he sure as hell was going to be lacking in the peripheral-vision department.

Dathan was at his back, working around to the females.

Eilor's next blow caught his blade edge, and the shock waves blew straight through his body. Brends retaliated with a well-aimed kick, and Eilor's left arm snapped backward, cracking loudly.

Brends spared a glance for their females. Right where he'd left them, more or less, he noted. Mischka's pale face had a whole lot of sorry written on it, because obviously, now she knew what he really was. A cold-blooded killer. It wasn't his fault if she'd romanticized the Heavens' guardians, but part of him mourned that loss of innocence.

Dathan's blade cut through leather and Eilor howled. There was blood running down his side now, but the rogue was still on his feet. And then he dropped the fyreblade. Mischka didn't hesitate, rolling, her hands reaching for the weapon.

Her fingers wrapped around the hilt and she went after the rogue like a dog after a bone. Raising the fyreblade, she jammed it deep into Eilor's throat, driving the sharp edge in with every bit of force she could muster. Hell, she didn't do things by half measures.

Eilor's roar of outrage was cut off as his hands went to his throat, clutching at the gaping edges. She'd torn him open, but she wasn't quite strong enough to finish the job. Brends was.

Not taking his eyes from his target's, Brends reached up and closed his hands over Mischka's, tearing the blade through the Fallen's skin and out the back of Eilor's throat. With a too-quiet click, the razor-sharp edge slid between the blood-slick vertebrae of the spine and severed the last bone.

Game.

Set.

Match.

Twenty-four

Taking a deep breath, Brends eyed the team waiting on the other side of the threshold. Christ, they all knew now. There was a bright stab of pain as he shifted his weight, not sure what he wanted to do. He felt all amped up. Powerful. Rolling his shoulders, he heard the crisp snap of his wings—his *wings*—catching the small updraft. This was going to change things for his brothers. It had to. So why him? Why not the others? He'd never done anything to deserve this opportunity.

Behind him, Dathan was sweeping Pell into his arms and taking her back to the SUV. So why was Brends hesitating?

The doorway to the Heavens was open and he had a long-standing date with Michael. Plus, the unseen watcher was already winging it up the gateway. Brends got an eyeful of dark wings and the sharp taste of power. Whoever had put Eilor up to murdering their soul mates had power. And lots of it.

What was surprising was the silence behind him. No more shouts or fighting. Just that eerie silence while his brothers stared at him, like they were waiting for him to make a decision. He snarled. He was missing something.

He wanted to pursue, and what the fuck was there to stop him? He'd lived for this moment, had lived and breathed and slept revenge for three millennia, and it was all being handed to him. By Mischka Baran, who was standing outside the gateway.

He looked back. Pell's hands locked around her savior's neck, but if those were endearments she was screaming at him, Brends would give up his wings.

The sensation of his wings rocked his world. He was flying up the passageway when he'd never thought he'd fly again. The heavy beat of the powerful wings shouldn't have mattered so much to him except, damn, he'd missed this. The air vibrated and shook around him as if the elements themselves were celebrating with him in a primal war whoop. He was whole again.

The gateway opened ahead of him and he remembered the liquid, golden light that shimmered briefly, flickering as the watcher shot through. The Heavens. A wing stroke away.

It could be a trap.

Or it could be home. Without Mischka Baran, because she couldn't cross the threshold until she was dead. She might have been part angel, but she was also part human—and that piece of her wasn't allowed to cross over while her heart still beat and she was dragging oxygen into her lungs. And damned if he didn't want to go back without her.

Shit.

This wasn't good.

He paused, half turned around and unsure whether he had to go forward or not. He braced himself and looked at Zer, who was still standing on the other side of the threshold. He couldn't cross over either, couldn't engage in this fight, and it looked like it was killing him. His sire hadn't found his own redemption yet. Fuck.

"Second thoughts?" Wings rustled as the watcher paused. Returned. The male was pale and silvery, almost as if Brends were looking at a transparency rather than a flesh-and-blood man. Scarred but still broad-shouldered, his dark hair hung to his lower back. Those strong biceps and calves were striped with scars and gouge marks. The man's flesh had been pitted where chunks had been torn away and the wounds had healed. It was not the roadmap of scars that held Brends's eyes, however. No, it was the man's eyes: flat, silver and utterly without life.

Cuthah. Brends recognized the bastard from his days as a Dominion. Something real bad had happened to Cuthah, however, because angels almost never, ever scarred.

Brends extended one hand through the veil. The liquid heat washed over him. It was a delicious pleasure that his nerve endings recognized, embraced. He could pass through. It wouldn't kill him. Reluctantly, he pulled back.

"Did you recognize me, Brends? From *before*? I watched you fall, heard you scream." Cuthah's laughter echoed mockingly from the other side of the veil as he wrapped his large hands around the blade. The silver armbands glinted, but otherwise, the bastard was naked except for a white loincloth. And the damned fyreblade. "Michael never did like violence, did he? Always a man of his word, your archangel, and so quick to choose a little dialogue over violence. If it had been up to me, I wouldn't have bothered with a Fall."

"You would have ordered us killed."

"Of course." Cuthah shrugged disdainfully. "But Michael, being Michael, offered an olive branch. He insisted that you Fallen have a chance at redemption." He smiled coldly. "And a chance to perish once and for all when the soul thirst got the better of you. How have you been feeling lately, Brends? That little problem all cleared up for you?"

"What's your point?" He was choking on the icy rage. *Control*, he reminded himself. *Breathe. In. Out.* He'd kill Cuthah and this problem would be solved.

"My point?" Cuthah's gaze flicked behind Brends. "Well, my point really is that Michael failed to consider the dynamics of the soul thirst."

Big surprise that Michael had fallen down on the job. Again.

"Yes," Cuthah continued. "Michael and you . . . well, together you've handed me a ready-made army of the thirst driven in these Preserves, all neatly collected and waiting for my call."

"You're planning a revolt." Hell. Cuthah was preaching sedition of the worst sort. If Brends had still been a Dominion, he'd have hauled the angel off for a little face-to-face with the archangels. But he wasn't a Dominion anymore and he couldn't afford to forget that. He was Fallen. He gripped the hilt of his blade hard. The bastards had framed him, had framed the other Dominions, and they'd gone down.

"A revolt? No." Cuthah shook his head. "Larger than that, Brends. I'll be using that army real soon, you see, and this awkward, barbarian world of yours is just a stepping-stone."

"You framed Zer. You set us all up."

Cuthah stopped his backward glide. "Yes," he admitted, "but that plan turned out to be rather too simple. I hadn't considered the larger ramifications. Frame Zer and your lot for a handful of violent crimes guaranteed to trigger Michael's protective instincts?" He shrugged casually. "It was effective, but then I understood that I could have more than just the Dominions." His eyes burned. "I could have the heavenly throne itself if I planned well enough."

"You got rid of the first line of defense." What else did Cuthah have planned?

"Yes. And permanently, as it turns out. When Michael made his vow, I admit I was worried at first. One or more of the Fallen could have found a soul mate, fallen in love and redeemed his wings. So I prevented it. Hedged my bets."

"I'll be back for you," Brends promised, and he meant every word. "You and Michael."

"Really? You and what army? No," Cuthah said, when Brends looked behind him. "Not them. They don't have soul mates. They can't touch me."

"Not yet maybe." But that didn't mean that there weren't other soul mates out there for his brethren.

"Not ever," Cuthah said, and he sounded confident. "Do you honestly believe that Eilor was simply targeting random women? I fed him names. I armed him. And then I loosed him, so he could do to them what was done to your pairling. Rather poetic justice, if I do say so myself." Cuthah paused at the edge of the gateway. Brends could see the familiar landscape of his home just beyond the edges of the other's still-beating wings. "Of course, you could step over this line right now. You could come *home*, Brends." And then he slid the catch in as if it couldn't possibly matter to Brends. "Of course, you'd have to leave *them* behind. They don't have their entrance tickets." He gestured toward the silent group of warriors fronting the gateway, protecting Mischka Baran from whatever else might come through.

He wasn't leaving any of his brothers. Not now, when they finally had something to hope for. He wasn't letting another brother lose his female. Worse, however, was the pain of knowing that they had already lost soul mates. Which of the brothers who'd fought alongside him today might have been redeemed if they had acted more quickly, had uncovered Cuthah's plot sooner?

"I worked a long time for this, Brends. I really couldn't allow you to fuck it up now."

"What do you want?"

Cuthah eyed him. "Let's just say that I saw an opportunity to get ahead. To get one step closer to the celestial throne."

"You won't get away with it."

"I already have. I live here, in the Heavens, and you—well, you live down below. With wingless, helpless humans. You're every bit as imperfect as they are. Angels, Brends, are perfect. We do not tolerate flaws. I wanted you gone, Brends, and Michael handed me the means to exile you on a silver platter. He was so very quick to believe the worst of you. I wonder why that was?"

"I gave up worrying about Michael long ago." Lie.

"True, although perhaps you should have cared just a wee bit more. He was the one who decided to exile you, you know. Oh, I wanted something more permanent. A punishment that not only would put the rest of the Heavens on warning, but something quite permanent. Instead, he voted for and got exile. Too bad, really. It meant that I couldn't just let you go. No, I had to make sure that there was absolutely no way you'd be coming back."

"Why? Why did it matter so much?"

"Truthfully?" Cuthah smiled slowly as he moved through the doorway and stepped out into the Heavens. "Why, because you were flawed, Brends. Some of the Dominions were flawed, right down to your very core. You're imperfect."

News flash. He'd known that since the Fall.

"You could *feel*," Cuthah continued.

Brends shook his head. "All angels can feel."

"No," Cuthah countered. "Most angels are unfeeling. Oh, our kind believes they *feel* perfectly fine. We insist on it. We've lived so long in our perfect little Elysium, defending good from evil, that we no longer have any conception of what evil is. What it *feels* like. We've bred every bad, dark, evil thought and intent out of our race and that, Brends, is our Achilles' heel right there. The dark is now reduced to a virus that contaminates our kind. Michael and his ilk have no idea how to deal with the tempestuous rampage of emotions. No idea whom to blame or how to place that blame."

"You showed them," Brends guessed. Cuthah's words had a terrible logic. Cuthah had shown them. And in showing them, he'd led them straight where he wanted them to go.

"Yes." Cuthah smiled slowly. "I did show them. I showed them that those uglier, darker emotions were a genetic flaw. A sickness of the soul so irreversible that nothing but the most radical surgery could cure it."

"By framing the Dominions for a series of murders."

"Yes," Cuthah agreed. "And then, after Michael had punished you, it was really quite simple to keep an eye on the situation. I already knew how to find your soul mates, you see. I knew the genetic marker that identified them and eventually I tapped into the unrelenting data streams that bound the inhabitants of the world below closer together than they could have dreamed. I could find them. All it took was time, and time I had in abundance."

"Michael never asked?"

Cuthah shot him a pitying look. "Who do you think reported back to Michael? Two millennia ago, Michael gave up on you a second time. He went into seclusion. It was better that way," he added thoughtfully. "I was tired of his constant questions. Had any of the Fallen redeemed themselves? And how long had it taken the redeemed to find his soul mate and fall in love? Of course, every time, I gave him the truth. None of the Fallen had been redeemed. There were no soul mates."

"I'll be back." Brends jerked a thumb over his shoulder. "And I'll have an army." He had the tools he needed now to *come* back. And he had the will, he acknowledged grimly. But not today. He'd finish sorting out his emotions later, but right now, seeing Pell wrapped in Dathan's arms was all the evidence he needed that they could—they *would*—succeed.

Right now, though, his place was still on Earth, so he turned and went back.

TWENTY-FIVE

His female was trying to torture him. The thin ribbons of the skimpy cocktail dress she was not-wearing slipped farther down her arms. When she inhaled sharply, the sensual scrap of black silk that passed for a bodice slipped completely. The dark shadow of a nipple peeked over the rosy material.

One brush of Brends's thumb and that sweet fruit was his.

"There could be benefits," Mischka whispered in his ear as she pushed him down onto his bed. "Of keeping each other."

A week had passed since they'd killed Eilor and driven off Cuthah. When Brends stepped back through the portal, he'd landed in a different kind of shit storm altogether. Zer had questions about the soul mates Brends and Dathan had found, and those questions guaranteed Brends had no time alone with Mischka. *His soul mate.* Just the word made the warmth blossom inside his chest.

The dress slid down her to her waist so easily. She watched his eyes, clearly understanding that he'd enjoy the show. "You promised to make *all* my fantasies come true, Brends." Her words shot straight down to his thickening cock, a verbal tease that made him want to take her hot and hard.

Hell, yeah.

Her legs opened and she draped herself over him, pressing the hot cradle of her sex against his straining flesh. He could certainly get used to this, he decided. But first he had to convince her to take him on. Permanently. Unfortunately, that meant showing some unwelcome restraint.

Carefully, he slid her off his body. "Restraint, baby," he chided. "We should talk," he added virtuously. But hell, he didn't want to talk. He wanted to hold her in his arms, worship her with his body until there was absolutely no doubt how much he had missed her.

Playing for keeps here.

Instead of thanking him for his chivalrous nature, she tested him further.

She slid back on top of him.

"I thought you were the big, bad seducer." Her husky whisper shot straight to his throbbing cock.

Being skin to skin with her did unspeakable things to his libido, and he was quite certain that she understood precisely how arousing he found her proximity. The little Cheshire-cat grin on her face gave away that knowledge—as did the massive erection he was now sporting. Her hair poured around them like a midnight-colored curtain, the soft brush of the unbound strands erotic torture against his heated skin. He groaned and buried his hands in her hair. She smelled like chocolate and cinnamon. Cool and yet spicy. Inviting. Like the scent of the woman herself.

Unafraid. Demanding. Sexy as hell. She took what she wanted—and she gave. She held nothing back. The sexy murmurs she made as she licked an erotic pattern across his throat had his cock tightening.

Can't come. Not yet.

He was playing for keeps, even if she didn't know it. Her hands roamed his body with a wanton familiarity that he found shockingly arousing.

Hands stroked under his shirt, tugging at it. "Off," she growled. "I missed you, Brends."

Pulling the shirt off in a long, slow motion, he reveled in the hungry examination of her eyes moving over the chiseled planes of his abdomen. Her small fingers found the taut circles of his nipples and tugged teasingly. A low groan was wrenched from him.

"Tease," he growled, pushing her dress down over the curve of her ribs. "I can see that you missed me." With a small grin, she shimmied free of the fabric, tossing it behind them in the shadows, where the warm glow of the light did not penetrate.

Her bra left him dry mouthed with desire. This was wicked. Black satin fabric cupped her skin, mounding the flesh for his enjoyment. Black lace straps. The shadow of a nipple peeking out of the cup drove him to distraction.

Her fingers skimmed tantalizingly over her own skin in a small caress. "Like what you see?" she asked in a throaty voice. He nodded dumbly. This was bounty beyond his most secret fantasies. Her fingers took his and brought them to the small plastic clasp that held the two sections together. "Watch and learn," she suggested.

She used his fingertips to brush against the hard peaks of her own nipples. When she moaned and her eyes drifted shut, he figured she liked what she was doing. Her sex shimmied against the thigh she rode in a slow, hot demand. He flicked his fingers and the bra slipped open, spilling her breasts into his hands.

She groaned a liquid demand. "More, Brends."

He wrapped one hand around the back of her neck, pulling her face down to his for a hot kiss. His tongue plunged boldly between her lips, stroking and licking the mouth that fascinated him so. He never knew what she was going to say or do next, he thought with amusement. She was a treasure chest of surprises. How would she react when he palmed her sex? Would she moan? He could smell the sweet, hot scent of her arousal mixing with his own. It felt right. They were more than a match for each other.

When he slid his hard thigh farther between her thighs, she parted, melting around him with a soft gasp, and she straddled the muscles in a rush of liquid heat. Patience, he reminded himself. He had a plan here. All rationality was dissolving into the white-hot passion that blazed between them.

His next discovery had him panting against her neck.

She was soaking wet through the gusset of her panties. Pushing upward into all that hot, soaked flesh was better than any afterworld.

His abdomen was a series of deliciously cut ridges and the stiff brown nipples practically begged for the touch of her tongue. Who knew that she would be so weak when confronted with such a spectacular example of the male torso?

Brends's heavy thigh pressed up against her aching pussy and Mischka bit back a scream of pleasure. There was no point in stroking his ego. Not, she thought with a wicked smile, when she could be stroking something else.

She ran her hands down his smooth stomach from his shoulders, wrapping her fingers around his erection. All smooth and satin hardness. Damp pre-cum clung to the tip, making her want to lick all that hot, salty skin. Maybe she would, later. If he was very, very good.

"Witch," he groaned, thrusting into her hands.

"Greedy," she whispered back.

"Something like that," he muttered, and his fingers stroked firmly between her legs. Even through her panties it was as if he had touched off erotic fireworks. Sparks of pleasure danced behind her eyes and she spread her legs wider. "Good," he said darkly.

Instead of ripping off her panties and getting down to business, his finger slid down her ass, delving between the cheeks and lower until his fingers rested against her, rubbing wickedly through the cloth. She moaned a small protest. He couldn't tell if she wanted more or less of the sensation. He decided to give her more. She was right. He was greedy. He was not ready to break the erotic spell that held them in its grasp.

He watched her face to gauge her reaction. Swamped with the sheer pleasure of being alive, with this woman draped over him, trusting him with her pleasure and her body. Deliberately, he traced small circles around her hard little clit. Stroking, testing her readiness. Dropping his head, he kissed her, simulating with his tongue what his cock wanted desperately to do. Stroking in and out of the hot, heated depths of her.

"Uh-uh," she chided him, freeing her mouth. "This time, it's my turn. Let's see if we can make you lose control," she said. She shot him a wicked look from underneath her lashes and the last thing he saw was her mischievous grin as she slipped down his chest.

Warm hands reached out to caress the heavy balls, stroking small circles over the full flesh with wicked fingers, weighing them. The soft pulling on his flesh and then the erotic release drove him crazy. Her breath moving across his stomach was his last warning; a hot, wet suction enveloped his erection and his world exploded in shards of dark red passion.

Long minutes later, he resurfaced, only to hear her say, "I don't think I'll ever get enough of you, Brends."

He didn't want to force her into his world. He *needed* her to accept him willingly. All of him, the good and the bad. "An eternity," he warned.

"An eternity of *this*," she countered, wrapping her fingers around his cock and stroking. Touching him was so damned right. "Not to mention, I get you. All of you. Tell me how I lose in this scenario, Brends, because I'm not seeing it."

He had to warn her, had to let her know what she was getting into. "It's not over between Michael and me. We've got battles to fight." A war to win. Cuthah was merely the tip of a very dark iceberg. He couldn't promise her safety, even if he could promise her love. Was that enough? "You can't walk away, baby. Not ever. So be sure. Be damned sure." His soul was in his eyes, in his voice. He'd never felt so naked before. Didn't like it, not one little bit, but damned if it wasn't worth it. If it didn't feel right. A ripple of pleasure shot straight to his cock as her free hand settled on the dark tattoo of his wings.

"I'm sure." Her wicked laughter surrounded him as she pinned him to the bed. "All I need is you. I love you, Brends Duranov. Bond with me," she demanded, cupping his head in her hands. She lowered her mouth to his.

Could you die from pleasure? From sheer heartfelt joy? Because the taste of her mouth was better than any damn heavenly ambrosia. "Agreed, baby." His eyes smiled up at her. "Ask your favor."

Behind him, the door opened and closed with a soft whisper as Zer slid into the room to witness their new bond.

"Love me, Brends." The fierce look of concentration in her eyes stunned him. "Love me forever, as I love you."

"With all my heart," he agreed. "I love you."

The darkest of ink swirls began to appear on their wrists.

He didn't need to look down to see the dark ink bands appearing on their wrists or feel the wicked smile forming on his face. Mischka Baran was tattooed deep in his heart and soul.

He'd fallen—and he'd found heaven.

INTERACT WITH DORCHESTER ONLINE!

Want to learn more about your favorite books and authors?
Want to talk with other readers that like to read the same books as you?
Want to see up-to-the-minute Dorchester news?

VISIT DORCHESTER AT:
DorchesterPub.com
Twitter.com/DorchesterPub
Facebook.com (Search Pages)

DISCUSS DORCHESTER'S NOVELS AT:
Dorchester Forums at DorchesterPub.com
GoodReads.com
LibraryThing.com
Myspace.com/books
Shelfari.com
WeRead.com